At the Time of the Pr(
Towards New Eden ©

Truth is stranger than fiction, but it is because Fiction is obliged to stick to possibilities: Truth isn't.

Mark Twain. *Following the Equator: A Journey Around the World*

There are alternative facts.

Kellyanne Conway Advisor to President D. J. Trump. *Meet the Press January 22, 2017.*

Foreword July 2021

This work was originally published in 2006 under the title *Towards New Eden*. I have changed the title because of some confusion about this being a religious work – which it is not.

Before starting to write in 2002, this novel involved several years of research, looking at a range of socio-economic, political, environmental and religious trends.

The central story starts on the east coast of England before the focus shifts to the United States. The work then becomes increasingly global.

Key themes, such as the conflict between Britain and the European Union were written around 2005. Some might say that my President Smith seems an increasingly likely figure given President Trump.

This is the 2nd edition. The novel is, hopefully, improved by removing any remaining grammatical and typographical errors. There are no changes to the original plot or characters though the first chapter has been slightly rearranged from the First Edition.

The sequels **At the Time of the Presidents' Wars Aftermath** and **At the Time of the Presidents' Wars: *Between Hell and High Water*** are available on Amazon and Kindle.

Chapter I
WashingtonWall
14.59 UTC March 18th

President Lopez stood, trying to control his emotions, on the lawn in front of the White House. The area was swarming with military personnel from different ranks and services, his Secret Service guards nervously viewing even their own as potential assassins. The wind twisted an umbrella held by a marine guard in a vain effort to keep the President dry, but Lopez hoped the lashing rain would hide the tears on his face. Remnants of the far east wing of the White House were still smouldering after a direct hit from a ground- to-air missile. The Secret Service had lied in their haste to get him to safety. His wife and youngest child had been killed before they could reach shelter.

Two large craters spotted the lawn, the debris from their impact spattered across much of the White House's shattered frontage. Outside the White House rails, on the far side of what remained of the gun emplacements, a Christian aircraft still burned, its last charge exploding an hour or so earlier in the heat of the blaze. *They were nothing if not determined* Lopez concluded to no one in particular, looking at an aircraft which had crashed into the lawn. There were no armaments visible on any of its racks and it seemed that it had been attempting to ram the White House itself, though the entire structure was so riddled with holes that it must have been flying on air itself for its last few miles. The pilot still lay slumped in the cockpit, the navigator sprawled backwards in his seat with much of his face missing. Lopez walked slowly to the cockpit, his slippers and pyjamas besmirched with a mixture of squelching mud and foam from the fire hoses. He reached in through the smashed cockpit. *Careful Sir,* cautioned a marine guard.

Lopez looked carefully at the still figures and then looked up the foot or so necessary to meet the marine in the eyes. *My thanks for your concern, but I don't think these two are going to cause us too many more problems. I just want to see …..yes here it is.* and he reached into the shattered cockpit and ripped the dog tag from the around the pilot's broken neck. *Oakdene W. Flight Commander,* he read slowly before the tears started to well in his eyes. There are times in the life of every individual, however powerful or glorious they may be, when the human replaces the image of super-human which may have been deliberately constructed over many years. So it was that a young marine colour-sergeant and a couple of Secret Service men witnessed the President of the United States of America burst into a torrent of tears. In their embarrassment they looked away, but their ears were filled with a torrent of oaths and curses as Lopez beat his fists in a mixture of anger and despair against the shell of the aircraft. Some of the larger audience ceased doing whatever it was they had been charged with, and looked on. Finally, there was silence and then a more controlled and dignified voice spoke. *My apologies. I realise that I am not the only one to have lost dear ones tonight. The main Wall has held, but I believe that there have been over twenty thousand military and civilian casualties counted to now. I am therefore not alone in feeling this anguish. But I promise you…* Lopez's voice faltered for a second before he continued in a tone which he had used regularly in election speeches and which seemed totally out of context addressed to a sodden group standing in a growing storm. *I promise you that tonight shall be revenged. I promise you that the deaths of our soldiers at Baton and elsewhere shall be avenged. This pilot and his like have brought our faith, our country and our democracy into disrepute. Wherever they have gone, our attackers will be pursued and destroyed using all means at our disposals.* And, to his surprise, Lopez found a ripple of applause burst spontaneously from his audience.

Chapter II
Foretaste: spring 16 years earlier

The re-designed *Endeavour* sailed effortlessly down the final stretch of the Humber estuary towards the North Sea. It was a first of its class, having replaced the old diesel driven *Rotterdam* that very spring. It still had conventional engines, but the vessel had been lengthened and masts installed housing enormous synthetic sails which could be automatically deployed on demand. Once on the open sea, and with a favourable wind, these were hoisted to save fuel and, once past 15 knots, the diesel engines automatically turned off. It wasn't a new concept. Ships using similar principles had been around since the 20s, but the new synthetics dramatically increased the surface area and mast strengths. As a result, the expectation was that most ships were going to be modified to this design, rather than based on nuclear power which had been so much favoured until the *Beijing's* explosion had destroyed Shanghai's. On current trends, sail would soon totally dominate near-land routes such as the Hull to Amsterdam crossing.

What do you think of her Bart?' Joel asked, turning to his son. *Impressive don't you think?*

Bart hesitated. His father had always been fascinated by the latest technology, especially anything with an environmental or energy - saving link. True, the ship was impressive and powerful in a rather awkward way, but Bart's interest lay more in the water lapping at the dyke wall. Over the years it had been increased by the local community in terms of height and width, and the bank down to the fields now towered some ten metres, with regular wooden steps allowing access to the top for further work and – unofficially- fishing and shooting. Scrambling up or rolling done the bank, things Joel had enjoyed in the childhood when the bank were much smaller, were now likely to result in a good beating.

She's certainly different dad, though a bit ugly, Bart finally replied. *But I hope it doesn't go any faster or we'll be drying out the house again tonight. Mum'll just love that.*

His father's eyes narrowed and followed Bart's gaze back to the Humber. The waves created by the *Endeavour's* bow lapped high against the Wall, leaving a thin film of vegetation, oil and other detritus. Clumps of vegetation, the occasional tree, and the impenetrable brown of the water bore witness to the scouring effects of the latest storms up-river. Joel's nose twitched in disgust. The Humber had been getting cleaner year-on-year during his childhood, but then London had decided that the area was to be left to the sea and responsibility for any continued flood protection left to the local Communities. Consequently, parts of York's sewage system had also failed sporadically in recent years, and he was not keen to guess the provenance of some of the items bobbing below them.

This area to the east and south of Hull had officially been a flood-threat area since the early thousands, and even those living there thought it was a miracle that it had not been abandoned years before. Sunk Island, where they were now standing, had been reclaimed from the sea through centuries of hard graft, much of the land becoming Crown property; the royal crest on the string of isolated farms stood testimony to the monarchy's repeated investment in the area. Cynics said that this was the reason that the local sea walls had initially been raised time and time again, whilst entire Communities to the north and south of the Humber had been allowed to slowly slip into the North Sea, or had been surrounded by salt meres. However, the last build had been five years earlier and it had been announced there were to be no more government of local funding – the community had been left to protect its own.

Yes, you're right about that, he chuckled *but they know what they're doing on this river. I bet this pilot and captain have been up and down here a couple of hundred times if they've done it once. It's not the ships that'll cause us more problems.*

What will then? his son demanded, his eyes still fixed on the *Endeavour*'s pulsating bow waves.

At eighteen, nineteen within days, Bart's substantial experience of the harsh coastlands had already sculptured him into a thin, tall, muscular young man with a mop of gingery-blond hair betraying his Viking blood. Older people kept telling him that he bore some resemblance to the American cartoon character he had been named after - something he found insulting after he finally located a worn DVD copy and viewed what he considered to be an arrogant runt with only vague similarities in profile and hair. He had a few weeks to wait before his final exams and then the plan was that he would study engineering in some form at one of the National Centres for Engineering Excellence – perhaps even in London or Manchester if he got the grades. He fancied the idea of adding something like politics or administration, or even law, to the course so that he could eventually try to get into politics in some way. Whatever his father might say about a straight degree being of more value, and opening business jobs, he was increasingly of the conviction that only links with the right politicians would enable him to make a go of things. Everyone he spoke to was of the same opinion -that having the right contacts was the way to get things done. Though his aunt had married a Manchester MP, his parents constantly refused to use the link. *Make your own way using your own skills!* was the family's dictum, and there was some considerable pride in the fact that everything they had achieved, and the little they owned, had been obtained honestly.

It's the rains and winds we need to worry about more, his father replied after a second's hesitation. *We can build to keep the sea out here, but when the summer heavy rains come it means we can't get rid of the water fast enough.*

Dad, why don't we just leave then? Lucy's shrill voice demanded. She was just over thirteen now, short for her age and dark haired, though a freckly face indicated the same Celtic roots which were so prominent in Bart. Despite the remoteness, she and had grown up happy in the flat fields and marshes of the area until, two years earlier, a combination of ferocious winds, high tides and heavy rain had flooded the majority of local houses. Nearly a dozen neighbours had died struggling in swollen ditches and newly-formed rivers to save pets and valuable livestock, and Lucy's closest friend had died in what some described as an archetypal young girl role -trying to lead her pony to safety. She had never been really happy in the area since. *Why can't we leave then dad?'* she continued. *Most other people have. Gail's mum and dad have gone, and Ab is going. Why can't we go too?*

What would we do with the animals if we left? Blurted Bart before his father could reply. *You can bugger off if you think I'm going without them Luce.*

Less of the bugger Bart! Joel snapped. *I know you think me old fashioned but I don't like that language used inside the family. Lucy, I'm afraid it's a bit more difficult than that. People like Gail have other houses to move to. Haven't they got a house near Leeds and a cottage in France or somewhere? All we have is our house, and since the last floods it's nearly worthless – it's gone down so much in value that we are really stuck here. Your Mum and I have looked into it, and at the moment we'd be lucky to afford a caravan to live in if we sold.*

A caravan! Lucy cried, almost slipping off the walkway in her excitement. *Great! I'd love to live in a caravan. Would be so cosy and we'd all be able to cuddle up and keep nice and warms if it's cold and ....*

And fucking kill each other after a few days. Get real Luce! Her brother snarled. *Do you really think we could live like that? And what do you think we'd do for food? Nothing but baked potatoes I bet you. That would suit you, but mum would go mad without her space and animals.*

It's better than living in a tent like some of your friends anyway! Lucy snapped back. *Some of your friends don't even wash – I can smell it when they come into the house. Disgusting!* she shrilled, whilst jumping back to avoid her brother's hostile lunge. Though many years older, and immeasurably stronger, Bart had yet to find a way of disregarding his sister's irksomeness and his own tendency to use force to silence her.

Joel caught her before she toppled back into the heaving water, and stepped between them. *Enough you two! Calm down both of you before you fall into the water again!* he snapped *and I'm not fishing you out like I did last time. Act your age Bart! And I've already told you to watch your language -I've just told you about that. Come on now both of you! Talking of your mother, I promised we'd be home to help her with supper and it must be nearly half six now. Come on now!* he added, holding Lucy by the back of her jacket as she tried to launch another attack on Joel, *it'll be dark soon, so you two can get the generator going. We just haven't had enough wind this week so the batteries are flat again - you'll need to use the rip cord.*

Flat again? Do you really think it was a good idea to spend so much money on that rubbish? Bart asked with concern.

There was no reply. Instead, his father cautiously led the way towards the steps, ensuring that he separated the squabbling pair. Much as they loved each other at heart, their incessant fights had proved dangerous more than once in the narrow confines of the Wall's top. Bart lacked the maturity to control his temper and Lucy still failed to realise how dangerous the waters and tides could be. Keeping himself between the two, and with the label on Lucy's jacket firmly hooked under his thumb, he herded them back to the steps they had taken up the embankment and down to the remains of the service road which lead still further out towards the marshes.

The road, heavily potted along most of its length and frequently deeply gullied on the field side where it was collapsing, epitomised the general decay of the area. This had once been valuable, fertile farmland producing a range of arable crops. Hence the Crown's – or more precisely national government's-persistent interest. Despite considerable past expenditure and continued efforts by the local

Community, increasing salinity and unstable weather had caused reduced traditional crop yields year after year. Over much of the past decade this had been offset by increasing demand and rising prices for both food and bio fuels, but there had been some kind of problem – the news had been less than explicit- with the Asian markets last year, and demand had fallen almost totally. This year? Well it had been a dry, windy spring and the wheat was looking straggly in the fields, the ears thin and limp in the late spring sun. This particular variety was a fast-growing genetic, bred for its flexibility and resilience, but it was still struggling. Joel had memories from his youth of protestors trying to tear up some of the early, similar, genetic crops. People didn't do that sort of thing anymore – they were too concerned with getting affordable food in their stomachs.

Further along the road, where the sweet water stood in a semi-stagnant lagoon, he slid effortlessly from the road and checked the rice. Though now well into his early fifties, a combination of hard manual work and intelligent control of his diet had ensured that he looked many years younger, and the children had been pushed to keep up with him as he had loped along the road. His own crops were not a great concern, he earned enough as a service engineer on the wind farms along the coast and out in the North Sea to buy sufficient food, but he smiled at the quality of their latest harvest before clambering back up onto the road. Rice could be boring, but they would eat well this winter if things continued like this and he would be able to sell the surplus to buy luxuries like clothes and shoes.

Despite their relative economic security, the issue which gnawed at the back of his mind was the growing isolation of the area. A lot of the local farmers, their neighbours, had quit their tenancies and the Crown Estates were trying to sell for what they could get. 'Holiday homes' had been a brief vogue, but the few people who had shown any interest soon lost it when the surveyor's flood reports came in. There was some spring and autumn lettings - careful times to avoid the summer rains- but these were mostly to the squeezed middle classes from West Yorkshire and Lancashire who now couldn't afford foreign holidays. Bird watching in the Yorkshire marshes, rather than the Turkish coast or Greek islands of his childhood, seemed a bit of a come down to Joel's mind. People came once - never to return. Most just stayed at home.

The result was a feeling of increasing isolation as all but the most determined or rooted – or those marooned by economic circumstances – had moved out. Many had moved locally to Hull or Beverley, or the safe villages on the high Wolds, where house prices had rocketed before Joel and his wife Mary had realised things were changing so radically. Family politics – all those bloody animals- had resulted in inertia until it was too late. Now, they could afford a bit more than the caravan he had lied about to Lucy, but anything they bought would be outside Hull's wall or inside the Beverley flood plain.

Not that it was all bad. The people who had stayed on the Island had been pushed together by circumstances and now, regardless of differences in occupation, age or interests, they constituted a dynamic and well-organised Community. Neighbours knew that they could rely on each other and, regardless of the season and weather, part of every Sunday was spent working on the embankments, or the roads, or building the new bridge which was taking shape to cross one of the newly-cut drainage ditches.

Turning the bend on the road, Joel caught sight of the wind turbine he had bought years earlier as a generator for his father's family. At the time, it had been a bit of a laugh and experiment to get the thing up and running. He'd found it on the Internet in America and had imported to play around with. *A small contribution to the environment,* he'd said long before Blair -and then Brown and Cameron- had half-heartedly, got on the environmental bandwagon. Not that he had been against what they tried to do, but even at the time it struck him as a bit pompous that the British government seemed to believe it could make so much difference when many of the major economies were doing nothing or little. However, he had done his bit. He could remember hauling the turbine up the tower with the family pulling on the rope and his sweating with a mixture of exertion and fear twelve metres or so up on the tower as he'd tried to get the first bolts located. It had been – still was - a good little machine too. They'd had a few problems, especially to start, but it had weathered storms which had brought down the company power lines and left then grateful for the feeble trickle from *'Old Sparky'* as they had named it with some considerable lack of originality.

Then *'Old Sparky'* had become more essential. Joel still remembered the day he had opened the letter from the local authority - it was still the East Riding of Yorkshire then -   and read with incredulity the list of services that were being discontinued or reduced. There was always a 'good reason', or so they explained, and that good reason was always market driven. Electricity was going because it was no longer economic, given the frequency of storm damage, to provide a service for an isolated, scattered community such as theirs. However, the letters continued, money was to be made available for solar panels, insulation, generators and the like, so the true implications were not fully appreciated until the first really bad, cold, winter.   Mail followed that same winter, with local deliveries abandoned in favour of a centralised delivery being made to the pub on the main road. When that closed, it was dropped at the multi-denominational religious centre which had opened in the old Anglican Church. Eventually, it was announced that collection had to be made from the Hull office some 20 miles away ' *…because it was no longer cost effective to deliver more than 2 miles beyond Hull Wall…'.* By then, people had already stopped writing letter, so only the bills were missed. The roads had been getting worse every year, so it was almost a relief to read that the council intended to give the Community a grant to maintain the road itself – part of 'Community stabilisation' they'd termed it. Water and collections from the cess pits had been continued, though cynics said that it was to ensure nothing nasty floated upstream; regardless of the reason, the service still worked and the trucks arrived regularly every month.

They were within a hundred metres of home, the silence complete apart from the cry of marsh birds, when Joel's thoughts were interrupted by the barking of his dogs, running excitedly along the road with their tails wagging. He had thought of taking them on the walk, but on several occasions one or both had risked death by jumping off the Wall in an excited, vain attempt to seize some passing water fowl. 'Getting old,' he thought to himself, 'they should have heard us miles off,' and he made a mental note to have a family conference about getting a younger dog which could act as a more reliable guard dog.

Not that there was much trouble out here. It was said that, apart from the military, most of those living inside the town and city Walls had relied so much on navigation systems that they could no longer find their way outside. For Joel the reality had always been that – fishing folk apart -Hullees had always kept to themselves or looked north towards Beverley and the dry lands going up towards the plateaux and valleys of the Wolds.

That said, there had been an attempt by some Hull lads to do a bit of thieving a few years earlier. It was agreed that they'd probably been after some chickens or lambs, and had come down the Humber in a large inflatable one night. Well, there wasn't really much to discuss really because the sole survivor had admitted that was their intent. Anyway, it was a big mistake for anyone who didn't know the waters like the back of their hands, because they'd snared themselves on some barbed wire hanging from a submerged post well out from one of the navigable channels, and the boat had been punctured in two of its main chambers. Apparently two of them had been thrown into the water by the impact and had been carried out to sea by the river and the ebb tide. Nothing was ever heard about them. Another couple had hung on to the remains of their inflatable and cried for help all night. The water was cold that night and one didn't survive until dawn. According to his mate, he eventually drifted away, leaving the last of the four to be discovered at dawn by a hunter out for birds.

There had been a lot of argument as to what to do with him after he'd been hauled ashore. Some wanted to hand him over to the police, but there was a feeling that would be a bit of a waste of everyone's time. There were a couple of extreme suggestions, rapidly scotched, that he should be thrown back into the water with some weights attached or strung up from one of the trees. Joel was unsure that the same suggestion would be dismissed these days, but at the time the decision was taken to give him a bit of a beating –nothing too harsh mind, and only after he'd drunk a good mug of hot tea to recover a bit from his ordeal. There was even some limited sympathy for the poor, scrawny thing, but giving him food could have meant Community children going hungry through the winter. After his RealTea - itself something of a luxury too far according to some- he had been dumped on the old, main road to find his way back to Hull as best he could.

There had been no trouble since, though that might have been down to the development of a well-organised Community system. Initially, on the suggestion of one of the older women, they'd called it Community Watch after the old police system. Mary's mother had been a member of something of this name when she was younger *A great chance to have a bit of a gossip and a cuppa,* she'd said, but then the Community Police had developed for a while with a semi-official, uniformed presence. Mary's mum said this reminded her of what she called *cardboard coppers*- some sort of community police with limited powers which had been created to make crime control cheaper. *PCSOs* she said, but she could not remember the precise meaning of the initials. The police didn't come out here now, and one of the great things about the new bridge when completed was that it would be swung out of position every night so that potential rustlers could not come in and take any of the Island's livestock. It was hard work to keep animals these days.

The results of this hard work could be smelled wafting along the road as the trio approached the house. There has always been an undefined potency in the smell of frying bacon which could lead even the most dedicated vegetarian into temptation. After struggling as a vegetarian in the Ecological Awareness Movement, Joel had been gratefully seduced by official figures proving the utility of the latest pig breeds as sources of protein, fat and refuse converters. Like most families in the Island, they had soon bought a breeding pair and, like most families, their inexperience had resulted in Mr and Mrs Pig, plus piglets, disappearing from their improvised sty. Initially, the resulting trips had caused considerable damage to the local crops and had been hunted down in a more or less organised fashion. Then, their value in snuffling up the decaying fish and general rubbish left by the floods had been realised, and a modus vivendi had developed by which the pigs were generally left in peace until they strayed into actively cultivated land, or were sighted and deemed fit for slaughter. Today's smell was the result of one such straying. True, the overly-heavy reliance on rotten fish had done a slight something to the bacon's flavour, but the children's brisk walk was almost a charge by the time they reached the door. They were stopped by mother's sudden appearance. *About time too! I told you lot to be back half an hour ago. Right, go and wash your hands – and use the soap this time- and then sit down before your food gets cold!* Mary's coldness was belied by the warmth of the smile she shot her tribe, but there was no mistaking the seriousness of her message. Food and energy were both too expensive to waste and food, once cold, would be eaten cold or given to the animals. The children knew from bitter experience that anything they wasted would find a grateful snout or beak.

After washing, they sat at the old oak table which dominated the combined sitting-eating room. On the south side of the room was a large door leading out to what had been the lawn, but was now the vegetable garden and orchard. This door was the main source of light for the room at this time, the setting sun giving a gentle touch of orange to what had once been white, florally decorated wall paper. This was now itself showing clear signs of yellowing. No lights were on, the darkness not justifying that yet, though the gentle background heat from the antique Aga used for cooking was welcome- unusually, it was already cooling rapidly outside. It was an archaically romantic setting, with the dying rays of the setting sun bathing the room with a weak light and the entire family assembled. Henry, the youngest boy, sat in his high chair with a spoonful of mash wiped across his face. Apart from this blemish, Bart thought to himself, this could almost have been one of the Victorian domestic pictures he had once seen in a book at school. *Water's fresh – boiled it earlier,* his wife started reassuringly. *Eat your food up, it's getting cold,* her voice sang out *and if you don't finish there's no pudding. No, not even for you Henry, and there's no good crying. Come on now, be a good boy and finish up. There are lots of little boys and girls who'd love to eat that tonight.*

At nearly three, Henry was already aware of the dangerous world outside. This, apparently, was inhabited by evil boys and girls who seemed to finish every bit of food whenever he hesitated. Consequently, with a cautionary glance out of the window, he returned to the serious business of finishing his rice and bacon as quickly as his dentition would allow.

So, what have you been doing then? Mary enquired after her first couple of spoonfuls. *Anything interesting?*

We saw the new ship mum, Bart answered immediately, aware that any hesitation could result in Lucy dominating the conversation for the remainder of supper. *She's a really interesting design, but I reckon the old ship....*

And it nearly flooded us!! interrupted Lucy, with the certainty that Bart feared. *The water came right to the top of the Wall when she went past, and dad said we should buy a caravan and move because of that.*

Mary shot a glance at her husband. *I'm sure he didn't say quite that Lucy* she affirmed decisively, whilst giving her husband an enquiring glance. *We have some very good friends here and dad has a good job and we have a house to keep us warm and dry – not like some people.* The hesitation, and final comment, were both inevitable. It was useful to have the tent and caravan dwellers as a reference point whenever the children started to complain. Whatever their own problems, it was easy for the children to see that they had many advantages, though Bart's friendship with a group of Tentlads had rather weakened that argument. Some of them seemed to relish the freedom of being able to pack up and leave whenever a problem arose, and the military tents obtainable on the black market were as warm and spacious as many of the houses on the Island.

Mary's thoughts turned to one of Bart's mates, a Tentlad called Phil who'd come round to help clear up after one of the floods. He claimed that the larger tents, made from intelligent materials designed to keep them at a comfortable temperature, had been manufactured as field hospitals. Phil had put Mary in what he deemed to be her place when she'd unintentionally launched into one of her social reform discussions about the merits and demerits of tents and fixed building. She'd been trying to convince Phil that his family would be much happier in one of the fixed houses for sale down the road. A lot of people were against the Tentpeople, saying they were no more than nomadic thieves, but Mary had always found Phil and his family very neighbourly and would dearly have liked them nearby. She was busy arguing the advantages of a fixed house during winter snow when Lucy raised her head from the table on which she was drawing.

What's snow? she'd asked, with the naivety of one who had experienced the cold of recent winters but was too young to have seen white flakes falling. Mary realised immediately the argument was lost, and by the time Phil had finished laughing –because he'd seen it once when he was really young - Phil had developed his own crushing riposte. *Mrs,* he'd said with the knowing certainty of a child about to destroy an adult, *just how long will it take you to pack up your house and move next time it floods? Me family can be packed and away in an hour. We've did it twice already in the last few years.* Mary glanced briefly at the carpet beneath her feet, its colours already bleached by exposure to sea water and the fabric thinning visibly. *OK, you win. But a day will come when you regret it,* she'd said laughingly. *Anyway, there'll always be a cuppa waiting for you here, but only if you give me a hand to shift this lot.*

Mum. Can I please have the water? Mary's thoughts were brought back to the table by Bart's irritated whine. It was the third time he'd asked, and wherever his mum's head was beyond his understanding. *Certainly not here and now,* he thought to himself. He reached forward to take the water jug and, as he did so, froze in mid - motion. Out of the corner of his eye he'd caught sight of something silhouetted in the rays of the setting sun out over the Humber. He glanced again at a bizarre contraption which reminded him instantly of something he remembered seeing in one of the old history books he'd help recycle at school earlier in the year. Long ago, in the 1920s and 30s - he remembered keenly because the book was full of fascinating pictures - the Humber had been one of the main training and launch areas for something called…….. *What was it again?* he demanded to himself. *A dribble? No, something more like a diri ….a dirigible, yes they were types of gas airships. And that thing was something like one of them but with something large slung beneath its belly.*

Bart do you want this water or not? His mother's irritated voice brought him back to the table.

Dad, what the fuck is that thing doing? he blurted out, ducking as his mother delivered a swinging slap to his head. Neither of his parents liked what he considered to be *'normal language'* and his mother had become totally unreasonable recently. He had already learnt that a bit of moderation with his tongue was beneficial. Rather than further teach him some moderation in his language, his father's reaction was to follow Bart's gaze. Mary always said that Joel gawked like a landed fish when surprised, and glancing at his father now Bart realised exactly what his mother meant.

Bloody hell. Joel muttered and then cursed vehemently as Mary savagely kicked his shin. She had become very religious over the preceding few months and was even less inclined to accept what she deemed bad language from her husband than the children. *Ok, sorry, but I've never seen anything like that before,* he gave by way of excuse. *It looks to me like someone is carrying a fighter under a balloon. Incredible! They must really be having problems if they are doing this sort of thing.*

What do you mean 'having problems' dad? Lucy queried, craning in her chair to get a better view. *And who is they?*

Who are they is better English Luce, replied her father gently *and they are the air force or the government or whoever is paying for the fuel and equipment getting those planes in the air. And the reason I think they are having problems is that they must be trying to save on aviation fuel. It's a clever idea. I can see what they are trying to do, save on fuel when taking off you can be sure , but I hadn't thought they'd be so desperate to save money and fuel like this.*

So where are they getting the fuel for the balloon? Mary asked. *And what are they using? Hydrogen or something like that?*

Joel hesitated for a second. *I heard that they were producing gases from the Hull recycling centre. It's going for house energy, but perhaps they are using some for this as well. Changing it somehow. I don't know, it's not really the right gas for something like this, it's all potentially too inflammable, but if they are desperate enough for fuel ..... Or perhaps they have another plant somewhere. Perhaps this is flying out of one of the old bases like Leconfield or, what's the name of the airport at Doncaster. The old military airport that they turned civil and then part military again?'*

You mean Robin Hood, chipped in Bart *but I heard that is cut off by floods. Isn't that why it was having money problems in the first place and then it closed down and I thought… wow, look at that!* he shouted, pointing across the Humber.

Hanging ponderously, the setting sun's glow dimly reflected off its silver skin. The dirigible had been some five hundred metres or so above the water when the aircraft dropped from a cradle system suspended beneath its belly, and fell nose-first like a stone towards the water below. To Jo's engineering mind, it was immediately evident that either the design of the cradle system or the timing was flawed. The aircraft's nose was released slightly before the main body and the entire carrying frame twisted violently as it dropped, the ignition flames pouring from the engines risking to engulf the dirigible itself, whilst the huge acceleration as the engine thrust the aircraft forward and downwards gave the pilot seconds to pull out of the dive before the craft crashed into the waters below. This potential for disaster was clear even from a distance of a mile or so, and Bart dashed from his seat to the window, obscuring the view of the rest of the family and causing cries of anger and irritation. Consequently, only he was in a position to see the aircraft level out perilously close to the estuary's surface and start climbing - and to realise that it was heading directly towards their house. Seconds later there was a deafening roar and the building shuddered as the fighter flew over them in an upward curve, clearing the roof by mere metres. Bart dashed to the front of the house to view the craft's path, while Henry frightened into a fit of screaming by the roar.

In one of those blurs which never ceased to amaze her husband, Mary shoved the last few spoonfuls of food into her mouth, rinsed it down with a glass of fresh water, picked Henry gently from his chair and held him to her breasts. Mary had worn the same perfume for years. It was one that Boots had developed - *Fleur de* something – when the local market for more expensive cosmetics had started to decline several years earlier, and she had bought several bottles of the stuff in a closing -down -sale when the company had gone bankrupt. Comforted by his mother's familiar odour, Henry's scream turned almost immediately into a gentle sob and he put his arms around Mary's neck before raising his head and giving her a snot-laden kiss on the cheek. *Me frightened by noise mummy,* he whispered before ducking his head down again. *Finish food now please mummy,* he added almost instantly, remembering the dangers of leaving his meal unguarded, and he lurched meaningfully in the direction of his plate. While Mary put Henry back in his chair and fought to wipe his face, Joel joined Bart with his bowl and continued to munch his food whilst following the dirigible's course over the estuary. The sun had almost set by now and Joel was intrigued to see how the craft was going to navigate back to its base. Suddenly he shot from his chair. *The animals! Where are the animals? Bart, have you brought them in?* Without waiting for a reply he strode to the front door and whistled clearly. Malaria had been a problem in the area for the last five or six years. A new form had first appeared in the south east and East Anglia in the teens and now it was essential to ensure everyone took their daily doses. There had been many cases of the mosquitoes entering houses on the fur of pets, so as a precaution you were advised to ensure that they were all in before dark.

It's OK Joel! Mary shouted. *Relax; I made sure the dogs were all in before we ate. They're in the bed in the other room. Bart, can you make a tea for us all now? And then we can watch the news.*

No, not the news again, Bart grimaced *it's always so boring and full of bad news. Can't we watch one of the old programmes, you know, one of the classics like Friends or 24, they're much more interesting and…*

And you have them recorded his mother replied testily *so you can watch them anytime. I know the news is not so good, but we need to know what is going on. There's an election next month and a lot of very important things need to be decided. What about watching one of the oldies together later? OK? We can do that before the power goes down. A deal? So what about that tea then?*

The BBC's *The News at Nine* had been running for about a year now. There had been a national outcry when it had been moved forward from the 10 o'clock slot, not least because everyone knew what the change presaged. Inevitably, some three months after the change, power down had also been brought forward an hour and everyone was encouraged to be in bed by 10.30 at the latest. In winter, domestic power would be cut around eleven and restored around five in the morning, though cuts were less severe in the summer if it were very hot. The aim of the exercise was to minimise energy use without wasting fridge food. It had been a tricky exercise getting it right - with the need for some new distribution equipment - and in many areas all the power had been lost when the local grid had dropped out. As an earlier contribution to energy saving, one of the Labour governments had introduced double summer time a few years before, and whilst that had not been a real problem for the south, the combined measures had left many in the north and midlands going to bed in broad daylight during the summer months. An economist at London University had even dared to write to *The Times Online* calculating that the energy saved had been more than compensated for by the increased birth rate. Despite complaints from the Scots, London had been firm and claimed nearly a 15% saving in national energy consumption.

Joel sprawled into the sofa nearest the screen and then cursed gently as he realised that the remote was on the nearest chair. *Don't worry luv, I'll get it,* said Mary, pushing him along the sofa. *And don't you forget our tea Bart!* she shouted just in time to prevent a disappearance though the door. The theme music for *News at Nine* was just starting as the screen came on. It was the usual combination of male and female presenters silhouetted against a London skyline. Joel had developed a suspicion that the entire programme was becoming increasingly choreographed, the female presenter always doing the really bad news – a way of softening its impact he believed – whilst the background was also part of the subtle manipulation. In the old days it had been Big Ben, but then somebody had decided that shots from different parts of the country would be good – perhaps a way of reassuring that all was well. Later still, a medley of smiling faces and shots of the latest 'achievements' had been introduced. Not that *The News* was lies -everyone knew someone who has experienced one of the events which had made national headlines so there was a degree of veracity in the reporting. It simply wasn't quite 100% truthful news – more like 90% with a twist of something extra.

The opening news shots were of the reformed police force, the national elections and the presidential elections in America. The national elections were important, but it was the American election which really concerned. The President's assassination the previous summer had been followed by weeks of violence between secularists and religious extremists, and white and non-white Americans. It had only been brought under control when regular troops had returned home from the last of the American overseas bases, though the situation was still tense, with many of the National Guard units and a few elements of the regular military refusing to accept the legitimacy of the Vice-President in Washington, and with calls for early elections to try and re-establish order.

They look like a lot of robots from the old science fiction series you used to like so much, Mary commented softly, pointing to shots of the national police with their new body armour. *What was it called again? The Doc or something like that?*

'*Doctor Who. I watched the last series and then the re-runs. But this lot is nothing to do with robots. Looks like a really heavy body armour to me. Why the silver though? Really strange,* Joel replied. Then, noting the inactivity in the kitchen, he shouted *Bart where is that tea!? Come on now lad, your mum is dying for a cuppa. And that's the religious nut who's trying to become US President isn't it,* he noted, turning back to Mary. *He's virtually split the States in three - one of the lads at work was saying anyway. Seems like the east and west coasts are more liberal and loyal to the President but the south and centre have really gone crazy on the religious thing. So Kev says anyway, you know, the old one in finance with a sister in Baltimore. And who is that with him? I don't …'*

Tea anyone? Bart demanded, brandishing two mugs of steaming liquid and standing deliberately in front of the television. Despite his age and size, Bart remained what his parents considered to be emotionally immature, and parental deprivation of *The News* was a pleasure which almost compensated for the loss of seeing his favourite programmes on the biggest screen in the house. *Anyone for honey?* he added, secure in the knowledge that neither of his parents took the same, and that there was none in the house, but that he could disrupt their viewing for several more seconds.

For some reason that Bart could not understand, the announcement from the voice from the screen that *Further clashes in the United States. Our North American correspondent Henrik Pierson reports that elements of the Virginian National Guard are fighting for control of the strategic town of….'* seemed to galvanise both the elderly ones. Both mugs were seized from his hands and his father thrust him brutally – or so it seemed to Bart – to one side. It was a pointless act. The power went at this point and his parents were left sitting in the dark with the barest of light from the rising moon and the remnants of sunset. *Shit!* he cried and bounded for the door to the generator shed. *Really sorry, forgot to turn the generator on – couldn't do that and make tea too could I?* The heavy door thudded shut behind him just after his mother's shoe flew past his head, but the thickness of the door was no protection from the cries of frustration from the other side.

Chapter III
WallWork

Sunday broke bright and with a warm breeze from the south-west. The forecast was for showers later in the day, so the entire family was up for six and down, eating breakfast, by half past. Henry had slept badly -yet another late tooth coming through – and both Mary and Joel snapped short temperedly as the children squabbled unnecessarily over breakfast. There was enough food on the table to ensure everyone ate well, yet an almost ritualistic bickering now characterised almost every meal as a means of protecting one's own plate against potential predators. Only Henry had been excluded from this to date, but he had already learnt that any hesitation in putting food put on to his plate into his mouth could result in its magical disappearance. Consequently, he ate as rapidly as his erupting dentition allowed, and the fact that eating was now painful resulted in his own variant of short-temperedness.

In medieval England males had been expected to spend their post-church Sundays practicing their longbow skills at the butts. Doubtless, some had enjoyed this because their prowess in archery had attracted attention from their peers or the local girls. Whilst the obligation was clearly there, there was little of the historical virility in modern Sundays, and by the end of the morning most of the family would all be covered in mud and soaked to the bone. Joel and Mary had avoided the temptation offered by the renewed power of the church, which excused church-goers sixty minutes of morning labour. Despite Mary's religiosity she could not bear to inflict evangelical church sermons on the family. Generally, she considered they had been written on a Saturday evening with an excess of alcohol evident in the vehemence of the preaching, and her morals made it difficult to accept that her own religiosity should excuse the rest of the family from work which would then fall on the shoulders of other. The law obliged all able bodied persons between 14 and

70 to spend a minimum of four hours on 'good Sundays' working on their local Wall *for the benefit of the Community* and she profoundly believed that her family had an obligation to *do their bit.*

Some areas had no need of a Wall, and in others there was more labour than was required, so there the convention had developed that work would rotate around different neighbourhoods. Neighbourhoods which were not required on a particular Sunday were expected to provide some kind of refreshments, but Highland areas without need of a Wall were legally obliged to provide rations for labour teams. This usually meant that vast amounts of rice, flour and tinned vegetables ended up being shifted from highland to lowland areas at the end of each month's reckoning. Joel found the entire process amusing. There were frequent stories of food coming in through YorkWall port, and being shipped to Sheffield and further up - only to be sent back to the coastal plain as WallRations a few weeks later. Sometimes there was, of course, a real surprise such as when Mary's work team had received a traditional cake shortly before the Christmas of the previous year. That had been a true labour of gratitude and her team had calculated that an entire family's dried fruit allowance for the year had been used in the cake.

Good Sundays had been re-defined in the latest legislation, so now they included all days with a temperature above 5 centigrade and less than 10 millimetres of rain. Apparently it was all connected with concrete setting and quality of work, but given the perversity of most of this spring's poorer weather falling on Sundays, several days' work been lost on their own Wall.

By seven, the entire family was dressed in their worst clothing and water boots with some chunks of bread and cheese, and some bottled clean water, thrown into a bag for the mid-morning break. Keeping the Wall good meant keeping the family safe, and whilst Henry would be left in the care of some of the younger children, the remainder of the family were all of work age and would do their bit.

They stood outside of the house enjoying the warmth of the sun as it emerged from behind the scudding clouds. They shared lifts and fuel with a neighbour further inland, and this morning she was late. Finally, about fifteen minutes after their agreed time, Hannah's old people carrier rounded the bend. The dilapidated Renault's arrival was preceded by much banging and followed by a plume of greenish-black smoke reflecting its reliance on cheap bio fuel. This time Joel decided he was not going to help clean out the jets.

You need to use cleaner fuel, he suggested authoritatively as he clambered into the front passenger seat *they've got some good stuff at the old Shell station on the main road.*

Hannah dismissed the hint with a simple smile, and, once everyone had crammed in, she crashed into first gear. *Perhaps you could have a look some time? I could let you have a couple of chickens if you sorted her out,* she suggested sweetly. Before Joel's mouth could form the *'No'* which his brain had planned, Mary's pinched him viciously on the back of the neck. *Sure, I'll try and have a look later today,* he found himself saying. Hannah's two chickens were a prize which Mary could use to feed the family for a week.

They arrived at their Wall section about thirty minutes later. It was far out on the Island only some five miles from the point where the estuary and sea met in a swirl of powerful currents where the Spurn Point peninsular had finally been overwhelmed by a winter storm some years earlier. Despite the weather and relatively light winds, the water was pounding high against their Wall. It was supposed to be low tide but the word 'supposed' was significant today, and the labour groups were standing looking doubtfully at the waves. *U late,* observed Pilling the unit manager in the truncated style which most of the youngsters seemed to have adopted. *Perhaps u want to do the wet stuff Joel?* Joel instinctively bridled at what he knew was an order rather than an invitation. The work teams were supposed to be co-operatives working for the good of the Community, rather than organised hierarchies, but powerful people like Pilling seemed to inevitably regard them as their own fiefdom. And they were late, so he had no basis to argue.

OK, where do you want me to start? He asked reluctantly, sensitive to the fact that Pilling controlled most of the paid work in the area.

Five minutes later he found himself in one of the protective wet suits tethered on the water side of the Wall. The work itself was simple and primitive in the extreme. There were no complex tools, let alone the energy to drive them so, so the next hour would be spent shovelling rocks, sand, shingle and any other solids from the estuary bed into what was basically a large metal bucket which functioned like a sieve. When as much water as possible had drained out, the bucket was passed across the Wall and then relayed to a selected spot where its contents were dumped into a concrete mix. Though the labour was definitely archaic, the greater plan was quite sophisticated. Years earlier the entire area had been laid with an extremely thick, plastic sheeting to prevent water seeping through under the Wall. Now the need was to build –up the land behind the Wall to form a firmer base upon which the Wall could be heightened. Eventually, soil was then added on the land-side thereby creating potentially good farmland, though the salt water content from the estuary meant that only certain hybrid crops would grow for the next ten years or so. With time, theoretically, they would be able to raise the land enough to justify a bid for a government grant to raise their Wall section properly. This implied a loan of power tools and a grant for concrete, reinforcing materials and the like. There would be enough assistance to make a real concrete wall with a life of over 30 years rather than the permanent need for patch- and- mend of their Community job. In his own mind Joel was unsure the entire thing would work, his suspicion being that the salt content in the materials being dredged from the Humber would be too high, but he was simply an electrical engineer and ill inclined to argue with the likes of Pilling.

Then he was in. Despite the season, and a reasonably good wet suit, the water was surprisingly cold. Work in the water was always done in pairs, and his partner today, Andy, was probably ten years younger and much tougher than himself as a result of labouring full time for local farmers. It was soon clear to Joel that Andy would be able to keep working more quickly and for much longer. After half an hour, and his best efforts to fight the sensation, Joel could feel a numbing fatigue creeping its paralysis from his legs upwards. It was not only that he could feel his body cooling, but the demands imposed through the sheer effort of heaving the loads from the estuary bed, whilst keeping his footing against the current, were proving too much. He slowed further. The cold in his legs started to give him cramps and the back of his neck ached from keeping his head above water and where passing branches and other flotsam had caught him. *You all right mate?* Andy enquired with a concerned look. He was known locally as a simple, honest, straight-talking fellow and he was so transparent that it was evident that something was troubling him *Of course he's fine Andy, aint you Joel?* Pilling called from above. *Joel here wants to make up for the time he lost this morning, don't you mate? In fact, you'd really like to do an extra half hour to compensate, wouldn't you?*

Neither man had been aware of Pilling's presence on the embankment, and Joel's immediate unease was increased by the malicious glint in Pilling's eyes. Just then, a cry from further up the Wall indicated a problem elsewhere in the works. Pilling turned away and disappeared from sight and almost immediately Andy immediately took the opportunity to wade through the current so that he was standing directly next to Joel. *You need to watch your back if you take my advice mate,* he whispered with one eye on the embankment rim. *He's really got it in for you- and you know what a bastard he can be.*

What's the problem here Andy? Why's he in such a shit mood or ...? Joel asked, though the question was unfinished as his foot slipped on a rock on the estuary bed and he slipped under the water with his full bucket. He was dragged to the surface by Andy's strong fingers gripping around his wet suit collar, though an unplanned consequence was that cold water rushed in to fill the gap between the suit and clothing underneath.

You ok? Look mate, seems like your lad has pissed off Pilling's eldest at school. Seems like your lad was better than his at football so he got selected for the team and Pilling's didn't so...

And you're telling me that's the reasons he's being such a shite? What a pathetic piece of work. I'll ...

You'll do nothing if you know what is good for you, Andy interrupted *or you'll have real problems ever getting work again. He's already had a word with your boss, so you'll need to be careful at work – any mistakes and he'll have you out and...*

Problem fellas? Pilling interrupted from the embankment top. Again, neither knew how long he had been there and the blood drained further from Andy's already pale face.

No, no problems. We're just trying to get a better footing, we've dug out most of the usable stuff here, he replied hurriedly.

Good, I'll tell you what then. Why don't you consider your turn done and I'll send Ralph in to join your mate. Ok with you Joel? Pilling purred, and without another word he ordered the woman at the end of Andy's safety tether to winch him out. Joel could see a note of protest form on Andy's lip, but then they closed as the rope tightened and the crane above their heads started to strain with Andy substantial weight.

Built like a bloody whale, no wonder he doesn't feel the cold. Joel muttered to himself, and then flinched in pain as a small pebble hit above his right eye.

Come on then neighbour; let's see you do your bit for the community. Only another half hour to go. In fact, if you work harder I'll have Hannah here pluck you out a bit early. You like that one do you? … Pluck you out like she plucks one of her bloody chickens! And he laughed hollowly at what he had passed for a joke.

Hannah was normally one of the most relaxed people on the Island. Whilst her people carrier was old and held together by a collective of help and goodwill from neighbours, the way she drove it showed an inner tranquillity which few could equal. Now, however, she looked down at Joel with a mixture of anger and concern on her face. *Isn't it time you go him out of there?* She asked Pilling quietly. *The rule is no more than thirty minutes in cold water.*

Says who? Pilling retorted. *This is my Wall and I have responsibility for it. If he turns up late that's anti-social, anti-Community, so he should suffer. Anyway, who says the water is cold? He does an hour in normal water, so shut it old woman unless you want to do his work.*

Without realising it he had raised his voice in anger, and the teams within hearing distance had stopped work and were watched with interest. It was unusual to see anyone standing up to Pilling, but then Hannah had no need to work and no dependence of kin or food on him. The idea of a free woman putting him in his place was one which secretly appealed to the entire Wall team, with the possible exception of Pilling's immediate family.

Hannah, where's Joel?! Mary shouted down the length of the Wall. She had been transporting material in an old wheel barrow from the Wall to a central point where the contents were raked into piles depending on their size and composition.

This bastard is keeping him in past the time. He's freezing in there! Hannah replied, and almost before she had finished the sentence Mary was sprinting across the works and up the WallSide. She paused at the top and looked down at her husband who waved up to her feebly. *Don't make any trouble Mary, I'll be all right – I'll be out in another twenty five minutes or so I reckon. Here, take this,* and he offered another full cauldron connected to the drag rope. Mary hesitated. Pilling had the power to make their life difficult if not impossible, but if he was allowed to get away with this humiliation he would make sure that every family in the area knew about it. Life would be miserable for the children at school, and as for Joel and herself – who would take them seriously again?

Listen everyone! She shouted at the top of her voice. *WallLaw says no more than thirty minutes in water except in an emergency. Am I right?* And there were a few mumbled agreements from along the Wall. *And is this an emergency?*

No bloody emergency here! Shouted Hannah. Several faces exchanged shocked glances at the atypical profanity. *And I've been on winch so I know how long he's been in,* she continued *so WallLaw says he should be out. Right?!*

Yea that's right! Came the shout from along the Wall, and Pilling looked around in concern at this unexpected turn of events. WallLaw was important- it was what kept many communities safe and the penalties for breaching it were severe. Even if it didn't get to the courts is almost always resulted in real social problems in the Community and, despite his local power, he had no wish to create unnecessary problems. Anyway, he'd already made the point.

Ben, for gaud's sake get him out before you make a fool of yourself. Pilling's wife was a thin, tall woman whose voice boomed surprisingly against the wind's current. Those who knew the couple also knew that she was not a woman to anger. It was perhaps a concern to avoid domestic strife which underlay the events of the new few seconds. Without warning, and with the barest, muttered *Get out of the way you stupid woman,* Pilling lurched towards the winch. There was no reason for him to do so, for Hannah was already starting to wind the ratchet which would pull Joel up. Opinion was later divided as to whether he intended to help, or to stop, Hannah, but it was also divided as to whether he intended to push Mary or not.

Mary hit the water about a metre down-current from Joel. He had seen her tip over the top, arms and legs flailing, and then fall from the embankment with a shriek of alarm. In normal circumstances it would have been an easy thing to have jumped sideways and grabbed her as she hit the water, but these were not normal circumstances. The signals from his brain met a sluggish response from arms and legs numbed by the cold water and, by the time he arrived where he had long before intended to be, Mary had disappeared under the surface for a second time. Stunned by her fall, and a good half metre shorter than Joel, she had scrabbled futilely to get a footing when she landed before the current took a hold. Now, she re-emerged spluttering for breath, but now she been carried further out into the main current which was ripping downstream.

Hannah, let out the rope, give me slack!' Joel shouted and, jumping out into the swirling water, he was caught and carried by the same forces as were carrying his wife. Mary was a fair swimmer and her first instinct was to swim back towards the Wall, secure in the knowledge that the water would be shallower and that someone would throw her a rope. But, however hard she tried, she found herself pulled further from the shore. Panic started to take a grip. Once she passed The Point, she knew the currents would carry her south into the open North Sea and then her only hope of salvation would be a lucky encounter with a small boat - the larger ones would more likely sail straight over her without even the slightest awareness of her demise. Then her spirits soared, and she almost giggled with relief, at the sight of Joel flailing towards her, the cumbersome yellow wetsuit buoying him along like some child's toy. Most importantly he was gaining, and in her confidence she relaxed slightly in her own efforts to swim against the currents. Then he was almost with her and she stretched out her hand to grab his. She felt her fingers rake through his just as he reached the limits of the safety line and came to a juddering halt.

Joel disappeared under with the force of the stop, and when he resurfaced his wife was already another twenty metres further out towards the open sea, floundering as the undercurrents dragged at her. *Cut the line!!!* He screamed, but his voice was lost in the wind and the line stayed taut. On the Wall he could see figures dashing about – they had clearly been relying on him - and within a minute a small dinghy slid violently down the Wall into the water. Two men clambered down hastily, threw themselves into the vessel. They paddled ferociously past him without so much as a glance while he was pulled slowly back by the winch, much like an exhausted fish is hauled in at the end of a line.

Chapter IV
Disintegration

Someone from the Wall had been carrying a working mobile and finally managed to contact the Coast Guard. Unlike the old days, there were no helicopters or boats scrambled to search –although these were available as a prohibitively expensive option. Instead, a simple request had been broadcast to any ships or boats in the area. Mary's body was brought ashore the evening of the following day. The dinghy crew had failed to find her in the choppy, fast-moving waters further out and had stopped searching when they risked being overwhelmed. Her body had been found floating face down by fishermen at morning nearly thirty miles out to sea. The family had been sitting waiting in the house with the hopeless optimism of those who know what the news will bring, but have suddenly developed a desperate determination that certainty will be denied today. Unusually, a police officer arrived in person with the news the following morning. It was good of her really because they didn't have to do it. Normally they simply sent a letter for collection with a picture asking for confirmation of the body's identity, but an officer had peddled out on her bike especially – apparently she'd known Mary vaguely through both having children in the same school. Joel had felt obliged to give her some tea and something to eat before the journey back, though her visit had not been without its stresses.

Despite his own anger and distress, Joel had been obliged to control Bart when he got back to the Wall. He found a young man suddenly brought back to childhood in a gush of tears and wailing and who, as soon as he'd learnt what had happened, had launched into Pilling with a flurry of punches, one of which had broken Pilling's nose. Despite his fatigue, Joel tried to interpose himself between the two, and a tense stand-off had developed between Pilling's family and some of the Wall crew. Both groups had armed themselves with axes, knives, spades, planks and whatever else lay to hand on the Wall, and there had been a herd determination to throw Pilling into the water with a heavy weight around his neck. He was rescued from this potential fate when his eldest daughter drove into the crowd with a fast pickup and Pilling, family and hangers-on had leapt into the back in a sprawling pile and sped off under a stream of stones and other missiles. Doubtless he would complain to someone he knew in power, but the consensus was that any retribution would be unofficial, and poorly supported locally.

Bart had stayed while Joel had given his statement to the police officer, he'd even asked why she was still wearing the old black uniform rather than the *'astronaught's suit'* – as everyone now called them – that the London cops were wearing. She'd smiled weakly, made some comment about budgets and levels of violence and then completed the statement. *What'll happen to im?* Bart finally demanded, with tears in his eyes. *Will it be prison or worse?*

The woman looked up from her notes and then looked at the two. *I'm going to have to take statements from everyone who was there,* she replied slowly *but the evidence so far points to an accident. Bart, your dad himself said that is seemed like Pilling was just pushing to get past your mum, and as for breaking Wall Law well….* her voice trailed off and she glanced around as though to ensure no one else had joined them. *Out here I would think you'd sort that out amongst yourselves and ….*

Almost nobody will do anything against Pilling out here! Bart snarled. *He runs almost all the bloody work! Are U telling me nothing is going to be done about me mum? You lot aren't much fucking good if …!*

Bart!!! Calm down! Joel interjected, seizing his son's arm. The boy had half risen from the chair and was shaking with fury. Despite his own grief and anger Joel instinctively recognised the danger of alienating the local police – having both them and Pilling to contend with would be disastrous- and he glanced anxiously at the old dresser where she had put her weapon. *The officer's right,* he conceded reluctantly. *I don't think we can prove anything against him, but we'll find a way -in due course. Now I think Officer Green needs to go before it rains again, and we should at least thank her for coming in person.*

After she'd left, Joel set to work making food for Lucy and Henry who were being looked after by neighbours. His mind could not focus and had already burnt the first two efforts when one of them knocked at the door with a vegetable pie and some cakes. Bart disappeared almost immediately after he returned to the house with the two children, and it was nearly three in the morning when Joel had heard the stairs creak as he crept back into the house. Joel thought of going to talk to him, but he had only just managed to get Lucy asleep and she was cuddled next to him with her young, tear-stained face on his chest. It was only when she had gone to bed and mum had failed to

appear to read her a bedside story that the meaning of 'dead' had become a reality. She had cried herself to sleep and now he feared disturbing her if he got up again. He decided to talk to Bart first thing in the morning. His night was spent alternating between near-silent weeping and a troubled determination to organise things so that they had the least impact on the children. The neighbours had already offered to look after Henry while Joel was at work and Bart and Lucy at school, but there were the immediate issues of arranging Mary's funeral and the logistics of getting her body transported back from the other side of the Humber.

Henry woke for a feed around five, and within minutes Joel was joined in the kitchen by Lucy. *Lucy love, do me a big favour and check see if your brother is awake. If he is, ask him if he wants something to drink or some breakfast or something,* Joel asked. To his surprise she turned back through the door without protest and he heard the creaking stairs as she padded towards Bart's room. *Not there,* she said, puzzlement written across her face when she returned minutes later. *And the dogs arnt there nether.* It took Joel five minutes to determine that neither of the dogs, nor Bart, was in or around the house. Normally he would have been angry – it was still too early in the morning to go out because of the risk from a stray mosquito – but this time he resigned himself to the fact that the lad needed some time on his own and Henry's crying brought him back to the immediate task of preparing breakfast for the youngest member of the family.'

Bart came come just before dusk that day, grabbed some bread and cheese from the store, and went straight to bed. The next morning he was gone again, much to Joel's fury. He'd arranged with the undertakers to collect them both so that they go to claim Mary's body – a journey he had no wish to make on him own. In one of those kind opportunities offered by providence, Hannah chanced to appear in a plume of smoke while Joel was standing outside the house waiting for the hearse. He waved her down and, it took only a matter of seconds to persuade her to keep him company on the journey. There might be local gossips who would think the thing rather improper, but neither of them were the type to give their prattle a moment's consideration. *Fuck their evil minds if that is the way they think,* Hannah declared with considerable vehemence, and she parked the old Renault on the drive to the house as though to declare her indifference to any passing gossips. Joel was still mulling over in his mind whether her eagerness to help arose from some feeling of guilt when, in a trail of smoke which dwarfed even Hannah's, the funeral director finally arrived.

It was dark when they got back. Unbelievably, the roads south of the Humber were even worse than on the north bank, and Joel found himself regretting that that he had not taken a friend's advice and had the body brought over by boat rather than using what was now less than affectionately called 'Old Shaky. There was a constant stream of bets as to when the entire structure would collapse into the Humber and fears had been re-enforced the previous year when a lane in each direction had been permanently closed by the owners. For now, he just couldn't bear to look at the water and had taken the risk rather than add another 40 or so miles using the roads running along YorkWall. He had made a point of closing his eyes when they had crossed the bridge and even when, to his disgust, the hearse driver had asked him to pay the toll, he had dug into his pockets with tightly screwed eyes and extracted a pile of notes which he handed to Hannah.

The house was in darkness when they returned home, the generator lying silent in its outhouse, and it took Joel some time to light enough candles for the hearse driver and his mate to carry Mary's coffin into the front room. She was going to lie there the following day so that friends and relatives could show their respects, and Joel had to be up early the following morning to collect Mary's mother and his sister from the new rail terminal they were building on the Wolds at Wetwang. Joel had vague memories of a school trip to one of the London museums when he was about thirteen– was it The British? – to see what his history teacher had told him was a very important object from Wetwang. He remembered feeling both disappointed and impressed by the display of skeletons of horses and people, a pile of wood which had – so they said – been a chariot. What had impressed him more was some of the metal work on display and the enthusiasm with which Mrs Wigley had explained how rare it was for women to have been buried in this way and how the wealth of metal and other artefacts marked the place out as having been very important.   The once-small hamlet had now been designated as a regional growth centre and was getting the best of the investment in the area – the advantage of height.

The coffin was placed with due dignity on a form of trestle the undertakers had brought, and with a respectful bow the two men withdrew from the room. They had removed the top section of the coffin in order for Mary's face to be visible. Despite their best efforts in masking her face with a cosmetic veneer, the abrasions and bruises from where she had been thrown against rocks or other objects were still visible. *I'm going now,* a forgotten Hannah said quietly, *unless you would like me to get the kids for you or cook something or...* and her voice trailed away with an unspoken suggestion that she would willingly stay to keep him company and share his sorrow. Joel looked up. *Thanks, but I'd better get the kids. Anyway, it'll be a good opportunity to check the car is still working. Haven't used it for weeks.* He deliberately disregarded the unspoken part of her message. He had once had a crush on Hannah, but that was long before, and certainly before he had met Mary, and now was not the time for ... for whatever she might be offering or not.

Joel stood and watched her car as it bumped its way along the pot holes, a thin vapour of burning diesel, vegetable oil and fats leaving an acrid smell in the night air. When the rear lights finally disappeared around the last visible bend, he found himself standing, staring at the rising quarter moon. Mary had never been a great romantic, but she had always enjoyed watching the patterns of the moon, especially when it burnt red with the dust from the summer harvest. It was under a quarter- moon such as this that they had met working on the local harvest, and five years later Joel had found himself standing at the bedroom window nursing a newly-born Bart in his arms.

The thought of Bart, and the first bite from a mosquito which had settled on his neck, brought him back to the present. *Where is that lad?* he asked himself with growing concern, but then a glance at his watch reminded him that he was more than two hours late in collecting Henry and Lucy. The garage doors groaned at being disturbed as he dragged them open, but he was relieved when the car burst into life at the second turn of the ignition. Pushing it into gear, he backed hesitantly out of the garage onto the drive and immediately stopped. The generator's familiar noise had suddenly disturbed the quiet of the night and the ground floor lights had come on.

....

Bart had left home at dawn of the first day. Before leaving the house he looked into his parent's room and struggled to stifle a laugh at the sight of Henry and Lucy draped across their father's chest. Their combined weight must have been causing Joel some breathing problems, for his mouth gaped open revealing a row of black fillings and his snoring reverberated through the house.

The sight of a pile of his mother's clothes on a chair immediately erased any humour of the scene from his mind, and reminded him of the task in hand. Silently closing the door, he padded as quietly as he could down the creaking stairs and into the kitchen. The dogs greeted him enthusiastically at the prospect of an early walk, and he fed them whilst warming some bread on the range, made a quick milk-tea, and then looked carefully around the room. The walls were lined with hanging pans and other utensils, and near the cooking range hung a set of carving knives. He examined each of them carefully, checking for sharpness and balance, and then selected two which he sharpened further with a wet stone he had brought in from the garden shed. The blades were quality Italian stainless steel which his parents had been given as wedding presents, and the meat carver in particular he was able to hone until it cut his skin with the slightest touch. He wrapped both blades carefully in some clean rags, put them in a pouch in his backpack, threw in some bread, cheese and an apple, and slipped out the back door with the dogs romping happily ahead.

Barny, Pilling's son, was in Bart's class. He had spent many happy hours boring his classmates by boasting of the buildings and boats his father owned, was doing up, rented or whatever. Bart had felt obliged to listen silently like the rest of his class – though they had no affection for Barny himself. They had already learnt from parents that his father was a man to treat resentful with respect. So it was that Bart had a vague mental list of locations and names of places where Pilling might have gone to ground. He was certainly not at home. Word had gone out that the police had called and found the place boarded up with a couple of watchman charged to secure the house and grounds against casual damage. The same word had threatened retribution, when Pilling returned, on anyone who might damage his property. He had obviously decided to lie low until tempers calmed down, but Bart calculated he would not have moved out of the area - he would want to keep an eye on his business activities.

Soon, home was far behind him, and he cut across the fields striking up to the north east. It was a sunny morning and already unusually hot for spring. Bart found himself tiring rapidly as he tried to keep away from the roads and tracks, skirting down into the larger drainage ditches so that he could not be seen across the fields. At times he regretted bringing the dogs. They were enjoying the unexpected game and were constantly chasing rabbits, pheasants and other fowl which rose squawking into the air in a manner guaranteed to attract unwanted attention from any hungry labourer. At other times he welcomed their company amidst the solitude of the fields and marshes, and by mid-afternoon he found himself sitting cuddling them in a ditch while they licked the tears from his face. His list of possible bolt holes for Pilling seemed to be nearing exhaustion, and as it did so the terrifying thought formed in his mind that his quarry might indeed have fled the Island and left him with no hope of revenge.

He had returned home late and exhausted the first day, getting into the house just before dusk. Any later and he knew his father would berate him for his stupidity in being out when the mosquitoes started to swarm, and that would mean a wasted evening washing the dogs, clothes, himself everything in a foul- smelling concoctions the local pharmacy sold to kill any hidden insects.

The second day started much as the first, though this time he turned to the west when he left home. He had spent most of the night mulling over the names he could remember from Barney's idle bragging before finally dozing off in a fitful sleep. As so often happens, in the hazy awareness before dawn he had suddenly remembered Barney talking about a new boat that his dad had bought and moored on the Western Creek. It must have been a big vessel - or Barney was boasting more than usual – because Barney had said several times that they would take *The Rover,* as it was called, down into the Mediterranean one summer. Moreover, anyone who was his –Barney's – friend could come along. Bart knew that the unspoken part of the deal was that they would have to help Barney with his homework, make sure he won at sport and – so some said – engage in what were rumoured to be some unwholesome and unusual male-male sexual activities. What his father possessed in terms of excessive money and power, Barney compensated for with a substantial deficit in almost all areas.

This time he left the dogs at home and by noon he was nearing the end of his sweep of the creek area. He had started near the estuary mouth on the basis that a large ship's draught would prevent it from making its way far up the creek network, but -as the morning progressed- he became increasingly convinced that Barney had been boasting of a phantom vessel, or a one capable of doing no more than bouncing up and down the Humber. His progress had been slowed by a group of Tenters who were slowly moving along one of the minor roads out of the Island. Their transport included old lorries with chattering engines belching out enormous amounts of smoke, and some fine - looking horses pulling state-of- the- art caravans. The poorest had tents neatly folded in carriers pulled by tri and quadricyles, but the thing that struck Bart forcefully was the air of dejection of the entire caravan. Lying securely hidden in a ditch, he watched their progress and pondered why they were on the move now, when the main harvest time was still to come. Then it occurred to him that they might have been one of Pilling's casual labour gangs and that, with recent events, they would move on before things became complicated for them on the Island.

Finally, towards noon, he reached a junction in the water systems and sat down, silently chewing a heel of bread covered in jam which he had taken from the kitchen that morning. Within seconds a small squadron of spring bees arrived and hovered eagerly around his slice, bumping into each other in their eagerness to access the sweet. Angrily, Bart swiped them away with his jacket's sleeve, though the growing swarm returned with greater anger and determination. It was then that, in the silence of the marshes which was almost total bar the buzzing insects, he heard another, distinctly human sound-music. He was sure one of the really popular songs at school was coming from what appeared to be a large hedge on the banks of the creek. Carefully, he brushed the angry insects from his bread and wrapped it again before putting it back in his bag. The bees buzzed around him threateningly and he had to wash his lips several times with water from his flask to remove the last remnants of jam which were drawing them to him. Then, rolling onto his stomach, he cautiously dragged towards the thicket and gently parted a clump of long grass growing at his base.

Almost immediately he let the grass fall back into place. A quick glance had been enough to inform him that he was looking almost directly into a porthole of a substantial vessel. Its size, the brightness of the interior and how it could possibly be so close to shore baffled him, and his first instinct was that the vessel must have been dragged ashore and covered in vegetation. That it was Pilling's he had no doubt. Even a split second's glance had been enough to recognise his blond hair with its developed tonsure, and he was almost convinced that he had also caught sight of Barney. Then he heard a women's voice and a younger person's – not Barney – both of them complaining about the wasps and other insects. These were apparently ruining efforts to cook a meal.

The presence of other people here was an unexpected development. Bart had imagined himself lying in ambush for Pilling and then jumping out, knife drawn, and enjoying the look of terror on the man's face before he embedded the knife deeply in his heart, or slit his throat - or a range of other variants which had crossed his mind during these past days . The presence of so many people was a complication which created the potential of being caught – not something which had previously entered one of Bart's hypothetical scenarios.

Now that his dream assassination had become problematic, Bart was unsure what to do next. For a split second he thought about abandoning the entire project, but that was instantly dismissed –not only did his mother deserve better, but the family also risked dishonour if her death were not avenged. He knew from the Internet and television all about the various forensic skills which were available, but he doubted if Pilling was so important that they would bother out here on the Island if there were no witnesses. People might guess, but guessing did not necessarily imply penalties and, in Pilling's case, guessing could bring substantial popularity. Consequently, several totally unrealistic options passed through a mind characterised more by fury than maturity. An early image included the idea of throwing himself, screaming, into the thicket in the hope of falling through it onto the boat's deck. He would land miraculously in such a way that he would surprise Pilling and immediately finish him off. He eventually dismissed this heroic plot on the grounds that his luck was more likely to carry him straight into the water. Finally, bereft of any meaningful plan, he decided to make his way further up the creek before crossing over and doubling back to get a better view of the boat from the other bank.

It took nearly two hours. The creek system was swollen with the same flood water from the Humber which had been so instrumental in his mother's death, and now reached nearly a half mile further inland than had been normal for the time of year. Even beyond that point the land was treacherously marshy. As a strong swimmer, Bart could have swum across at a number of points, but -despite his anger - he still had enough cool rationality to avoid risking infection from the fetid waters of the creek with its bobbing Nottingham and York turds. These bore witness to the dangers of the water and a potentially early death or bankrupting the family paying medical bills. He had finally found a spot where the creek narrowed between high banks, and here someone had wedged a fallen tree trunk to act as a primitive bridge. From this crossing point he had struggled back through the undergrowth to the place where the boat was hidden.

It was a wasted effort. Double checking against the features he had registered from the other bank, he realised that the boat was no more visible from this bank than the other. From his new vantage point he could see where the banks started to curve in, making what he estimated to be a small basin of some twenty or so metres in length. Whether this was natural or man-made he had no way of knowing, but a considerable amount of skill and time had clearly been exercised in camouflaging the location. Without his chance stop, Bart would have walked straight past and spent the rest of the day in a fruitless hunt for a quarry he had been within feet of.

But now what? He looked at his watch. It was already nearly three. If he left immediately he could still be home before dark, but would Pilling still be here in the morning? Waiting any longer would mean close questioning from his father and, for the first time, Bart started to question the wisdom of what he was doing. 'Would his mother have approved? What would be the consequences for the rest of the family?' were amongst the questions which flitted through his mind. Finally, he decided that his best plan was to make straight for home, see the family – that would allay any concerns and close questioning from his father – and return the following morning. 'Sooner or later Pilling will come out on his own.' he rationalised, though part of him knew that in reality he was cooling from his initial anger and that revenge would have to wait – or perhaps be abandoned forever. He was in the process of wriggling back from his vantage point on the bank when fate intervened as Pilling's voice erupted from the piled vegetation on the other bank. All thought of security and hiding had clearly been abandoned, for out here in the still of the marshes his voice would travel for a mile or more. Amidst the stream of expletives, the word *beer* could be heard repeatedly. Sometimes it was *bloody beer*, sometimes *fucking beer*, sometimes milder *ruddy beer*, but it was clear that Pilling wanted ...*me beer*... and ...*some fucking twat*... had forgotten to buy enough. Pilling's wife responded with her own torrent of insults, and there was much shouting and banging as though the entire ship was being searched for a hidden store of ...*me fucking beer*.... Bart settled back into his position, well hidden by the grasses around him, and prayed fervently that this domestic drama would result in Mrs. Pilling doing his work for him.

....

It was dark when he reached home. He'd covered himself as best he could with his clothes to protect himself against mosquito bites and, despite the pain from his shoulder, he

had managed to slip a spare sweater over his head. Consequently, only his eyes showed between his clothing and the hat he had lodged firmly on his head. Despite these precautions, he could feel the occasional pin-prick as one of the larger, or more determined, insects penetrated the material. Meanwhile, the swarming clouds before his eyes reduced him to swinging wildly with his good arm and bag in an effort to drive them away. The clotted blood on his face probably made him the most attractive meal on the Island that night, and he felt a surge of relief as he rounded a bend in the track to see ships lights bobbing along the Humber. 'Ebb tide' he made an automatic mental note, and grimaced again as a fresh wave of pain swept down the side of his face from his left eye.

Twenty minute later and he was at the door of his home. 'Home' – the word had always held a special meaning for him, and there was still a small corner of his mind that believed he would open the door and find his parents holding hands, sitting in the darkness. Once, two or so years back, he had caught them doing something more, and he had backed quietly out of the door. As with almost all children, even now he found the thought of his parents doing *that* brought a mixture of deep amusement, revulsion and embarrassment. He stopped with his hand on the knob, tried to remove the image from his mind and -without a conscious effort on his part- he found himself slumped, weeping in a corner of the porch.

The tears both stung his face and seemed to instantly galvanize his winged escorts into a fresh wave of attacks. Struggling to his feet, he closed the outer door, turned on the porch light and –taking a deep breath– swept the area thoroughly with the insecticide which lived on the ledge by the porch window. After a minute he breathed out again and savoured the spray's faint perfume – it was strange how many bad things seemed so good. When he felt sure that the last mosquito was dead, he opened the main door and was greeted by the dogs whose leaking bladders revealed how desperate they were to toilet themselves. Disregarding every rule in the house, he opened the door and let them sweep past him into the night. Closing the external door again, he walked straight into the house before closing the inner door. It took only a few seconds to realize the forms dancing around the light bulb were evidence of his failure to spray a second time. *My parents -my dad,* he corrected himself *will kill me,* he muttered aloud, but instead of using the insecticide again he strode directly to the bathroom.

Turning on the mirror light, he recoiled in shock at the face before him. Pilling's second blow had left a huge area of bruised and cut flesh which encircled his left eye and joined with a stream of dried blood which had flowed from a subsequent blow to his forehead.

Taking off his hat, he carefully inspected the open gash beneath his hair and then gently touched his nose. *At least that isn't broken,* he reassured himself, sliding his fingers down both flanks. He wasn't sure if two or more ribs were fractured but, if they were not, Bart wondered if it were possible for the pain to be much greater. As for his shoulder, Jacob had fired from maximum range and, because of this, the shot was lodged relatively superficially in his skin. He managed to prize most of the pellets out with the help of a pair of tweezers his mum had used for picking her eyebrows, and felt some satisfaction as one-by-one they pinged onto the porcelain of the sink. He was so absorbed that he failed to notice the bathroom door opening silently behind him until a voice boomed in his ears: *Bart, what the fuck have you done?*

....

His injuries were, of course, a result of his own stupidity. Pilling had suddenly appeared from the other side of the creek like a ghostly apparition after his drunken row about his *bloody beer*. His wealth, or power, was such that he had managed to acquire sophisticated camouflage used by the military, and whilst the far side of the creek appeared to be a simple continuation of the vegetation and water elsewhere, this was simply a mimic of the surroundings. Pilling exited from this and clambered unsteadily into a small motorboat with a clear determination to …*go and get some more fucking beer*! as he shouted back to his wife. Bart had almost laughed openly when her head also appeared suddenly, as though from a bramble bush, and then an arm broke out and threw an empty bottle in a symbolically inaccurate attempt to hit her husband.

That's bloody slow Bart mumbled as he found himself calculating Pilling's speed. Whether from lack of haste, or drunkenness, the craft's throttle was barely open and it was proceeding at little more than walking pace. Checking that Bev Pilling's detached head had disappeared, Bart slid away from his vantage point. He made some quick calculations. There were only two places locally Pilling could buy alcohol. One was a rundown shop up on the main road called 'Tesco *Conv Sto'*, a name which the older people appeared to understand but which baffled Bart and his mates. Another, and the more likely destination if Pilling were to keep to the waterways, was a floating barge on the Humber which traded with both passing ships and Island folk. There was no need for Pilling to make a choice until after he had passed the old road bridge, so Bart made his plans accordingly.

Keeping to the ditches and low ground, and using the undergrowth to screen his progress, he pulled slowly ahead of the chugging boat. Once or twice the engine seemed to falter, and Bart's heart missed a beat at the prospect of Pilling turning round and giving him the dilemma of how to attack a large, apparently crowded, vessel whose camouflage system he was still struggling to understand. Once, he pulled so far ahead that Bart totally lost the sound of the engine. He crept up onto the embankment in time to see Pilling appear round a bend in the river, steering erratically and apparently struggling to keep his head upright in a drunken stupor. His condition irritated Bart considerably. The idea of a Pilling being unaware of his impending death was not appealing - his dream was that of *the bastard* being fully conscious of his imminent fate and consumed by fear. There was nothing about avoiding fear and pain —and some remorse even?- through some drunken cloud.

Moving further ahead, he came to the remains of the road bridge about a mile along the river. There were still people who were brave – or stupid- enough to use it, but the side furthest from Bart's approach was clearly totally dilapidated and he paused to assess the bridge's condition before starting to cross. How anyone trusted to drive over this was beyond him. A section about a metre wide and two long had totally collapsed and fallen into the river - Bart could see what appeared to be its tip protruding from the water below. The collapse must have happened recently; the debris blocked some of the navigable channel and a passing vessel would have been obliged to do its duty and shifted it to the side, or even dragged it out. For Bart, the good news was that Pilling would have to slow even further to navigate his way round it, and with a new certainty he decided that this was the place where his mother's death would be avenged.

The sound of Pilling's boat could be heard clearly again now and, lying low to avoid being seen, Bart opened his bag and carefully unwrapped the bundle of knives he had stolen from the kitchen. The largest was an old meat knife his father had used from time immemorial. Nearly thirty centimetres long, it was – as always – honed to a fine cutting edge and Bart decided that he would use this to finish Pilling as he passed under the bridge. If his first blow was not fatal, he reasoned, he could jump through the gaping hole and complete the job. There was nothing heroic about the plan -a cowardly way of dealing with Pilling he admitted to himself - but in a fair fight Pilling's greater strength and experience would prevail. Fairness would not kill the bastard.

Exactly what happened next remained something of a mystery for the remainder of Bart's life. Lying tensely on what remained of the bridge's surface, he slowly became aware of a rumbling sound and a slight trembling of the tarmac under his head. Looking up, he realized that a horse and wagon were slowly approaching the bridge from the landside, the horses' hooves and wagon wheels spilling a cloud of dust into the air. This was an unwanted complication. The plan was to kill and to get away with the act, but not to find the Island littered with witnesses whose gossip might reach the authorities. However, the Waggoner appeared not to have seen him yet, but was absorbed by Pilling's eccentric navigation downstream. With luck, Bart calculated, Pilling would be under the bridge- and dead- many minutes before his own presence was even noted. He hugged the surface as though it would make some difference to the possibility of being seen and briefly popped his head through the gaping hole, confident that it would be hidden by the deep shadows under the bridge.

He looked back upstream towards the approaching craft. Pilling seemed to have sobered slightly, for at that moment he suddenly looked around, checked his watch, and opened the engine throttle fully. Bart cursed quietly to himself- the new turn of speed would make his attack more difficult. Drawing back slightly as the rusted steel and tarmac surface creaked ominously under his weight, he checked the progress of the wagon and then looked back into the creek. 'This is no good,' he thought to himself, realizing that he would be able to see nothing from that angle until Pilling was directly under the gap - this would give him little time to act. Momentarily, he was reassured by the thought that Pilling would have to slow to clear the debris below, but the boat's constant speed caused him to question whether Pilling was too drunk to see the hazard and would plough recklessly past.

Now, the roar of the engine appeared to be almost directly beneath him and, leaning forward again, he looked down just in time to see the dinghy's front enter the shadow of the bridge. Then, without warning, he felt the surface beneath him shudder and he found himself tipping forward as the section on which he lay pivoted on some hidden fault. Desperately, he attempted to lever himself backwards, dropping his knife in the process, but it was to no avail and he suddenly found himself flapping his limbs wildly like a stricken bird as he slid with uncontrolled speed through the gaping breach and towards the water below. Out of the corner of one eye, he saw the blade drop loudly into the water just ahead of Pilling.

Pilling was universally considered by the Island to be 'an intelligent bastard' and, despite the alcohol haze, the glint of the falling object was sufficient to alert his drunken senses to possible danger. However, even if he had been totally sober, there was no way that

Pilling could slow or change his course with sufficient alacrity to avoid the falling mass, nor was it possible for Bart to stop his fall. The two impossibles coincided with Pilling's attempt to change both speed and direction. Bart fell clumsily onto the front of the craft where he lay sprawling and winded. The impact of his fall was such that Pilling was almost thrown into the water, the boat rocking violently and momentarily threatening to capsize. He had been standing upright at the tiller when Bart fell, and the boat's motion caused him to sway, pulling the tiller sharply to the left and directing the craft straight into the mangled debris from the bridge. The bow immediately rose into the air, throwing Bart towards Pilling who had been even more unbalanced by the impact. Momentarily, Pilling's jaw dropped in surprise, then confusion gave way to alarm as recognition dawned. *You're that woman's lad, what the fuck do you think you are up to?*

Unthinkingly, Bart's hand reached for, and drew, a knife he kept in his boots for everyday use around the house. Seeing the danger, Pilling immediately clenched his fist and swung viciously. The blow scraped across Bart's scalp, gouging deeply through the skin where a ring dug under the flesh and tore out hair in its transit. His eyes streaming with the pain, Bart scrabbled to his feet just in time to receive a second blow directly on his left eye. Concussed, he staggered back, desperately aware of the fact that, despite Pilling's drink, he was proving no match. However, through the pain Bart had kept a firm grip on his knife and, grasping it firmly, he lunged forward.

The sweeping blow met only empty air and, totally unbalanced, he fell forward. In so doing he opened himself to another blow aimed again directly at his face. The fight would have ended if this had found its target, but the boat suddenly settled back into the water, carried off the debris by the combined weight of the two fighting at the stern. Pilling, who had raised himself to his full height and drawn back his arm to deliver his punch, was thrown off balance by the motion. Arms whirling in mid-air like a crazed windmill, he tried to regain his balance before staggering backwards. In so doing he caught the tiller a glancing blow, tipped over it, and fell headlong towards the water.

In his drunken stupor Pilling had largely disregarded the obstruction under the bridge and kept the engine throttle nearly fully open. Now, despite the drink, he realized the danger posed by the propeller blades churning a substantial froth on the surface. He twisted violently midair, pulling his legs back in an attempt at a backward somersault which would pull him clear of the slicing blades. His body cleared the back of the boat and he sank headfirst into the water, but his attempt at a somersault had failed and his right leg crashed down into the water directly by the blades. There was a monetary splutter, and change in the beat of the motor, before the water turned red. Seconds later, Pilling's head burst through the water's surface, screaming in agony. This was not one of Bart's planned or imagined scenarios, and instinctively he pulled himself to the edge of the boat and proffered a helping hand. Instead of taking it, Pilling backed off, fear and pain in his eyes and a growing pool of blood marking his progress through the water. *Come on you bastard, I'm trying to help you!* Bart shouted above the roar of the engine.

Almost immediately the surface of the water next to him exploded into a dapple of small vortexes and he felt his right shoulder sting as though he had been simultaneously attacked by a hundred wasps. Puzzled, Bart look down to see blood oozing from a collection of small holes in his jacket. He had spent time enough hunting out here in the marshes to immediately recognize them as a gunshot wound. Looking up, he saw Pilling's eldest son Jacob seated on the cart. He was struggling to shove a new cartridge into an old shotgun and Bart cursed himself for his stupidity in not recognizing him earlier. Then, concluding that he could nothing for Pilling if dead, he jumped into the water and swam desperately for the shelter of the reeds on the far bank.

Chapter V
Frontier stuff: fifteen years later

BailriggWall Strategic Reserve Area. Northern wastes. Northwestern stormbelt.

Complement: 1 Commander, 1 Captain, 2 Technical Lieutenants, 25 other ranks. 60 mobile and static robotic defence units.

Annual rain 450 c.ms. Annual sundays 185. Average summer day temperature 25 centigrade. Average winter day temperature 14 centigrade. Average wind 30 knots. Maximum recorded wind 280 knots.

Data Courtesy of National Military Met Service with the support of Channel 8.

Remember: Channel 8 brings you the best of adult 24 hours a day.

March 2nd

Lieutenant Gary Brown hated the north. More precisely, he had hated the northerners since most of his unit had been killed in an ambush near CarlisleWall around three years earlier. It wasn't that he lacked sympathy for northerners - his mother could actually trace her roots back to Scotland - but he felt that it was their struggle which had resulted in his being selected for military service. It really wasn't fair. Most of the military were paid professionals - maniac thugs if his opinion was asked, which it never was - and it was only his misfortune to have studied electronic communications at university which had got him into this mess. He complained even more bitterly because his parents had sacrificed everything to pay his fees and to see him trained properly, and it was this training which had got him conscripted. And now he had lost five years of his life to a poorly paid job at Bailrigg I defending against rebels on the frontiers of civilization. *'Only another two months to go and this nightmare is over!'* he shouted to himself once more. Most of the day was spent with this single thought.

His posting was on a tall tower which had once been part of the University of Lancaster, Bowland Forest and the Lake District. At low tide, an old, rusting sign was still legible, welcoming to the university which had been built on a small hill outside the city during the 1960s. Now, much of the land to the west was covered by water from Morecambe Sea or consisted of treacherous marshes which changed constantly under the influence of sea and river currents. To the east, efforts continued to persuade the hostile soil to yield commercially viable arable harvests rather than yet more mutton. His understanding was that some of the newer modified strains had shown promise, and this probably explained the increase in raids from northerners seeking supplies of fresh food. The marshes provided a more secure frontier than the open sea to the west from which Bailrigg had been attacked more than once – with little success - by Scotties and Free Fishers alias *'pirates'* (government information service Monday) alias *'Dutch terrorists'* (government information service by Friday).

What remained of the university buildings had been heavily fortified and circumscribed by a Wall for protection against storms and raiders. From Bailrigg 1 it was possible to see westwards directly to the tip of the Blackpool Tower automated fire station sitting further out to sea. To the east and south lay a chain of support stations on a series of islands collectively called Bowland's Tip. Each station was automated and controlled from Bailrigg I. The entire complex constituted a dedicated weapons support and intelligence centre for the remnants of the old gas and oil collection facilities in the Morecambe Sea area, and - more importantly historically - for the remaining facility behind Heysham NuclearWall. It had once been a strategically important post with an initial garrison of over a hundred technicians and troops. However, in recent years the Morecambe fields had been deemed totally exhausted even allowing for the critical demand for carbon fuels, and Heysham's facilities abandoned after the damage of the last Great Storm. Consequently, the defence systems had slowly decayed in both quality and personnel.

London said it was lack of money, but Brown saw it as more a problem of corruption and priorities. It was just like the area commander - Anderson - a big, vicious Midlander who everyone knew sold preserved foods and sandbags and other essentials to the local fishers in exchange for regular nights with their wives and daughters. He had a good crop to pick from too- his command ran up through Bowland's Tip to the high ground of the Pennines and then 80 miles both south and north as far as ManchesterWall.

Apart from some jumpy, porno stuff from Channel 8 on an old commercial satellite -which had somehow survived stuck in geostationary orbit- and some odds and ends dragged from the Internet, Brown had not seen a woman for half a year. Brown was amazed that Channel 8 was still there. How a commercial satellite was still up and functioning when the last of the British military capability had been lost years before was beyond any logic. Again, he attributed this to somebody having enough food or other valuables to have pleased somebody somewhere. It even suggested influence with the Americans, as they had been the ones – probably their religious crazies - who had been busy blowing things out of the sky and space for years.

Talking about women, which was the main theme in Brown's head when he was not bemoaning being in a decaying Wall facility, there had been an available blonde private in one tech group. Inconveniently she had been drowned months ago in a tunnel collapse. Recently, life had been spent crawling through the tangles of cables which constituted the spine of the control systems, linking them both physically and electronically to the cameras, sensors and fire control systems which constituted Bailrigg I's defence net. He resented the time spent struggling with components which had been scheduled for replacement years before, but he knew his life might well depend on nursing them along: for another 60 odd days.

Days had passed uneventfully enough for his first year - boringly so at times. It had been a soft posting - the Manchester clubs and brothels were only 10 minutes flight time away. But then there had been more cut-backs after Treaty II and the loss of revenue after the failure of CarlisleWall during the last raid and the death of most of its inhabitants. Combined, they had left the zone isolated and exposed to raiders. Another 60 days and he could return home to his parents. When he had last spoken to them on his mobile they had talked about getting him a job and a local girl who wanted to marry, and how - with the money and bounties from the past 5 years (not to mention what had been made on the side) - he might afford a small place in one of the higher parts outside London, or perhaps even within LondonWall itself. 59 days from tomorrow.

Today had been unusual. Not dangerous -there'd been no attacks for weeks and Captain Henderson said that the Scots didn't have it in them for anything else after Carlisle. But Sergeant Hussein had always reckoned that was a load of toss and he's always said that he knew the Scots better *Cos me family lived with them in Dumfries afore the troubles.* Hussein reckoned that they had taken lots of computer stuff from the Companies before they had pulled out from a place called Silicon Glen before it was lost to flooding, and that the Scots were shit hot with the electronics. But Hussein was dead now, so his views didn't count. No one listened to an idiot who got his brains blasted when he forgot the old saying *'Never put your head up when there's a Scottie about.'*

Today was unusual- and very difficult. Yesterday hadn't been good either. Usually the system went down totally and the problems was fairly easy to find and get the system back on. But now there were more general - diffuse - problems. Images and data kept breaking up and then ghosting back, so it seemed that the entire area-sea marshes and land - within Bailrigg 1 control was on the move. Initially, the alarms had treated it as a sneak attack from across the marshes and numerous islets to the north and west, but a visual scan had shown nothing. Then the same problem has started on the eastern perimeter. Brown had been working fruitlessly on the problem for about four hours before he broke for a revolting drink of LikeCoffee, and now he was back on the job he had become even more convinced that it was some problem with oscillation. Perhaps one of the submerged buildings had collapsed onto a field trip as had happened only the month before- or it was perhaps something to do with a gas eruption from the water's bed. There had been plenty of those in the old days caused by injecting water under pressure to vent the gas and oil. But then, that didn`t seem to explain the problems from the land. Consequently, instead of being in fresh air and sunshine which was today at the top of the tower, he was in the gloom and fetid air of a control tunnel two levels with water seeping in from Morecambe Sea. Down meant cables, dim lights and the usual stifling, sweaty heat. Being at the top usually meant wind and rain. Not much of a trade.

His current monitor was an old VIP which, like everything, should have been replaced years before. The fact that it hadn't, and the reduced garrison, served to reinforce the general feeling that Bailrigg I was increasingly expendable. It served no purpose now except to provide some oil and gas from the dying storage tanks for Manchester - when it could afford it. Without an income, the post was simply a drain on the national government, so things that broke got mended or stayed broke. For the garrison, the reduction of chopper flights to Manchester from a weekly to a fortnightly service spoke volumes - aviation grade fuel was too expensive a commodity to spend on a loss - making garrison.

'Only 59 days to go,' he found himself thinking yet again as he gazed into the monitor. The chaotic data suggested movement or sorts - of comings and goings, of sighs and groans and creaks. The visual monitors indicated nothing but the odd fish and eel swimming past, though a few fishers had been spotted out past the most distant

islands. Perplexed and fatigued by constant staring into the monitor, Brown scratched his head and ran his hand through his damp military cut.

Damp? It was hot and sticky yes, but not enough to justify his soaking mat. His mind froze for a second as it took in this new fact. *Henderson, bring me a flash. Be quick willyu!* he shouted to a trooper further down the dimly lit corridor. Henderson looked up from his own monitor before meandering over with a large flash gun.

Whatup? he enquired. The trooper, another Londoner, had no respect for conscript lieutenants. Like most professional troopers he thought them a waste - nothing more than time servers.

We got a leak' retorted Brown.

You joke? Through two metres of armoured concrete? That aint possible. The two men peered up, following the powerful beam of the flash. There, almost immediately above them was a glistening sheen of water droplets slowly seeping through the concrete. *You the technical expert. What the hell causing that?* Henderson demanded in Londoneese.

As if in answer, a tiny jet of water flew spurted into his face. He squealed in pain almost instantly and jumped back, pulling madly at his face. Finally – swearing profusely – he made a gesture as if throwing something to the floor.

You lost it? demanded Brown, both alarmed and amused at these antics. Going crazy was an occupational hazard in the military, and he carefully checked Henderson for any arms he was carrying.

Get lost your fucking self!' Henderson blurted. There was no trace of the respect owed an officer, though out here on the frontier troopers had been fatally beaten for less. *That not water. That's acid or somit – really hurt me face. There must be a leak in a battery system somewhere.*

There's no battery around here. But what the ....? Peering down in the gloom, Brown had caught sight of a tiny, silvery form flashing as the lighting caught it. With a screwdriver he gently stirred the pool of water until he felt a gentle tug at the end. He lifted the tip into the beam of the torch and, as he did so, a small form was revealed grasping the tip of the driver and rotating slowly whilst the light caught the glistening grooves on its body.

Is that a fish or some sort, or an insect? Never seen anything like it before, but it bloody hurt.' grunted Henderson, embarrassed at his own apparent weakness- troopers did not feel pain when attacked by tiny creatures. Grabbing the screwdriver, he stamped viciously on the twisting form. It simply continued to twist - and started to gouge the slightest furrow in the dirt beneath it.

If Henderson had been watching, he would have seen Brown's face whiten and his eyes look around apprehensively. *Insect? That's no insect!* he snapped. *That's a flaming nano - you know, micro machine. Look, it's trying to bore into the floor. That explains all the monitors going crazy it's picked them up eating away at the concrete. That's why nothing is working! The bloody Scots must have set them things on us. With them at work the whole place will collapse into the sea, and we'll drown like sewer rats down here!* He turned without a second's hesitation and fled towards the upper levels stairway.

Perhaps he would have made it too. Perhaps less time spent thinking about another woman, less time counting his days would have resulted in his identifying the cause of their problems and reaching the surface. As it was, Technical Lieutenant Gary Brown and Trooper 2nd Class Lee Henderson had made it to Level 5 when the external wall collapsed and a lethal wave of water swept them back into the bowels of the building.

Chapter VI
LondonWall

LondonWall - Strategic Governance Area
Military Complement:
1ˢᵗ, 2nd and 3rd Divisions National Security Service.
1ˢᵗ and 9th Divisions Armoured Tactical Corp
1st and 2nd Guards Regiments
Eastern Fleet Headquarters: Navy of the Federal United States of America
2 Battalions United States Federal Marines
Squadron of the New England National Air Guard
Annual rain 600 c.ms. Annual sundays 130. Average summer temperature day 29 centigrade. Average winter temperature day 12 centigrade.
Average wind 27 knots. Maximum recorded wind 168 knots
Data Courtesy of National Military Met Service with the support of Channel 8.
Remember: Channel 8 brings you the best of adult 24 hours a day.

March 3ʳᵈ

From his window on the sixth floor, John Macgregor had mused over such scenes every morning since his appointment to London. Standing at the window often reminded him of his youth at a Manchester comprehensive; he had always arrived early each day in order to savour some solitude before the arrival of the bullying masses. Manchester had been called the Windy City even before the GreatWinds started, and he unwisely cherished vivid memories of cycling to school in the rain and storms of winter, dripping up the stairs to his class room on the third floor, and gazing over the adjacent houses whilst the heat from the radiator steamed him dry. He had never liked -or been liked by - the other children. They had regarded him as too bookish -"a right little book-worm" or a "stuck-up black bastard"- and Macgregor had always cherished an illogical satisfaction in feeling himself dry and warm whilst they struggled through the rain in a vain attempt to avoid being late yet again.

Getting to Cambridge had saved his life. Another year in the slums of Manchester and he knew he would have killed himself- or so he seemed to remember thinking.

It was March. It was a beautiful morning. They had almost all been beautiful mornings for months -or was it years? Almost every day seemed the same - a thin screen of clouds dashing across a blue sky. Then there were the other days. The days when the wind came screaming in from the south or west and drenched everything in incalculable amounts of water. From his armour plated window it was possible to see across Hyde Park Parking as far as the burnt-out ruins of Buckingham Palace. The west wing, which had survived the fighting, was again shrouded in scaffolding in an attempt to repair it after the winter storms. Even at the highest levels there was now a debate as to whether the building should be abandoned or placed in one of the protective environments —essentially storm-resistant domes- which had been constructed around a number of the other important cultural and politically significant sites. In addition to the new glass, Macgregor's own building had been topped by ten floors surrounded by new landscaping which —the engineers assured — would change the aerodynamics and leave the building less exposed to the winds.

This had always been one of the most attractive areas of London, and rows of serried tulips still gave it a touch of brilliant, spring colour. They were one of the latest genetic strains and were doing well — fortunate in that no further resources were to be allowed for non-food research. A gardener was busy spraying from a pack whose fine brown mist spoke much for the efficiency of the local sewerage recycling system. *'I wonder if the Prime Minister's turds are in that lot?* he found himself asking the figure seated behind him. *Bloody waste of time anyway, that area will have to be converted to food production. Looks bad for government to be producing flowers while people are hungry.*

He turned and looked thoughtfully at a much younger man who

sitting busily scanning the wad of documents on his hand lap on the far side of Macgregor's desk. In his early thirties, Bart was a good six feet tall and built as one who spent several hours a week working hard in the staff gym. His blond-ginger hair was always trailed across his right forehead in order, as Macgregor had quickly realized, to hide a jagged scar. When they had first met, Macgregor had been struck by his resemblance to one of his heroes from his youthful reading, in books his grandfather had adored as a child, about a young wizard with a special mark on his forehead. *You know*, he continued *when I first visited my grandfather in London I swore I would never live here -never get sucked into the rat race. I was right to follow my first instincts - but soon realized that instincts have never paid any bills. Anyway, we have a good Wall here.*

It took some seconds for the younger man to register that some kind of reaction was expected of him. Nervously, he lifted his head. *Yu what sir? I'm very sorry but I wasn't listening – I was studying the documents again.*

I was saying that I never wanted to come to London. Macgregor replied tersely. He hated the way La Fontaine always said *'Yu what?'* It wasn't that he was unique in this. It had been accepted English for years now, and was almost de rigueur amongst the under 30s. But he did feel that it somehow cheapened La Fontaine. He liked him intensely, unwisely given the difference in rank between the two, and couldn't help but feel that the coarseness of the southern England dialect ill-suited someone with La Fontaine's claimed French pedigree. Claimed was the operative word if he chose to be precise, but he really liked him – perhaps was attracted to him? That was – he would admit reluctantly to himself on Saturday evenings after a bottle of whisky -part of the explanation, though Macgregor kept pushing this thought to the back of his mind and preferred instead to admit only that he was reacting against his own experience of prejudice. He was the non-white first to have ever held Interior and Environment and his career had always been marked by the constant need to overcome the racial barriers. He had always felt the need to be perfect in everything just to be accepted as an equal, and that included his spoken language. It hurt him to find such skills irrelevant in a *Yu wat* society and it hurt even more deeply to know that someone like La Fontaine had to dissemble linguistically in order to achieve what he considered to be *'conformity'*. Not, he reminded himself, that his dissembling stopped at the spoken word. He had an interesting background including a false name – what had he started life as. Brian? Barry? No, it was…Bart. And there was the outstanding warrant for attempted murder from some irrelevant security unit in the far north. It was an old case and the potential victim had been murdered by someone else years before, though the dead man's family kept pressing for action over the first case. La Fontaine had proved to be a highly effective assistant and Macgregor was happy to keep this, and more, useful information in case it could be used at a future time.

Why was that then sir? enquired La Fontaine. He had noticed the irritation in his master's voice, attributing it to stress and a lack of sleep. *Natural, given what he is dealing with. Try and keep him sweet Bart, Henry, whoever you are.*

Because I was ambitious but didn't want to be corrupted replied Macgregor. *I was trying to do the impossible- to be powerful and to prove myself without getting involved with the seedier side of politics. You know something? I actually used to believe that we should tell the truth. For me London seemed to epitomize what needed to be done -too big, too fast, too corrupt -too everything. You'll remember that it was here that the government had to establish the silvers don't you? What was it, about fifteen years or so years ago?*

Mmm, so I believe sir. I remember seeing them on television news about the time when… His voice trailed away as though other memories were of greater importance. *No*, he re-started *I think it must have been longer ago than that -may have been more than fifteen when I think about it. Would eighteen make sense?*

Yes, well, whenever that happened I really felt that something had been lost. My great grandfather told me that he came to Britain in the 1950s partly because the living standards were better and partly because this country had a reputation for being...for being somehow gentler in the way the people were treated. So now I have the power, I've proved things to myself and everyone else, but I had to compromise so much on the way. And now near the top? Well, it's like standing on top of a very rotten manure heap.

Why's that sir? La Fontaine queried. He already knew the probable answer, and the question risked irritating his boss even further, but he needed more time to clear his head and think more clearly simply after what he believed was the ultimate in hangovers. *'Must have been something wrong with the bottle,'* he mused to himself and felt again in his pocket for the packet of pain killers he was sure he had brought with him that morning. He had memories of the local farmers talking about manure heaps when he was younger, but that was years ago now and before his breakdown after he had left home and spent time in hospital – well, that was what he called the first year at his aunt's Manchester house. After that he had thrown himself into a new identity and working night and day to ensure he got the possible grades from his studies- he felt he had erased so much from the last two decades or so of his life.

This is a problematic manure heap?' he queried tentatively with a pathetic attempt at humour. Manure heaps could, after all, be damned good. There were associated with increased food production, reduced waste and keeping the urban population busy doing minor, useless tasks, so there might be something of significance in the report that he'd missed. *The report, that damned report!* he found himself shouting internally. *Is it what you feel about the reaction to the report sir?* he voiced.

Macgregor gave La Fontaine a withering glance, thought better of making yet another comment about the quality of modern training and made a mental note to simplify his vocabulary in future. If La

Fontaine's hangover had possessed the speed, he would have recognized the scornful response. *It most certainly is Henry. What do you honestly think about it?*

La Fontaine furrowed his brows as he customarily did when wished to appear deep in thought. The action revealed the scar running beneath his fringe into his hair line. *'Must have fallen badly when he was young to have got that,'* Macgregor found himself thinking, and then cursed himself for his growing tendency to drift away from key issues being considered.

La Fontaine certainly wasn't the most expansive person in terms of his vocabulary, but he lacked neither the perception, knowledge nor intelligence to give a more immediate response. However, experience had taught him that it was unwise to appear too intelligent -certainly no more intelligent than senior officers-and the appearance of deep concentration gave him time to consider the wider ramifications of anything me might say. *Never trust anyone,* his mother had once told him, and he had found the advice invaluable in rising through the ranks of what was now called the Administrative Corp – so much more efficient in its implications than the old Civil Service. He treated even Macgregor, for whom he had more respect than any other minister, with an automatic, and considerable, caution. He had worked hard, and paid much, for this post and had no intention of losing it despite his not infrequent battle with alcohol.

However, this morning he had a clear problem -he had not actually finished reading the report. He looked again at the papers in his hand, each page filled with neatly processed graphs and data and let time give greater weight to his pause. He should have read it the night before, but it had been a long day at work and Rachael had already opened a bottle of fine Chateau Worcester '19 before he'd had the chance to say *No.* So that, and the invitation of an amorous early night, had resulted in him neglecting the report until he had made an early start at five. It had been a fantastic night of eroticism –what couldn't that woman do with her tongue?! But whether it was worth risking his post....

He stalled. *I think it isn't really telling us anything we didn't know - I mean it fits in with all the long terms trends and projections. I think that the main problem is the usual one - what do we do with the information? We cannot persuade people to cut-back any further at present, not if we really intend to hold proper elections next year as the Premier promised.....*

You don't think we can swing the '...for the sake of the country and the world...' bit again? interrupted Macgregor.

No, not really. That got worn a bit thin years ago when we had to prop-up the Welsh provisional government by sending extra troops – Americans at that. People took that because they were worried about energy and food supplies, but I can't see them voluntarily taking much more .....and that is certainly what the intelligence is saying. There is already a lot of moaning about the companies not having to make the same sacrifices and people are saying that we plan to reduce their living standards but protect the rich – though even most of the employers and farmers are united against us. As for the fishers!! They'll work with the Dutch, French or whoever allows them into their fishing grounds with the minimum of bribes. Politically, it's an impossible situation. Henry found himself relaxing slightly. Somehow the conversation had drifted back into areas which the two men had already evaluated a hundred times, and whatever was novel in this most recent report seemed to be of less immediate significance

The desk that dominated the centre of the room was a large one, which Macgregor had described as *Victorian* in one of their first meetings. *Ornate, and made from real oak...* Macgregor had proudly proclaimed, using historical terms which had cost La Fontaine another thirty minutes or so researching when he was already hard pressed for time and data access. It had belonged to Macgregor's grandfather - or great grandfather according to one family tradition - who had bought it from a London antique dealer in the 1950s or 60s and had been purchased with money he and his new wife had received as a wedding gift from relatives in Trinidad *So you can study hard and get on,* they had apparently said. At the time it had appeared overly large and ostentatious in a dilapidated semi-detached terrace in London's Brixton, but the hours sweated over it had born fruit in slow promotion from tube driver to a traffic manager for an organisation La Fontaine remembered Macgregor calling London Transport- another mini-research project. In Macgregor's office its age seemed incongruous with the harsh modernity of concrete, steel and glass, but it served as a comfortable perch from which he could lecture or discuss and -unwittingly- give notice of the seriousness of any issue. This had served La Fontaine well. He had long ago noticed that when Macgregor became tense or agitated he would wrap his ankles and calves around the scrolled legs of the desk and use them as an anchor whilst Macgregor engaged in the gentlest of rocking- to and fro, to and fro- of his entire, imposing frame.

From this simple observation La Fontaine had learned to judge both mood and the seriousness of the issue and had out-witted his more able but less observant peers. He was now Primary Advisor in Macgregor's office and had found his ability to adapt to his master's moods result in the imperceptible development of more personal sentiments- more suited to those of father and son. Perhaps Macgregor's greatest weakness was his lack of natural children. Macgregor gave a final glance through the window and then assumed his customary position astride the corner of the desk. La Fontaine noticed he was becoming increasingly slow on his feet. *'Never takes his medication. More than just weight and age, perhaps a touch of arthritis,'* he thought to himself.

The idea brought with it a mixture of feelings. Macgregor's retirement or death could mean loss of position or possible promotion. It would all depend on how the game went, and La Fontaine knew he had made many enemies over the years serving Macgregor.

How old are you? His boss demanded suddenly.

Thirty. La Fontaine lied, surprised by the unexpected shift in conversation and trying to remember the details from his very expensive fake documentation.

And your son?

John will be three this summer. Mind you, he looks older – very tall and strong. Rachael claims it was all the breast feeding that made him grow so...

And I ask you again, what difference do you think the report will make to you and your family? interrupted Macgregor tersely. *Have you given that any thought? I'm sixty nine, so I've had a reasonable run for my money. But you. I would have thought that you would be much more concerned. What is it about you Henry? Have you lost the ability to show concern ? Is it your professional veneer, or could it be it hasn't dawned on you yet what is starting to happen?*

Unusually, La Fontaine found himself lost for words. He had seen Macgregor angry before, often in a stage-managed tirade intended to press-home a point, but he had never before seen such genuine emotion in the man. The words themselves were too vague to give him any real inclination as to Macgregor's perception of the situation, and he hadn't finished reading the damned report. So what was so important? The conclusion? No. He'd read that first. So Macgregor must have heard something from his intelligence people or simply have a keener perception of the implication of the content. Or had the conclusion been doctored in some way and didn't accurately reflect the contents?

Don't you see Henry? Macgregor continued. *People will not be prepared to accept these measures if they are seen as being imposed from outside and we have been so busy lying to them that we cannot publicly change policy. It isn't that the coalition government would collapse, they –and I include myself - are all too scared for that, but there are a lot of people out there in the streets who already use violence to earn enough to keep their families. Many of them were once very decent, law-abiding citizens. If we lose them, what hope is there?*

But Sir, we have the National Security Service and the army. They put down the troubles on the Scottish frontier without too much difficulty. You aren't suggesting that we can't rely on them are you? They have the best rations in the country and got a pay increase last year. They have the least to complain about. Put down the Scots without too much difficulty! Macgregor exploded. *Christ man, you know as well as I do that the Scots have been a thorn in our side for years since then, especially when they get together with the Dutch. They are worse than that Irish lot used to be in the past - what were they called again, the IRA in various forms or something? Come here!* he demanded, walking to the window. Henry jumped anxiously from his chair and joined his master at the window. *How long have you been working with me now?* Henry immediately felt a surge of unease. Clearly he had been rumbled- the old man realised that he hadn't been keeping up with things and that he had failed to understand something in the report, or that it was really a bit beyond him. Well, perhaps it was, but he'd paid a good price on the side market for this post and he wasn't going to lose it easily. He almost found himself thinking the old term '*black market'* but found it insulting in Macgregor's presence. Attack was the best form of defence he decided. *Three years Sir. And I have found it a real pleasure and very stimulating. I hope that I have provided good service Sir.*

And what kind of changes have you seen in that time? retorted Macgregor disdainfully. *Down there for example?* He demanded, jerking his thumb in the direction of Hyde Park Parking.

Well... Henry paused, suspecting he was being led into a trap. *Most managers were still allowed to car to work until Directive 23 .... something. I can't remember the exact details. I must say it seems a bit desolate down there, though the air is much better for it. I can provide the technical figures to prove that.*

And how did people react?

Badly. There were protests and riots all over the place. We were forced to abandon our love affair with the car and other forms of private transport in just two months. Then there was the unemployment and logistics chaos which followed.

But you appear to have forgotten about Scotland? You remember Scotland I assume? Macgregor demanded with considerable irony.

Well yes, of course, Henry replied, attempting to hide the testiness in his voice. It was not only that he couldn't really understand the full drift of the conversation, but he felt insulted to be asked such a stupid question – surely he wasn't doing that badly. It was just before he had come to Interior and Environment, in fact it was before the security side of Environment had even developed -so it was just good old *'Environment and Regions'*.

You seemed to forget them a few seconds ago! Macgregor barked. *Controlled them without any difficulty? What a load of rubbish! How can anyone forget the Scots? They are a permanent threat to national security. What was the name of that idiot? Was it Hardy? He and his team claimed to have solved the southern water problem by tapping some of the Scottish lochs, but got the figures wrong so the salt content changed. Probably an irrelevance because the weather up there was already getting impossible, especially in the west, and the weather and winds had caused the harvests to fail – as had the transport system.*

No justification for invading us though, Sir Henry ventured hesitantly.

Invaded? Well yes, they were nominally partly independent, but I wouldn't call a mass migration in search of food an invasion. Personally, it was totally opposed to the use of the army - should have been left to the NSS police. And then the Highland regiments mutinied and there was one hell of a blood bath. Almost the entire Scottish Parliament shot!

But sir, that was years ago. I was just coming out of University for Industry and Enterprise, so it would have been about six years ago or even more. At least Hardy had got his reward -assassinated by a mad Scot a year or two later….His voice trailed off as the drift of Macgregor's tirade dawned.

So you really think there will be another Scotland? A wider spread Scotland? Is that what you are thinking Sir?

Macgregor put his hand on Henry's shoulder. *You don't know it, but we lost Bailrigg I yesterday. The report came in late -after you had gone. Some kind of attack it would seem. In itself the place was no longer of any real value, in fact the garrison was really kept there to test the Scotties, or so the PM insists. Personally I think they were left there as a soft target for whoever wanted to have a go at them – lots of time and energy spent destroying something only symbolicly important. I don't have the details of the garrison composition, but if I know our current military you can be sure it was stacked full of military creditors –we don't like paying our troops- and obsolete equipment. A brilliant way of saving on the budget I must say. But Henry, if this report is accurate don't you foresee the entire system folding?*

There was no opportunity to respond as Macgregor continues his tirade. *Error after error! We needed to protect ourselves against the sea -so we effectively flooded Holland and other areas of the Confederation – and we got a war for our troubles. Even with the limited intelligence we can get it appears that the United States is splitting into independent republics. The Americans are doing a pretty good job in jamming our systems and controlling information flows, though we do have some other sources. But it seems some areas have gone what I consider to be totally mad - some kind or religious - zeal- revenge thing. The - what are they calling themselves again? - Evangelical States, or sometimes they call themselves the Christian Confederacy, are threatening all sorts of death and damnation to anyone who infringes 'The Lord's Word' whatever that happens to be. If there are Federal elections next year, and if they do mean anything, it could well be President Lopez standing against, and possibly losing to, that fundamentalist Christian Smith. You know, he of 'The hand of the Lord is punishing you for your evils.' fame. Frankly, I don't think there will be elections because intelligence indicates the place is in a state of near civil war. Washington puts a brave face on it, they have done for years now, but we do know for near certain that some of their military have mutinied against the federal government. The units here are still appear to be loyal to Washington, but they must be desperate to get home and they are an enormous drain on our budget. I believe it was you who got the figures on that – wasn't it one US military personnel cost the equivalent of four of ours? As for the Chinese and Russian areas, well, we really have no clear idea what is happening there. Since we lost control of Europa VI last year we've had to rely on the Americans for satellite intelligence, and they have been none too helpful. Mind you, it was really a Confederation satellite but we managed to take control for a while, so the Americans blamed us. What an irony. We incur the wrath of the Americans with Europa VI, then it fails so we have to go cap in hand for data - and they are not helpful. What a surprise!*

Henry finally found the opportunity to interject. *To me it seems this is all really Foreign Service work. What has it to do with us?*

Macgregor's frustration was evidenced less in the tone of his voice than the swelling of the blood vessels in his neck as he fought to control a wave of intense irritation. *This conversation is proving totally unproductive.* he blurted. *Are you on something illegal? Because for me it seems like you cannot even grasp the basics. We have seven million under-employed out of a population of around fifty million, and endless transport, water and food restrictions. And now this report talks of a further ten percent cut in all areas. What has it to do with us?! You earn too well my lad. You clearly are not suffering enough. I am not -I repeat not- convinced that we can sell this package to the cabinet let alone the population as a whole, and if we cannot sell it to the people I am not convinced we have the capacity to enforce.*

Henry was still struggling to formulate a response when Macgregor continued his tirade. *Just to take one simple issue, exactly where do the American military stationed here have their loyalties? If they sided with any one rebel group we would be in danger. So now, I need your brains – not the primitive model you've brought with you this morning. I suggest you go and get some real coffee and clear your head. It might also be a good idea to re-read – or is it read?- the bloody report. We have a major cabinet meeting in two days, and I am not impressed by your current powers of perception. Do not fail me now Henry. I may need your specialist skills -but you need me if you want to keep your sweet life. Now get out!!*

Macgregor was still shaking with anger when the door closed behind La Fontaine, and he made a mental note to have another look at his file in the near future. Henry had always been an enigma, but it had taken security less than a day to destroy what amateurs had clearly intended as a complex, elaborately fabricated history. Taking a brother or sister's name was a hallmark of more than half such fabrications, and was generally regarded as a subconscious attempt to maintain some kind of link with the family. Why he had taken the risk of applying for such a highly placed post puzzled Macgregor – if he had stayed in the lower ranks there would not have been such a rigorous check. Again his emotions were confused towards him. He did like him – and he asked himself again the question he dared not answer: *'Do I find him attractive?'* In the past he had been able to justify employing him because of his analytical skills and knowledge, including his real experience of working in the Confederation states. More recently though he had appeared to lose some of his focus. *'Getting too confident? Problems at home?'* Macgregor mused, but then asked himself why he continue to employ someone whose CV was a pack of lies, and was wanted for attempted murder, if Henry couldn't deliver? Not that the intended victim was of any great note - apparently some local crook who had ended his days on a prison labour gang. Politically La Fontaine was a potential liability whose value had to be proven by a better performance than he had been able to muster this morning and Macgregor sadly decided that he would have to act on that basis unless there were some major improvements.

Chapter VII
Louisiana

Baton RougeWall and floating facilities.
Headquarters: Navy of the State of Louisiana.
State motto: 'God Will Avenge'
Christian Republic of Louisiana Records Service: Annual rain 490 c.ms.
Annual sundays 100. Average summer day temperature 39 centigrade.
Average winter day temperature 26 centigrade. Average wind 26 knots.
Maximum recorded wind 290 knots.

March 4th

Admiral John Christian Monroe stood, surrounded by his fleet officers, on the deck of the Christian Confederation aircraft carrier *Genesis*. Previously the United States Navy's George Washington V, *Genesis* had been justly seized from the Federal navy yard at Norfolk in May of the previous year. It had involved a firefight which Monroe had fervently prayed could have been avoided. Even now, he could not fully come to terms with the ferocious opposition mounted by the Federal troopers and sailors and the gun battle which had moved from the dockside into the bowels of the ship. Fighting had continued for more than three days until the last pockets of resistance were eliminated. One of the Federal troops had survived despite her wounds, and had explained that the determined resistance arose from rumours about the terrible torture meted out to prisoners by the Louisiana Inquisition. All lies of course. Typical Federal lies. She had been executed humanely with lethal injection according to Louisiana martial law: *Those who oppose the work of The Lord shall die...* 'stated the state military code - and there was certainly no spare food to waste feeding prisoners.

The fighting had caused considerable damage to the ship itself, and it was only now that she was ready to put out to the high sea. Moving her from Norfolk to RougeWall had not been easy, and several small vessels and a number of precious aircraft had been lost in a vicious rearguard action with pursuing Federals. The Lord had rewarded the Christians in their righteous actions with calm seas and the eventual abandonment of the Federal's pursuit. December was a dangerous season in these latitudes, and it was the stupidity - or was it part of some yet unknown mission?- of the Washington's captain in sailing, in these waters, that month which had obliged the ship to put into Norfolk for repairs. She had indeed been a Gift from God.

Monroe glanced seaward and surveyed the other elements of his fleet. Despite its anchorage further out to sea, the *Genesis* was equaled in size by the heavy battle ship *Ark*. The largest oil tanker in the world at one time, *Ark* had been seized from the Saudis years previously. She was not a pretty sight. Irregular sections had been cut in her sides to house gun emplacements, whilst lines of portholes and ventilation grills testified to the extensive below-deck accommodation enabling *Ark* to carry up to five thousand troopers and their equipment. The forward decks were lined with rows of missile launchers and facilities for balloons and even aircraft and helicopters -when there was sufficient fuel. Other ships were minute by comparison, though some - such as *Matthew* and *Luke* had been regular federal navy ships whose crews had seen the truth of God's word. Their sophisticated weaponry, and the quality of their crews, partly offset their lack of value as troop carriers. Only *The Virgin Mary* and *Our Lord* were nuclear equipped. There had been an attempt to requisition other federal ships in the Baltimore Federal Floating Yard in November, but that had failed with the loss of over 500 Christian lives.

'*God will avenge.*' Monroe found himself thinking again, and his spirits rose as he thought of the steady flow of families, ships and animals which daily crowded behind the Wall and its floating booms. *This will be one of the greatest testimonies of the Lord's hand ever seen,* he observed to the captain standing at his side, but without waiting for a reply he turned to address the other officers mustered on the bridge. *Crusading*

Officers! He addressed his commanders. The term was one which President Christian Smith had instigated only that week as Commander in Chief. As a former federal naval officer Monroe found some difficulty with the novelty of the term, but his spirits soared as he admired his commanders, with their new red crosses sewn above the heart on the old federal navy white. Some wore civilian clothing with Christ's red cross tacked on - civilian captains who had joined the cause. Most of their ships had no military value, but many would be able to carry hundreds of passengers in the migration.

Crusading Officers! He repeated. The term clearly caused some confusion. *'Was it discomfort amongst some of the lesser believers?'* he asked himself. *I have called you here this afternoon to make an initial announcement of our intention to abandon Louisiana.* Louisiana had been home to the Christians for some seven years, and the shock of the announcement brought an immediate ripple of protest and questions from the normally disciplined – some might save fearfully passive – officers assembled around here. *'The President was right to keep this a secret,'* Monroe thought to himself *'too much prior knowledge would have allowed opposition to develop and the news would have spread quickly through the lower ranks.'*

His thoughts were disturbed by a demanding *Abandoning Louisiana for where admiral?* Monroe made a mental note that Captain Henderson was a man who needed careful watching. He had strongly opposed the raid on Baltimore, and the heavy losses there had brought him support from other weak believers. For the time being, his experience as a former federal officer with nuclear weapons experience, made him invaluable as captain of *Our Lord*, but it had been reported more than once that he had called the ship by its old name of *USN Arizona*. Such slips indicated a fundamental disloyalty which would require his removal at the first possible opportunity, and a thorough inquisition- but now was not the time.

Abandoning Louisiana for God's new home, Captain Henderson! Monroe exclaimed enthusiastically. *Louisiana will not endure many more winter storms, and we are not safe from Federals here. The Lord has spoken to President Smith and told him it is time for us to establish a new home, safe from those who would seek to frustrate the Lord's cause. The Lord has provided us with the ships, the crews, and the people to found a new community in The Lord's image. What I am asking of you here, is to re-double your efforts over the coming days, for the time is fast approaching for us to leave. Our President, God bless him, is awaiting The Final Word from God. Then we shall be setting sail -God willing, within this week. I ask each of you to ensure that any captain —but only captains -who could not be here today know of this. Go from here with this great news and await detailed orders. Fleet Dismissed! The Lord's Will Shall Be Done. Amen!*
A roar of approval swept through the bridge, though something in it left Monroe sensing that the unease extended further than Henderson. Another good reason for him to be replaced at the earliest opportunity. *And where will our new home be admiral?* demanded one of the civilian captains with less respect than Monroe felt he deserved, and after some officers had turned away. Monroe's pervasive paranoia caused him to make a mental note that, in due course, he should also inquire into the loyalty of *The Savannah's* captain.

That is something is currently known only to a few of God's elect captain. All will be revealed in due course as Crusading Officers need to know, or as the Lord reveals His Will to the President. In the meantime, you will also appreciate the need for strictest security. There are many Federal spies even here, and you were in Virginia were you not…?

Peterson turned white at the question. His wife had been lost, probably killed, when Federal forces had retaken VirginiaWall. Virginia had been a good Wall with hundreds of square miles of land -wet enough to be fertile but dry enough to be safe. The man seemed to shrink within his clothing and set his face in a manner which indicated no further questions - or answers - could be expected for that day at least.

Washington FederalWall

Government of the Federal United States of America
Federal motto: In God We Trust
Annual rain 370 c.ms. Annual sundays 193.
Average summer day temperature 37 centigrade. Average winter day temperature 22 centigrade.
Average wind 19 knots. Maximum recorded wind 280 knots

19.10 UTC March 4th

WashingtonWall was the antithesis of logic. It should already have been abandoned to the waves which each day lapped ever higher at it. Federal Americans saw its survival as one of the greatest wonders of the modern world, though it survived largely because of its symbolism as the historic home of the United States of America and because its survival was an affront to the evangelical rebels, freedom fighters or whatever they might be called and to the forces which had called them into existence. The Free Christian Republics - The Evangelical Republics they were called by some -considered its continuance as a slight on The Lord's name and a perversion of the Ultimate Destiny. However, even they regarded it as a startling feat of civil and military engineering.

Standing some 80 feet high on their eastern side, the Walls were supported vertically by a honeycomb of flying buttresses. At the end of each lay a network of similarly inter-linked, horizontal, honeycombs which served both to take the pressure from the Walls, and to provide protection for the land area within each of the honeycomb's cells. Each cell - some four miles square- could be sealed to provide protection in the event of Wall failure. From the sea in the east, the Wall stretched west to the Appalachians, reducing in height as it rose with the ground. To the north it stretched fifty miles, joining with BaltimoreWall, but only ten to the south. There had been plans to extend further south, but building had met armed resistance from the early Virginian Christian Militias so the plans had been rapidly modified.

Within the Wall lay not only old Washington and the Pentagon, but mile after mile of intensive farming units. What could not been grown through genetically modified planting lay under glass, whilst protected lairs on the seaward side supported another 50 square miles of cultivated sea foods and engineered edible weeds. Above these, remnants of the Federal Atlantic fleet lay moored to floating jetties, whilst a series of missile batteries on the slopes of the Appalachians supplemented the air defences provided by the aircraft carriers below. The centre of Washington including the White House itself and Capitol Hill had its own 'miniWall' to delay the waters in the event of the major Wall failing –delay them long enough to evacuate the President and other key figures. It also had its own defence complex including a dedicated anti-aircraft system and a battalion of marines which had been stationed there since one of the anti -government groups had parachuted in a squad of assassins some five years earlier.

The Pentagon lay towards the southern side of the Wall and on its -3 level the Federal Government maintained its Strategic Command Centre. It wasn't that the levels below could not be used, but maintenance cut-backs meant that there was a growing sense of clammy dampness which basically meant *'O.K. for emergencies, bad for daily hygiene.'* Such ironies were not lost on older staff who could remember when the Pentagon could spend millions of old dollars an hour without the slightest hesitation. Third level rooms had all been a relaxing sky-blue, but this had faded to a duller sky-something which needed urgent attention. This seemed even truer of Room 303, where a group sat, focused on a plasma display headed *'On-going Capacity'* on which a number of red dots circled a globe whose fixed reference point was the Americas.

Is that all we've got? was the question which finally broke the cold silence. *I thought we had at least double that.*

That is what we have General Lall. Six fully operational, two very iffy, four over which we are still tussling with the Christians. We also have control over an old Brit bird whose orbit is useful to us for about a couple of hours a day. We could take full control and re-position it, but that could make things a touch more hostile so we'll leave it where it is for now. Anyway, it gives us some coverage over the eastern Atlantic and western Europe, which may be very useful. We also have their Europe IV – they thought it had failed after they took it back from the Confederacy. The Brits don't know we have their codes, so it might be as well to keep them in ignorance. The commander of Federal forces in England hasn't been informed, so no communications on that. Clear gentlemen? Karl Nielsen's English was as curt as his blond hair was short. Despite generations in America his Scandinavian origins were as distinct in his complexion and features as Lall's Asian origins some fifty years earlier. Lall's chronic diabetes made for a marked difference in build between the two. Even Marine Corp generals had had problems getting good health care since the main biotech plants had been destroyed in the fighting two years earlier.

Karl, you can almost certainly rely on the current Marine Corp and Army to obey orders. They are my responsibility. And we have some good men left in England. A bit disorientated perhaps, but good, loyal troops to the core. What is worrying me in this situation is how we continue to maintain intelligence and air cover with such limited resources and satellite cover. I knew things were bad, but not this bad. I don't want to criticise the air or space defense people, but what the fuck happened?

Despite his best efforts Nielsen turned a distinct red. He paused for a few seconds. *What happened was simple. Some of the Strategic Air Command in Colorado, including some central control staff, went over to the Christians. Simple as that. We still don't know how they accessed the command and control systems, but in reality they were our people, working with us, and knew as much as we did. It took them less than ten minutes to destroy the majority of our satellites and cause chaos in the missile and air launch systems. We managed to get them back under control before it was too late - they had assigned us as a primary target – but by that time our surveillance capacity was crippled. What happened to the attackers, Karl?* Admiral Andrew Cutler had quietly watched the tension between the heads of the other two services with some vague amusement, but the fate of traitors and their intelligence value was a serious issue. The federal navy had been badly mauled during the past eighteen months and Cutler was keen to avenge the loss of some thirty ships and submarines. In many cases the fate of loyal crew was unknown, but he knew with chilling certainty what had happened to those on the *George Washington*.

Andrew, when they realised there was no escape they simply blew themselves up, taking as many as our people as possible with them - the old jihadist Islamic fighter's tactic transferred to Christianity. I think we can assume that they will use similar tactics again in the future – they were certainly effective enough. Which brings us back to the issue in question now. Not that I want to hog the meeting. We have these intelligence reports of the Evangelicals planning some big move, but we don't know what. From the information we have, they seem to be massing in a number of areas including the southeast. Now, what are they planning? Scenario one is that they plan to attack us, but there appear to be too many women and children for that. Scenario two is that they simply find the communications and supply lines too difficult over distance, so scenario three is that they are going to relocate. Smith has this thing about a 'New Eden', and 'New Genesis' – name any 'new' in the Bible and he has used it. We have had some intelligence reports suggesting that they are storing food for a long journey – some sort of mass exodus. We've had them going everywhere from the old Holy Land area – which would fit them – to the Argentinean and Chilean Highlands. Not exactly Biblical, but damned good for food production, no need for many Walls at present and not so well defended.

So what do you propose gentlemen? President Lopez's distinct New Jersey accent carried across the room. It contained what many perceived as a unique blend of suave reassurance and cold, latent threat. These were possibly the essential contemporary requirements for a President of the United States. Like millions of Mexicans, his grandparents had come to America – California to be precise - in search of a better life. His had been part of a small minority who had enjoyed almost immediate success. They had been staunch Republicans supporters, believing firmly in the free market, enterprise culture, and confident that anyone could succeed through hard work and drive. Work had taken his parents to the east coast, and it was there that Lopez had moved towards liberal Democratic policies under the influence of an east coast university education, and a perhaps inevitable reaction to the conservatism of his up-bringing. The final push had undoubtedly been the murder of his Catholic grandparents – then in their 90s – during one of the earliest religious troubles. He had been elected President some four years earlier in elections as fair, transparent and ordered as possible, but since then he had seen the Confederation slowly fragment to an extent that he now exercised his powers largely through the writ of martial law. *This whole situation seems to be increasingly uncontrollable.* Lopez continued. *A key advantage we had over the rebels was our intelligence, and that relied heavily on the satellite surveillance. It seems to me, as a non-military, that no satellite equals no intelligence. Is that right, or do you have other systems?*

There was a long pause during which a number of enquiring glances were shot between those sitting at the table. *What we do have Mr. President are a number of very brave and loyal Americans who are risking their lives by working inside the Evangelicals.* It was Lall who had spoken, breaking what had seemed a glacial silence. *There are not many of them, and the information is often old by the time it reaches us. But it is generally good quality. And, of course, we also have reports from our forward positions and from occasional aerial surveillance. The latter is a bit limited given fuel limitations and, I regret to say, increasing losses from the rebel defences..*

What have they got? interrupted Lopez.

Some of our best I regret to say Mr. President. Nielsen replied. *They captured some of the old Stealth bombers when they raided Montana-vintage stuff. We are not really sure what happened to them because they lack, to the best of our knowledge, a landing strip large enough to accommodate. However, they also took a couple of squadrons of XT71s from Vandenberg during the fighting there. They are the best we – or anyone else for that matter – has. If they have the fuel and the pilots, they can match us in the air unless we mobilize our resources en masse for an attack – and that would be possible but an enormous drain on our fuel reserves. Until we regain full control over the Texan and Carrib oil areas I we suggest we nurse those reserves unless we are really obliged to engage in large-scale combat. But…*

The navy can help there Mr. President. interjected Cutler. *As you know, we have been working on new synthetic sails to increase speed and reduce fuel consumption. This means that…*

Which means you cannot use most of your guns most of the time, or launch or land most aircraft, retorted Nielsen. *If you think I am going to let you have my valuable aircraft to serve as a shooting gallery for rebels, you need to think again. Putting sail back on ships is like asking us to fly gas balloons like they did what, back in the 1920s and 30s I believe.*

Which you may yet do again! Lopez barked. *And if I may remind you, while I am President of the United States of America, and nominally head of the armed forces, those aircraft are mine to do with as I see fit.* He paused. *Subject to advice from you good officers,* he added as a conciliatory afterthought. *So what are you suggesting the navy do Admiral?*

I suggest we hit them and hit them hard Mr. President, Cutler replied immediately. *We need some clear victories to raise the morale of our own forces and of the population as a whole. The more these Evangelicals win, the more people are convinced that they do have God with them – it's a vicious circle for us. Just how do you convince a young conscript that he is fighting for right when right seems to lose all the damned time? Hit them now with everything we have and finish this thing.'*

When you say 'everything' admiral what exactly do you mean? You aren't thinking of nuclear are you?

In the last resort Mr. President, yes, Cutler replied emphatically. *The balance of power is slowly tipping against us, and the last thing I wish to see is the United States, and that means the entire world as well, sliding into some kind of religious zealotry like Europe in the Dark Ages.*

If you authorize nuclear weapons you shall have my resignation in the morning, Mr. President, Lall exclaimed, his face red with semi-controlled fury. *One thing we have avoided to now is the use of all non- conventional force on our own people. I am not prepared to serve an administration which would do that. You know why? You would simply unleash the craziest of the crazy. These people are already prepared to explode devices knowing full well they will die – does it make a damned difference to them if it is nuclear or conventional? No. They simply have not passed that point, and I don't believe they will unless we do so second – I mean first.*

There was a momentary pause before a slight ripple of laughter - which included Lall himself- swept the room. *Gentlemen, it has been a long day, and we are clearly all getting tired,* Lopez said emolliently and smiled despite his fatigue. *I shall sleep on your advice and comments. General Lall. Rest assured I have no desire to nuke my own people. Unless we are attacked with nuclear weapons, we shall stay conventional. However, I am not clear as to the other policies to pursue. I shall let you have my decision on general strategy in the morning. For now it is clear that we lack the intelligence to formulate any real coherent, detailed strategy or tactics. To that end, I would like recommendations from all of the services as to how we can acquire some hard intelligence. Can we hit one of their Walls or bases and extract some senior figures for example? I want to meet again tomorrow at 11.00 and to receive your suggestions then. For now gentlemen, I bid you good evening.*

Lopez rose slowly from his chair. He was stiff from the injuries sustained in an assassination attempt the previous year, and rose only with a bodyguard's assistance. *Until tomorrow then gentlemen,* and he limped slowly from the room.

Chapter VIII
Hanging On

Bordeaux Forward StrategicWall. French state.
European Confederation of Democratic States
Motto: In Diversity Unity – In Unity Strength
Annual rain 190 c.ms. Annual sundays 270. Average summer day
temperature 36 centigrade. Average winter day temperature 14 centigrade.
Average wind 11 knots.
Maximum recorded wind 240 knots
Garrison: Elements of the Free Dutch Marines
3rd Division European Tactical Corp
1st Franco-German Strategic Corp
3rd and 7th European Confederation Air Corp Squadrons
Elements of the Confederal Atlantic Fleet.

March 5th

Bordeaux sat like a concrete carbuncle in the western marshes, protected by two decades of flood defences, and furnished with the best naval facilities for over three hundred kilometres. Strategically, culturally, symbolically and- to an extent- economically, the city was an icon of Europe's resistance to both climate change and external enemies. The French areas had maintained the tradition of flying their flags above the civilian and military administrative headquarters, so the tricolour flew alongside Europa. Since '25 the Confederation flag carried the gold star of the thirty three states in a circle on the azure. Now there were only thirty gold and two red stars in remembrance of the lost states. The British star had again been removed.

This was still good land. In the past it had supported industry and agriculture in seeming harmony. To the north and east small pockets of viniculture continued alongside wheat and sweet corn. Nearer to the main urban settlements, pockets of soil supported figs, fruit trees and whatever else could be coaxed to grow rapidly and with maximum nutritional content. Far to the east, Clermont Ferand, Puy de Dome and a host of other settlements rose like a series of French chateau above the waters on the Safelands of the Massif Central. Where the land had proved too low to resist the in-coming sea, huge walls had been constructed topped with rail and road linking the Safelands in a network extending over hundreds of square kilometres. The Safelands housed the heavy industry, strategic installations, garrisons and even the occasional - rarely used - airstrip, all laid out in the neat, hygienic style which had come to characterise European architecture during its peak in the 30s. These newer areas clung to the older, dis-organized urban core.

'Clung' was literally the case in areas where huge concrete bastions supported housing suspended over the sweet water reservoirs constructed behind the external wall. Intelligently, Brussels had linked the higher areas in the area with the dams, thus ensuring both that stored sweet water was not contaminated by the incoming sea and that land communication was maintained. Clinging was also the case on the far north side of BordeauxWall where the old rail link to Paris lay abandoned in twisted sinews. The sea had finally breached the early western defences the previous year. Scavenging teams were systematically reclaiming the metal and other precious commodities – nothing could be lost here. Communications with Brittany and Normandy were generally by boat – by flights in emergencies. To the south, the Walls joined Safelands and cities as far south as Toulouse and the Pyrenees. Thereafter there were huge expanses of Safelands across Spain, though the term 'safe' was sometimes a misnomer in the searing, desert heat.

East of the Massif Central were huge fertile Safelands stretching across central German into Austria, though to the north the GreatWall protected much of northern German from the threat from flooding by the Danish and German marsh wastes. The Black Forest area extended protection eastwards as far as Stuttgart and

Ulm - thereafter, there was Safeland to Munich, the Alps and the Central European Highlands. The construction of these enormous structures over a 20 year period had strained the economy of The Confederation to near-breaking point, and had eventually required the use of forced labour and military personnel - to date they had ensured the survival of some sixty percent of The Confederation's population despite The War and climatic extremes.

BordeauxWall thus lay at the hub of a huge communications, economic and military complex whose spokes ran in almost all directions. Its importance was clearly signified by the security screen provided by vessels from not only the French and Germans, but the former Dutch, Danish and Belgian navies which were now embedded in the Atlantic Fleet. Weekly, dirigibles were launched to scout the sea - sometimes out to the 200 km radius limit and even farther if wind conditions permitted. Similar importance was given to Porto and Granada which played major roles in protecting both the Atlantic further south and the western Mediterranean zones.

Squadron Leader Marie-Claire Heinz's blonde hair fell across her epaulets as she released it from her helmet's webbing. She stood on the tarmac of the Confederation Air Force's Bordeaux base as technicians swarmed over her craft. It had been an uneventful reconnaissance until they had been hit by a Downsurge only 50 kilometres or so from home. The scorch marks on the reconnaissance aircraft and the mangled remains of an engine bore witness to a life and death struggle which had lasted less than a minute, but which she felt she would never forget. Turbulence had always been a risk in flying, but SuperSurges were relatively new, becoming more and more common and increasingly violent. Being carried in an Upsurge at speeds of over 200 kilometres per hour was bearable and survivable if the aircraft and balloon were properly connected, though the experience was enough to cause even some seasoned aviators to vomit. Downsurges could leave a pilot seconds within which to deflate or abandon a balloon and switch to jet power or risk being smashed into the sea or Dryland.

Today, caught in the worst Downsurge of her flying career, Heinz had lost her balloon and used almost all fuel reserve in saving her craft and its crew, though she had committed the cardinal error in igniting the engines almost immediately after jettisoning the balloon. The explosion, as the hydrogen met the jet burners, had sheared off most of one of her port engines. She was still shaking and trying to remember exactly what she had done to bring the aircraft under control to survive the experience. Clearly, elements of her training had instinctively kicked in, and she found herself saying a quiet prayer of thanks for both the grim colonel who had spent hours teaching her apparently useless drills while training, and for the quality of her craft. European fighters had long lacked the sophistication of their American counterparts, but they still had their strengths. Whether this particular machine would ever fly again was the main concern of the on-going engineering examination.

That was a bad one Maam. Flight Lieutenant Aznar had all the stereotypical characteristics of a Spaniard from a hundred years or so earlier. Born on the Zarragothan Safelands he was swarthy, dark-skinned and carried himself with immense dignity. He also had a great sense of humour which made him immensely popular with all the air crews. To trump everything, he had a 10 kilo weight advantage over most of the northerners and – as Heinz had learnt in basic training -the energy savings were enormous. All air forces now found themselves in a similar position to the early days of the old space programmes, when ability had often been disregarded and astronauts selected using weight, size and photogenic qualities as decisive criteria.

14.20 UTC March 5th
LondonWall Strategic Area

It was after two when they finished. One of the more obvious social changes in recent years had been in the nature of the working day. At one time the Administrative Service had worked a standard 9 - 6 day, though Macgregor had still had bitter memories of a time -soon after he had joined what was then called the Civil Service- when they had been pushed into an 8-6 day. This was part of a process called competitive tendering which had become very popular at one time, but -fortunately in his opinion- had been abandoned. This was partly because of legal pressure from the old European Confederation and then the first Environmental Protection Accord had been signed. The government had suddenly realized that there was no point pushing everyone to work harder when they were also being told to produce, and use, less. Consequently, magically, leisure had become the stated objective of government policy. One of many overnight, and increasingly incoherent and desperate, changes.

Both men agreed that one of the most welcome changes in recent years had been the development of the midday break -very much on the lines of what had once been the traditional Mediterranean siesta- and the movement of more life out onto the pavements and then into the road itself when the restrictions on private transport had actually been enforced. This was a trend limited by two factors. The first was the obvious one - the weather. Even on the warmest of days the wind -and there was always wind now -had a tendency to suddenly veer. And, when it suddenly blew from a northerly direction, even the warmest February day could suddenly become too uncomfortable for sitting out. Climate change had not resulted in any magical change in the day's length, and whilst the weather might have encourage more outdoor activity the length of the winter nights and the growing cost of energy had always acted as drags on the *Continentalisation of Britain* -so the media had called it. At a more fundamental level, increases in unemployment and the introduction of rationing had caused many pubs, cafes, bistro and the like to close. In this way, Continentalisation had been slowed dramatically, in some areas abandoned, but not brought to a total end in pockets of greater wealth.

A –by now illogical - consequence of recent reforms had been moving cabinet meetings to five in the afternoon. The intention had been to allow the most up-to-date intelligence to be assessed in the morning before the meeting, but the entire intelligence-gathering machinery was now creaking to the extent that some important information could be weeks old before it reached London. All the late meetings now served to do was to stretch the day unnecessarily and – for at least four months of the year- to negate some hard-won energy savings as the entire Cabinet Service worked late into the evening and night.

On this day, both men had agreed by two that they could make no further progress. La Fontaine determined to redeem himself for the earlier debacle by taking his master to a little bistro he knew called *'Chez Paul'* near Lancaster Gate. He and Macgregor had eaten there before, and Henry knew his master liked it. The restaurant was a relatively unassuming place some ten minutes walk from Environment and Interior. Paul, its owner, had been a Met Police officer before it was disbanded. Though he'd been offered a place in *The Silvers,* he'd been intelligent, or opportunistic, enough to realise that the constant changes were an indication of the political system's inability to deal with a whole range of fundamental problems- the future would, he foresaw, be very violent. That this was also the thinking of the political classes was clearly signalled by the equipping of the new force with even more powerful weapons, in addition to their seemingly medieval body armour.

Paul and Henry shared a certain warmth, in part generated by their mutual appreciation of French language and culture, though Paul found Henry's apparent French ancestry a mystery. His police training suggested this was best left unexplored in one so close to the powerful, especially given his decision to use his side-market contacts to ensure - what had been for some time -a good living in the food trade. The links he had developed over the years in the Met served to ensure a magical supply of the rarest foods of the highest quality, and at least once a week one could be sure of finding pork or even a fresh, milk-based desert at *'Chez Paul'*. His French image was at least partly based on reality- in the distant past he had briefly worked with the   Police Nationale   and the old Europol in Normandy. There, and this was one of the crowning glories of his business success, he had developed some good links with both the legal and side-market. Even now, he managed to trade across borders which were sealed to lesser mortals- or certainly those with fewer important links and less money to lubricate greedy palms. Grace a dieu, or to a climatic quirk if one wished to be more scientific, he was also lucky in that Normandy's climate was usually still gentle enough to support outdoor cattle and milk production, though the farmer had to maintain sufficient vigilance to heard the cattle to their bunkers when the storm fronts heralding the SuperWinds started to develop.

They collected the usual contingent of bodyguards on leaving Macgregor's office. More accurately, a contingent of ten body guards attached themselves to Macgregor who loathed this constant interference with his privacy. Each man —all men in this team Henry noted- was dressed in loose-fitting blue-black trousers, crisp white shirt and blue-black body jackets. *'Clean, sporty and bullet-proof throughout.'* Henry mused. There was a general consensus that the government should invest in some different dyes to break the monotony of the blue-blackness, but rumour had it that the armour's quality was degraded by most other dyes. Good rumour was rarely wrong. The trendy, dark sunglasses also suggested that this team had been excessively exposed to old American secret service films, though it struck Henry that their violet ear pieces again spoke much for government penny pinching and little for any attempt at discretion.

Macgregor's sudden, announced intention to walk over to *Chez Paul's* was justified by *Need some fresh air and exercise after this morning* and was followed by consternation and a minute or so of dark mutterings as the ten went into a consultative huddle. Their commander, a lean, sallow-skinned man called Faz (Henry remembered from the records that he was third-generation-removed Iranian) emerged from the pack, pulled out the standard black, pocket-recorder and walked across the reception area towards Macgregor and La Fontaine. '*They don't want us to go*', he thought to himself. All the security people used recorders - either overt or otherwise - to make records and cover their backs to the maximum. It was generally accepted that they were equally adept at modifying the records later, but at least there was a pretext of following the system. There was something ostentatious, and vaguely threatening, about the way Faz had drawn this one and was pointing it towards Macgregor as though he wished it were a weapon.

Sir, we don't approve of your choice today, Faz said distinctly for the record. *This would be the fourth time in six months you have visited Chez Paul's, which constitutes a habit in security terms and habits pose a security threat. Might I suggest an alternative venue? The Ministry Restaurant has fresh roast chicken and real custard desert today if that is of interest.*

For Faz the temptation of fresh dishes and a real milk dish should have been sufficient to persuade Macgregor, and to have made his own afternoon much less stressful. The security at the Ministry had not been breached for some five years, not since some environmentalist from the German lower provinces had got through the outer cordon with a bag of grenades. Consequently, if Macgregor stayed inside they could all have a nice, relaxed time and enjoy their custard- and there were apparently some good vegetable roasts as well according to one of Faz's team. Macgregor hated custard, and hated even more the near-certainty of having to talk work with someone from the Ministry in the canteen- if they were important enough he would have no choice.

Comments noted, was his terse reply. *I want to go to Chez Paul's and I want to walk. Please make the arrangements so that we can leave in 10 minutes.* Faz's face barely controlled his disappointment. With a curt *As you wish Sir,* he turned away, barked-out commands to his squad, made some radio checks and within minutes they were walking down the stairs to the main entrance. Ministers were still allowed to use lifts -energy saving had not become that extreme- but Macgregor seemed determined that this was an exercise day. However, as they left the building the body guards had to slow their pace as they were reminded that Macgregor could at best manage a leisurely stroll. Faz looked around in a manner which barely concealed his tension, and ordered his team to space out further to afford Macgregor at least some minimal security. The ten minute walk was going to take much longer.

They plodded across the gravels of The Parking. As he had been reminded in the earlier meeting with Henry, Macgregor was old enough to remember when all of Hyde Park had been covered in vegetation. That had been slowly lost to roads and then parking spaces so the whole area had come to resemble a patchwork of parking bays with the odd clump of trees and grass and flowers preserved for aesthetic reasons. With the onset of the restrictions it had lost its function as a parking area and nature had since made a determined effort to reclaim its lost acres. So it was that the tarmac had sprouted a fine growth of grass blades, whilst here and there more established growth had succeeded in flowering where the maintenance people had missed with the annual kill-all spraying. Reaching he main control gates, documents were flashed to the guards who were sufficiently surprised to see a Minister out of an armoured vehicle to be unable to hide their bemusement. Then they were on the pavement, Faz's men roughly pushing aside any beggars who had the temerity to stand their ground, and ensuing that the lunchtime crowds kept at least a minimal distance from their charge. It was clear that each man felt a considerable degree of tension, and it crossed Henry's mind that any assassination attempt would likely cause himself considerable injury or worse. Inwardly, he cursed Macgregor for his naïve determination to take risks with his, Henry's, life and found himself joining the body guards in scouring the way ahead for any threat. They arrived at *Chez Paul's* in the resulting silence some ten minutes later. Henry had the impression that even Macgregor, sensing the tension, had found additional reserves of speed. Faz cleared their entry with the door security and within minutes they were sitting at *Chez Paul's* best table, discretely separated from the other diners by what Henry suspected was a copy of a nineteenth century changing screen.

Today it was chicken, with custard as a speciality dessert. Henry noticed the contortions as Faz and several others tried to control their laughter as soon as they spotted the menu. Faz disappeared from sight for several minutes and Henry found himself digging his nails deeply into the palms of his hand in his own effort to avoid laughing - glancing at Macgregor's face warned him that there lay no amusement at the unfortunate coincidence. Two of the body guards appeared totally unmoved. They were both several centimetres or so taller than the average for the squad, a heavier build, and had chiseled features and sandy blond hair which immediately distinguished them as being distinctly un-English. *'Could be left-over from the American gene programmes, or even real robots,'* he mused in an attempt to distract himself. *'Let's see if they can eat or drink. Mind, they could even be real American troops, plenty of those around, but what are they doing with our security. I need to…'* His train of thought was broken by sight of Macgregor's face, which revealed a poorly disguised fury.

Your contacts are not what they used to be Henry, Macgregor whispered coldly. *Not your fault I suppose, but I do object to the humiliation of facing down Faz and his brainless friends – much as I appreciate their willingness to die to protect me – only to find the menu here the same as the Ministry's. But tell me, were you thinking what I'm thinking? Isn't there something a bit strange about some of our body guards today?* Though not a religious man, La Fontaine found himself thanking an unknown god for Macgregor's shift of focus. His mind had been filling with images of advertisement placed on hard and electronic advertisements. *'Free man. Vast experience of government service. Analysis and support skills,'* was not likely to attract much interest in a country of, how many millions unemployed was it Macgregor had said this morning? *What do you think? American Federal Security?* Macgregor whispered.

Before La Fontaine could reply, Paul himself dashed over, his eyes brimming with tears. Seeing a mature man in his 50s so totally stripped of dignity unsettled both men, though the more observant of Faz's squad noted the dilemma and blatantly smirked. Theirs was not a world of any mercy. *Minister, Henry, I am so, so sorry for this poor offering,* Paul blurted and Henry found himself wondering if he had either been in touch with the Ministry canteen or had even obtained his food from there. *I had,* continued Paul *ordered the most delicious veal and some fresh farmed salmon for today, but my consignment was ambushed by Dutch pirates just outside DoverWall. The escort all killed, and no one in the least interested. No one at all! I pay my taxes and* what do I get, no protection whilst some representatives of the government – and he looked feebly in the direction of Faz's squad – *sit and enjoy my real coffee. I really cannot go on like this you know, this is the second time in as many months and …….*

Macgregor cut him short. *I'm sorry for your loss Paul. Sadly, you are not alone in dealing with these problems, and I only wish I could promise you with some certainty that the criminals will be punished. However, as you know, our resources are widely spread and – well, let us just say that these relatively minor crimes are not at the top of the government's priorities at present. You were insured?*

Insured Minister? Paul's face showed a wave of surprise and then settled into a more composed frame. *Perhaps the Minister is unaware that a consignment like this with a value of over 50,000 costs almost half that amount to insure. If I insured, this place would be almost empty – who could afford to eat here? And my men were killed. Does murder now constitute a minor crime?*

Mmm. Yes, I see you point murmured Macgregor. It seemed to Henry that his mood had changed yet again – *'What was happening with the man?'* – and that the mellower side of his character had won through as usual. *I'll have a word with the Governor for – DoverWall area wasn't it? – and see what we can do. Perhaps we can get on the track of these people and use them to set a good example. We haven't quite returned to the 'good old days' of putting pirates in gibbets for a warning, but some of my colleagues do believe that public executions are starting to have an impact. But one small question. If all the escort were killed, how do you know they were Dutch?*

A couple of a Faz's squad, who had been half listening to the conversation, suddenly showed a deeper interest and turned attentively. The sniff of mystery – another potential fraud here?- was also the sniff of promotion and better rations and accommodation. It may have been Henry's imagination, but it seemed that Paul blanched before replying in an unconvincing whine. *Did I say Dutch? I don't know where they came from. Could be English for all I know. There are bad English after all. But everyone says the Dutch are the worst for killing and the most involved in pir – raiding. Personally, if I were Dutch I would be happy to kill lots of English if I thought that they had flooded my country, so…*

For the second time that day Macgregor silenced him. *You know that we never accepted responsibility for the Dutch dikes - and that is almost old history now. It's as fruitful a conversation as the eternal one between the Jews and Arabs about the Jerusalem area. I suggest we focus on food now, and, as I said, I shall make enquiries and see if I can use my influence to help. Now this thing about chicken. Are you sure you have nothing else you could offer. Even real bread and real vegetable soup perhaps? And as for dessert, an apple – perhaps even a banana if you can locate one. See what you can do, I know you are a man of many skills.*

Paul smiled broadly looking like a man relieved to have escaped from a self-dug grave. Whatever his game had been —a claim for compensation perhaps?- he'd shown remarkably little foresight in his planning, especially given his previous career. In the back of his mind Henry has an inkling that Faz and his crew would be back to see Paul later that day. *Minister, my thanks for your help. And, it just so happens that I do have some fresh bread. Fruit? Well, I shall have to see what we can muster. Are you in a hurry? There may be some delay.*

Reassured that half an hour or so was a reasonable time to wait, Paul scurried into the recesses at the back of the restaurant. As soon as he was out of sight, the younger of the two body guards walked away some distance with his mobile. La Fontaine had a vague feeling that he was a Smith – boring old English name, but a boringly reliable type who did his job well. This Smith was supposed to be getting married soon La Fontaine remembered, and a conviction carried a nice bonus. He had the strongest of feelings that this communication was about the recent loss of a meat consignment in the DoverWall area and whether it had paid taxes and been insured. Fraud now carried a minimum 10 years on a WallGang – dangerous places to be, but vital to protect the economy and land areas- and La Fontaine remembered that the loss rate for detainees on most of the walls was around twenty percent per annum. If for no other reason than continued access to good food, he found himself hoping that Paul's distressed state had a genuine cause.

Chapter IX
Omens?

Headquarters: Navy of the Southern Christian Confederation.
Baton RougeWall and floating facilities.

March 7th

It was a glorious March morning and Monroe founding himself surveying his fleet from the bridge of the *Genesis*. It was probably the hundredth time he had done so since the year had changed, each occasion witnessing new ships having joined- some old, useless inshore traders, others large ocean going vessels with space for thousands of Christian souls.

There had also been today's destruction of the *Minneapolis,* a Federal vessel. Some of the crew had mutinied and signaled their location before being overwhelmed. Through the grace of the Lord, a squadron of the Christian navy had been nearby and managed to locate the heathens and sink their ship. Several Federals had been rescued from the sea and, before dying, one had confessed to their being on a spying mission to determine the size and disposition of Monroe's fleet. For Monroe, this was proof that Washington's satellite surveillance capacity had deteriorated even further than he had dared to hope. He took it as a sign that The Lord had blessed his marauders sent out into Federal waters to disrupt and destroy communications and any military capacity they came across. Their mission was clearly going to be blessed, and if doubters needed any further sign of the Lord's will they need look only at the tens of thousands who had flocked to RougeWall during the few weeks since the last call had gone out. Communications were not always good with Texas and the Carolinas because the Federal were jamming transmissions, but it appeared that they were now having great success in bringing their people in, and that the combined fleets would have nearly a quarter of a million Souls, not including fighting men.

Not that all could be taken. Many would have to be left here as a diversion for the Federal forces, something which he and the President had long pondered over. Ultimately it was a non-issue, as both men had conceded; anyone killed in a Federal attack would have the honour of meeting the Lord at an earlier date. However, for a reason which Monroe could not fathom, President Smith was insistent that all fit, remaining personnel were to leave RougeWall the day after their departure and make their way to Amarillo in Texas. Smith had even sent a crack reconnaissance battalion ahead to bolster the local garrison, a move which Monroe considered an evil squandering of resources – not that he would dare voice such an opinion. His thoughts were interrupted as the bridge com rang shrilly and the duty officer responded. There was a silence before he handed the piece to Monroe. *The President for you Admiral.*

Louisiana Marshes.
2 miles north east of the Headquarters: Navy of the Southern Christian Confederation.
Baton RougeWall and floating facilities.
11.13 UTC March 7th

The Rangers traced their origins to units formed during the Independence War against the British during the 18th century. Their specialism had always been advanced scouting and unorthodox warfare. Now, wearing the most sophisticated and intelligent battle armour available to the Federal government, and so blending perfectly into the monotony of the landscape to escape the attention of the circling dirigibles, General John Martinez and a part battalion of the 1st Rangers lay silently in the mud flats which surrounded RougeWall at low tide. They had sailed out in some fifty kayak-type boats from the *Minneapolis and Jefferson* the previous day, and then floated in with the in-coming tide before grounding as the sea retreated. The boats had been camouflaged in a hollow on the mud flats some five miles to their rear and they had waded or walked to their current location. They had taken much longer than planned to get here and Martinez realized with alarm that within hours the tide would be turning and would soon be racing back in.

Born in Buffalo New York state, Martinez had left college and volunteered for the Federal army as soon as the troubles had started. Like many Latino immigrants – even four generations down the line – he loathed the puritan rhetoric of the new Christians, and their hostility to the values of the society he had been raised to admire and respect. *Catholic laxatives running head-long into bigotry,'* was how he had tried to explain his decision to his parents. He had never forgotten his mother's howls of laughter in his confusing *'laxity'* and *'laxatives'*. Words had never been his good point, but he had proved a highly effective field officer, been decorated for bravery at Wilmington and seriously injured at Dallas. He was – some said *'loved'* – greatly respected by his command. Some commanders led from the rear, but Martinez was famed for his willingness to be *'in there'* with his soldiers and to face their dangers and privations. He was also regarded as a good command to be under – his casualty rate was low given the missions on which the Rangers were generally sent.

Martinez had been briefed by Lall himself before leaving. It appeared that their current mission arose from the President's urgent need for up-to-date intelligence on the Christians' intentions, and Martinez and his men were to *risk all* in trying to snatch a number of senior Christian officers.

A casual onlooker from the Wall would have seen nothing, though a more careful scrutiny might have detected a slight shimmer – doubtless heat rising from the wet surface in a warm March sun. Sophisticated Christian electronics would have detected them, but Martinez's electronic warfare team had detected nothing but a few primitive systems on this side of the Wall. There were also a few, primitive booby traps, but these were being rapidly disarmed. What had proved an unexpected problem were the concrete-lined moats which had been constructed around the Wall- like those around a medieval castle. It had taken some time to ensure that nothing *'nasty'* had been left in these waters, and then to devise a system of crossing without being detected. To avoid ripples of splash being seen as they swam across, a system of simple, smart bridges had been constructed and then carefully swiveled across. The process had resulted in some very strange scuffing in the mud, but the hope was that these would be over-looked or attributed to water action. Martinez also hoped that they would not be obliged to retreat across the bridges under enemy fire; with room for only one trooper at a time, re-crossing would be a long process.

Now, the advanced units were almost at the Wall and awaiting his command. Immediately to his right, specialist sergeant Rodger Lang from Ohio was peering into a small screen which controlled the flight of several micro drones – *buzzers* these were affectionately called - on the far side of the north Wall. Each buzzer resembled a small insect, and only close scrutiny would reveal their tiny cameras and sensory devices. Privately, Lang was a bit worried about their use. There weren't many insects around at this time of year and he had a suspicion that some technicians somewhere had enjoyed doing a paint job without any consultation with the ….. *'What was the word for the insect people again? Ornithologists was it?'* he asked himself. At the moment they were sending back pictures of a surprisingly empty Wall. True, there were many people still milling around, but far fewer than they would have expected. *They moving out,* Lang concluded in a barely audible whisper. His speech was typical of the cryptic style which the military increasingly used, though Martinez's father claimed that it had developed many years earlier amongst young Blacks and been further refined with the use of private mobile phones. *Our intell had it right on that. Many of the people here old or have some problem. From conversation seems their main fleet is sailing out and these either chosen to stay here with kin or been obliged. Not enough room on the ships for all of them. Orders sir?*

Sergeant, our brief is to get intelligence on where their fleet is going and why, Martinez replied softly. *We are also to kill Smith if we can find him here. I think there is a good chance he is here somewhere, but probably safely on one of the ships. These southern religious people are his natural supporters. You just try and identify some of their leaders using the buzzers. Is there anyone there in uniform or who seems to be controlling things? Have a good look around the Wall and then see what is happening Seaside.*

In response, Lang sent each of the buzzers soaring to a point some hundred feet above the ground, and surveyed the area beneath them. RougeWall was typical Wall in retaining traditional buildings and street layouts. Useless, public buildings such as bus stations had been converted into accommodation, and some buildings had makeshift extra floors of accommodation added to the flat roofs. Though these were less than perfect in the heavy rains, they were better than living at street level where flooding was likely. In RougeWall however the former parks and open spaces had clearly been used to house thousands of people, for row after row of tents stood empty, apparently abandoned *Why didn't they take the tents?* Lang murmured. *What you say?* whispered Martinez.

I was asking why they hadn't taken the tents. Are they so rich in stuff or are they planning on finding accommodation where they end up?

Or they haven't space on the boats. Martinez replied. *Look at that pic. They seems to have stuffed them as far as they can. A miracle some of them can still float and ….*

We have a target! Lang interrupted. *Looks like what they call a Field Major from the uniform. I'll close the buzzer to that target so we can get better data. Not a good position though. He well inside the Wall - nearly on the Seaside and moving further that way. That gives us about 2 – perhaps 3 - miles of hostile ground. Some other senior people in the area too, I'll take a closer look at them.* and he directed four of the buzzers to these allotted targets whilst the remaining three were ordered to do a general recon of the area.

Martinez lay enjoying the sun warming his left side and back. *A Field Major,* he mused *he'll know what is going on. But how do we get him to come to this side of the Wall without having to fight our way to him?*

He didn't want to risk radio messages being intercepted this close to the Wall, so after a few minutes further thought, he sent a messenger gliding through the ditches and mud flats to a forward unit. Some twenty minutes later the messenger returned and reported simply *Message understood. Zulu company will occupy the building on the far side once the Wall is breached and wait as instructed.* Martinez knew he lacked the men to take a fire-fight across RougeWall, but a lot of noise might bring his prey to him.

Long legs

One of the targets Lang had identified from a hundred feet up were a pair of long legs protruding from the a balcony's shelter. The long legs belonged to Helen Murphy who was sitting on an old rocker nursing her son William. She had just decided not to join the .. what had they called it again? The Armada or something of that sorts. Her husband John was a good, caring man and they should have taken him. Some very un-Christian thoughts and vulgar terms passed through her head as she thought of the selection committee which had refused John a place. *'Too few skills and too old,'* they'd said. *'Since when was man too old at 45?'* Helen had asked herself every day since the decisions had been communicated to them. He wasn't *'too old'* to sire a child and he wasn't *'too old'* to fight for his beliefs. He'd taken a bullet for the cause in a fight with the state police in the Early Days, so he'd done enough. *'Too few skills',* well that might be something else. John had never been one for studying, though he could make a good piece of furniture given the wood. Not like Helen. Her love had always been of nature and she been doing her doctoral thesis at New Orleans -on some obscure insect whose name even she had forgotten some ten years later-when things had started to get really bad and she'd decided to come home. She flicked away a strand of her long blonde hair which the wind had blown into her mouth. Remarkably, she found that she had now forgotten the name of the obscure insect she had studied for some two years, but she still prided herself on at least recognizing every flying creature the southeast and was still – despite near universal criticism for time-wasting - adding to her collection. That Lang should have chosen this target was just one of those events which can shape the course of history. Almost anyone else in the Wall would have disregarded Lang's buzzer as long as it stayed away from their food or infants, but when it came flying down to inspect her Helen's interest was instantly aroused. She looked at the brightly coloured insect as it hovered low in front of her and William. If Lang had been less frustrated after weeks away from his woman, he would have been less interested in getting a better view of her heavily laden breasts and might have noticed the net at her side. These were all the *'ifs'* of which personal and universal histories are made, and she was about to shape her own history with a swift flick of the net lying next to her chair, which ripped his buzzer out of the air and left it whirring helplessly trapped in the mesh. Gently, she shifted William against her breast and groped for a large magnifying glass she had been using the previous evening.

Within each ChristianWall neighbourhoods were organized around their chapel, and next to each chapel was the local Security Office. The system was simple and predictable, and repeated itself across all the Christian States. Some said that President Smith had taken the idea from his reading of the Roman cities, others that it was an idea sent to him by God. A few minutes after her examination of her new prize, and with a screaming and frustrated William slung hastily in a papoose on her back, Helen could be seen running with her net towards her local SecurityOffice. Dashing in, she proudly presented her find to the desk sergeant. Only minutes earlier she had been pondering the criteria President Smith had used in selecting who would stay with the Wall and who would sail with him. Within the briefest period of time she concluded that intelligence must be a criterion and this was her chance to reverse, the earlier, unfair decision.

Sergeant Harrison had been excluded for that reason- intelligence. His slow brain finally absorbed the reality that this was indeed not a true insect, decided to challenge the bearer as to whether it was she who had actually manufactured it, and then suggested it might be a sophisticated toy for William. Only when finally convinced by Helen that this strange object might possibly be a Federal spying device did he reach for the phone. The line to the main office was engaged and so, eager to return to his RealCoffee, Harrison told Helen to be seated until the line cleared.

Baton RougeWall and floating facilities.
11.38 UTC March 7th

For days WallSide had been busy with the loading of supplies – armaments, food and a limited number of live animals as well as precious cargos of thousands of cryogenically stored animal embryos and preserved plant seeds. With some misgiving Monroe had even allowed the stowing of some genetically modified life forms. His beliefs held these to be wrong, but both the President's senior scientific officer and the President himself had insisted they be allowed. They were more pragmatic than Monroe, arguing that, if The Lord had provided such things for their new home, they had a duty to accept what could be a useful bonus in ensuring the survival of God's flock in their new home.

Each ship now lay deep in the water, laden as fully as was dared. For the past two days people had been filing aboard, and most of the outer garrison had been systematically pulled back in preparation for boarding. Monroe had felt deeply uneasy about this, fearing that Federal troops might use the opportunity to breach his Wall. Consequently, he had ordered a couple of heavily armed dirigibles to patrol on a twenty four hour basis – an excruciating use of energy, but one which might avoid enormous loss of life. He had also decided to keep these craft aloft as long as possible to help pilot their course out of RougeWall. The waterways were a complex labyrinth of shallows and submerged buildings. Most had been cleared to provide clear channels, but there had never been an attempt to move so many ships in, or out, simultaneously. Monroe feared that some of the vessels might be caught up in the sweet water currents which swept out to sea at this season. Full of sands from the central Badlands, their speed and trajectory was clearly visible – as was their capacity to wreak havoc should any ships be poorly piloted or lose power for more than a few seconds.

Despite some new additions to the fleet, *Ark* was still the largest merchant-type ship in the fleet, and Monroe had thought long and hard as to which ship should carry his flag. Finally, after discussing the issue with President Smith, he decided to stay with the *Genesis*. It seemed to both men that the name fully captured the meaning of their mission, and that her multiple capacities were well suited her for a leading role.

Monroe's only concern was the ship's relative slowness, but this had been increased in recent months through the addition of extra sails and by fitting a new bow profile which, in trials, had sliced through the water with remarkable ease. Overall, it seemed that an extra 2-5 knots could now be coached out of the enormous hulk. A similar experiment had been conducted on *The Virgin Mary* and *Anna-Maria*, even though they were already amongst the fastest ships in the fleet. In both cases the gain in speed had been minimal, though it had been decided that the new bow sections would serve as useful protection against mines- so they had been left welded to the ships, despite protests from their captains that the vessels were now less maneuverable. Both men were to be replaced with more loyal, and obedient, commanders now that the President was coming on board the fleet. Both ships had a key role in the mission, their nuclear capacities potentially being crucial to success; so, there could be no doubt whatsoever about the loyalty of captains or crews.

Mr. President is waiting to come aboard, admiral, reported a young lieutenant whose name Monroe could never catch, but whose tone he found over-enthusiastic. High-pitched and piercing, it spoke of the semi-hysterical even in the calm of the harbour. '*What will he be like under fire on the open sea?*' Monroe reflected and he had visions of the man being either a perfect Christian martyr or cracking under pressure. Both, and the lack of certainty, disturbed him greatly. He had become accustomed to '*knowing*' men within minutes, yet there was something about this man he could not fully fathom. Despite the epaulet clearly marked *Adams*, he made a mental note to call him '*Lieutenant Who?*' until he had time to investigate further – he should be able to remember the name of an officer of this rank on his own flagship. *Signal to his party that he is welcome aboard immediately and ensure that ship's security is informed of this Lieutenant. Captain Wilson, please take command here until you order an officer to relieve you. Then, please join the President and myself in the chart room.* Unlike '*Lieutenant Who?*', Wilson was man who could be read and was a man who could be trusted to the end. It was therefore important that he should fully understand the nature of their mission, as far as any lower ranking officer would be allowed to do so, in case something should befall Monroe himself.

Baton RougeWall and floating facilities.
11.46 UTC March 7th

Martinez prayed silently that the Christian's dirigibles would be distracted elsewhere. They would, he reasoned, be charged with scouring outside the Wall area and – with luck – would be distracted by whatever was happening SeaSide. As ordered, beta and alpha companies had been first through the Wall once it had been silently vapourised. Zulu company had taken up position in a large house just within the Wall, whilst Charlie and echo companies had been ordered to provide flanking cover for the two forward units. Delta company – composed mostly of raw recruits -had remained behind to provide covering fire when they retreated across their bridge, to ensure the security of their rear. Lang and the other specialists stayed with it, attempting to provide the forward companies with regular intelligence up-dates.

To their amazement, there was no opposition - as the buzzers had indicated, almost the entire population was assembled SeaSide loading the vessels there. A few locals did emerge by chance from nearby buildings but were shot down before their brains could fully register their surprise. Martinez had ordered the best sharpshooters in each unit to fit silencers to their weapons- an enormous reduction in power, but potentially a way of penetrating deep into the Wall complex before their presence was noted. The stealth armour they were wearing was also intended to assist, even though it was not designed for fast movement and now provided poor cover as they moved forward rapidly through the deserted streets. Indeed, in a near - comic scenario, a small child was left gaping in bewilderment outside his front door as a bush – where a trooper had paused for a few seconds –ran past him. Such comedy would be over - the portable power supplies on the units were near exhaustion following their slow progress across the marshes.

Baton RougeWall and floating facilities.
11.49 UTC March 7th

Leaving the bridge, Monroe strode down through the ship's decks to the enormous pontoon bridge connecting *Genesis* to RougeWall. For some of the winter period the ship had almost grounded at low tide this close to dock, but the spring rains had swollen the river networks and she now floated freely in the mixture of fresh and salt waters. He arrived in time to see the first of the Smith's bodyguard come aboard, struggling to negotiate their way in bulky body armour.

As always, President Smith was escorted by both his personal security and a squad of heavily armed marines – even here there was no sure safety from Federal assassins. Monroe knew the head of Smith's security, an Alabaman called Tuckman, well. He had fought alongside him during the first wars when Tuckman had been an evangelical preacher attached to Monroe's command. Tuckman had not only preached with zeal but had fought with the deadly fanaticism and lack of fear of one who was keen to meet his maker at the earliest possible opportunity. In Smith's opinion The Lord had spared him for great things which, in the divine order, might be revealed through his serving the President as a truly dedicated and self-sacrificing security chief. The two exchanged a brief, Christian hug before Tuckman's obligatory *All secure?* and then President Smith himself could be seen walking with his usual dignity up the pontoon bridge.

To Monroe, it appeared he had lost weight since their last meeting a month earlier, but he knew the President had been busy traveling back and forth across the Confederation to organize men and materials for the mission. There had been a rumour that he had been ill though exhaustion whilst in Arkansas- another rumour was that the illness resulted from a Federal poisoning. Monroe intended to ask Tuckman about this when the possibility arose. As it was, President Smith still appeared with all the charisma and personal magnetism which had attracted millions to his cause, and a spontaneous roar of support and adulation arose from the crowds lining the port decks. Smith raised his hand in acknowledgment and beamed at the waiting crowds, but Monroe noticed a distinct edginess amongst his escort and several nervously rechecked their weapons.

Finally, Monroe and Smith were in each other's arms. The Kisses of Christ exchanged, Monroe led the President and the rest of his party to the chart room some two decks down. The room was large and well lit. At one end a crucifix dominated the wall, whilst at the other one of the latest electronic projection systems salvaged from a Federal ship had been installed. Smith took his place at the head of the table and after a brief, sweeping glance at the assembled captains, beckoned they be seated.

This was of course only a representative cross-section of senior officers. With some three hundred ships positioned at various distances around The Wall, it had been deemed logistically difficult –and poor security - to bring them all together. It had therefore been decided that each of the captains attending – men especially noted for both their loyalty and ability – would brief another ten from ships moored close to their vessels. There were, consequently, thirty of the fleets most trusted and experienced officers assembled in the room. Monroe had initially had some misgivings about potential mistakes arising from this cascade system of communication, it conflicted profoundly with his concept of military order and discipline, but he and Smith had ultimately decided that this was the most secure and effective means of communicating.

Monroe had ordered drinks and light refreshment to be served upon arrival and he and Smith exchanged polite conversation whilst these were served and the officer corp. engaged in the opportunity to engage in dated gossip. Finally, after some fifteen minutes, Smith and Monroe exchanged glances and Smith addressed the meeting. *God bless you*, the President beamed. *It is a true pleasure to be able to meet so many of you today. May the Peace of the Lord be with you and your families. God willing, this day will be recorded by future historians as one of the most important in the experience of mankind. However, I feel that I should start by apologizing for the secrecy of recent days. Undoubtedly some of you will have been puzzled by the nature of events in recent times, possibly even offended by an apparent lack of trust, but this is not an indication of a lack of confidence in yourselves. But –* and he hesitated *it is true that, despite our best endeavours and the guidance of The Lord, some traitors and doubters remain in our midst. It has therefore been of the greatest importance that the nature of our mission be kept within the counsel of God's most select. It is clear to you all that we have amassed here what is without doubt the largest fleet every assembled.*

Smith paused, looking around to gauge the reaction. *But we are vulnerable* and he looked around the room to ensure his words were given due weight. *We are very vulnerable* he repeated for emphasis. *We carry within these ships many tens of thousands of children, women and non-combatants - as well as the cream of our fighting forces. This is no fighting armada however, and our ultimate objective is…* He stopped mid sentence as the Genesis shuddered, and the occupants of the room shot enquiring glances at one another. *That is not a Federal attack, or if it is it enjoys a most fortuitous coincidence with our own plans.* Smith laughed. *Admiral Monroe. Correct me if I am wrong, but I believe that we our casting off and that we are even now being towed from our moorings. Our voyage to meet our destiny has begun! Correct Admiral?*

Correct Mr. President! Monroe replied. Though he had ordered that *Genesis* leave her moorings during the course of the meeting, he was still somewhat surprised that they were now actually moving.

Mr. President, may I speak? The stunned silence was broken by Captain Harding of the *Oregon*, a large fuel carrier. He was a man of the utmost loyalty and piety, as was befitting the commander of such an important vessel – only human life could almost equal fuel in value. *Certainly Bill*, Smith replied, and the captain glowed red with the honour of being recognized by the President himself.

Mr. President, Harding continued after a few seconds composing himself, *you doubtless know the Lord's plans for us- and it is clear from the supplies we have been loading these last months that we are not going for a weekend picnic.* There was a ripple of laughter through the room and a visible relaxation as Harding continued. He was asking the questions which hung on the lips of every man and woman present, but few dared utter. *May I ask our destination Mr. President? Thanks to God we have amassed a huge armada here, but the ships in it vary greatly in speed and capacity. All we need is to meet a spring storm and we could be scattered far and wide, so surely we all need to be taken into your confidence now. And, as I haven't used a telephone for some ten years now, so I promise not to phone Washington with the news.* There was another ripple of laughter, but neither Monroe nor Smith smiled. *Could you also tell us what is happening to our vessels at the moment. Are we all on the move?*

Bill, replied the President *the vessels of the Christian Confederation are in good hands. Admiral Monroe has placed the best pilots we have on each ship, and they are all putting to sea according to a carefully arranged timetable. Shortly, you will be returning to your vessels, and you may tell your crews and passengers what you are told here – no more and no less. You may not have telephoned Washington for ten years, but there are those less loyal than yourself -and we cannot risk this mission. For now, all you need to know is that we intend to establish a new home – the New Eden as many of us call it - safe from the Federal government and its profanities. Our families will be able to prosper there with the help of The Lord and, as many of you have doubtless seen, we have loaded these ships with that in mind. We, or our descendants, may ultimately return to these shores if the Lord wills it - but, when we return, they shall have been purified and freed from the Godless Wuccies. I shall tell you now that God has made me mindful to inflict the most terrible punishment of those feral heathens, and with time you shall witness this punishment. For now, we are not alone in this voyage, for in due course we shall be joining our brethren from the Carolinian wastes, from the Virginian highlands and thousands from beyond. There are many tens of thousands who have heard our call -even in the Federal lands.*

Smith stopped and looked searchingly around the room, sensing the deep unease of his senior officers. *You look troubled. What did you expect? That we were going to stay here until over-run either by the waters or the Federals? Or were you expecting some vain-glorious attack upon WashingtonWall or some other heathen stronghold? Or do some of you find the idea of punishing the Federals too much?*

There was a long pause and then *None of these things Mr. President.* The speaker was Julie Stark, the only woman present and the only female to still hold senior rank in the fleet. At 55 she was just old enough to be past childbearing age with the medical technology available in RougeWall, and her courage and devotion had ensured her a love and respect which, perhaps, emboldened her to speak so directly to a President long noted for branding any opponent as a heretic. *I believe I speak for many here Mr. President when I say how honoured we are to have you amongst us. I believe I also speak for many when I ask if we are being required to do the impossible. We already have some eighty thousand or more souls crammed on these ships, and I see no way we can carry more. Like the other, I have no idea of our ultimate destination, but I have been a captain for some thirty years now and I know the ferocity of these seas. Loading any further will cause some of the ships to founder and ....*

Captain Stark interrupted Smith. *We shall not be taking further passengers aboard. Thanks to God, and a bit of borrowing from the Federals, the Carolinas have their own ships and there are others from the Christian lands who have - shall we say borrowed – from far and wide to boost our numbers. Enough to carry another fifty thousand I believe from the Carolinas alone and close to a total of quarter of a million including those from other scattered points on the east coast. And your maths are somewhat awry Captain Stark. Admiral Monroe assures me that we have closer to a hundred thousand souls here alone – perhaps one of the advantages of having produced many children during the past two years! Small, beautiful, pure Christians who are light and compact. What better cargo!* There was a roar of laughter from the assembled officers and Stark relaxed visibly. Even she had feared speaking so frankly. *I remain convinced that you do not need to know our ultimate destination,* continued Smith with a reassuring smile, *but you will find details of your immediate rendezvous point when you return to your ships. In the event of our being attacked, or separated in a storm, you must ensure that you reach those co-ordinates at the time and date enclosed with your sealed instructions. May I remind you that each set of instructions is security sealed – make an error with the security protocol in opening and you lose more than a hand. For now, I believe it is time to see how our departure is progressing, is that not correct Admiral?*

Baton RougeWall and floating facilities.
12.03 UTC March 7th

Some minutes later the two men were on the bridge with some of the more senior captains. Monroe immediately tensed as soon as he looked out to sea. Despite the skill of the tugs fretting around it, *Genesis* was being manoeuvred with difficulty as the strong river currents pushed it back towards the Wall. Though more than fifteen minutes had now passed since the ship had cast off, it was barely fifty yards from its berth. He cast an anxious eye further to sea, and immediately felt that his unvoiced misgivings over calling the vessels' commanders together at such a crucial time were being vindicated. A clear bottle neck of ships was developing in the narrow channels leading to the open sea and deeper water, and a number of ships of various size and power were all attempting to hold their positions as others negotiated the channels. *Mr. President, please do excuse me for a few minutes,* Monroe said hastily.

Problem John Christian? Smith enquired.

No, Mr. President. Not a problem - but a concern. We are far too tightly bunched at present. If we continue like this, the least we risk is losing some vessels through fouling or holing, and if the Federals chose to launch an attack at this time the consequences would be catastrophic. We simply have no space to maneuver.

Smith's eyes narrowed. *An attack now? Do you think they would be so rash? And surely we are still protected from air attack by Wall defences.*

No Mr. President, we have stripped most of the Wall's defences for our own use. Seeing Smith's reaction Monroe hesitated before quickly adding *As wisely instructed by yourself. Mr. President, an ungodly man like Lopez is capable of anything. It will depend on his interpretation and understanding of our intentions. If their intelligence has concluded that we are abandoning this Wall they may decide that destroying it before we leave is an appropriate response — they would probably suspect that our intention would be to destroy their Walls at this juncture.*

Smith laughed quietly. *A purification which will have its time John.* Not one to accept responsibilities for his own orders he immediately shifted responsibility. *But what are you proposing to do now to get us safely away?*

Before Monroe could reply, *Lieutenant Who?* appeared at their sides, a slight flush on his youthful face. *Christ Lieutenant!* Monroe blurted out the profanity without thought and immediately regretted his error as a dozen faces, including Smith's, turned disapprovingly. Captain Wilson was standing next to the main communications console and the lieutenant was greatly delaying a response in his enthusiasm acting as a runner. *My apologies Lieutenant,* he continued in a lower tone, *but Captain Wilson is what …let's say about ten feet away from us? Do me the honour of informing the Captain that the President and I, with your agreement Mr. President, intend to make this long journey and will join him shortly. Now, please scurry back.*

The lieutenant flushed further, saluted and strode briskly to Wilson who stood peering out through the bridge windows. Before he could utter a word, all heads turned as cries of anguish swept the side of the bridge closest to the open sea. A small personnel carrier, the *Greenville,* appeared to have lost power and, regardless of any efforts made by the *Montgomery*'s crew, was carried by the force of the currents against the bows of the *Montgomery,* an old, regular navy destroyer. Monroe had secretly feared the consequences of loading each vessel to its maximum – and beyond- but Smith had put him under pressure to maximize the fleet's carrying capacity. Whilst his professional judgment had dictated otherwise he had bowed to Smith's will and this, and some sloppy stowing, doomed the *Greenville.* Rolling violently under the impact, the haws holding the deck cargoes stretch under the strain and then snapped, whipping across the deck and cutting all in two. One sailor, who had recognised the danger, was struck by the snaking haws which instantly cut through him. Arms stretched, fingers pointing and mouth wide open in an unheard warning, his upper torso was spun, frozen in time, into the sea. For a second it bobbed in the water, then up-ended leaving a trail of blood in the water. Smith blanched visibly and turned away, while Monroe found himself praying fervently that what could next happen would be avoided. It appeared that The Lord had abandoned him that morning. Without sufficient restraints the remaining haws snapped as the vessel rolled back to right itself, and the carnage was repeated.

The *Montgomery's* crew appeared immobile with shock and the larger vessel continued to bear down on the *Greenville* until it reached a critical point on its roll when the cargo visibly shifted. Initially, the movement was slow but then, as the slide gathered momentum, the vessel listed fatally before coming to rest with its port side submerged to a depth of ten or so feet. Monroe could only imagine the terror ship as the water flooded into the decks. He knew the innards of the vessels were lined with hundreds of bunks each containing one – or in the case of infants – more occupants. Unless someone had managed to close the bulkhead doors – most unlikely in the circumstances – seawater would rapidly be filling the lower decks and there would be no hope for those trapped. He was not alone in his thoughts, for several small craft vessels were struggling against the current to come alongside the stricken ship and boarding parties could be seen scrambling onto its hull. Their efforts were impeded by civilians and desperately sailors trying frantically to escape from the stricken hulk, and Monroe saw several lose their footing and fall into the swelling waters.

He turned. Smith's face was not contorted with unrestrained fury. *How did this happen Admiral? Why are my people dying within yards of our own home base? The Lord cannot be punishing us, not here in this way. I smell treason here John, and believe me, when I detect treason The Lord's vengeance will be without mercy!*

Chapter X
Carnage

Baton RougeWall and floating facilities.
12.11 UTC March 7th

Helen Murphy crossed her legs for what was probably the hundredth time and gently rocked William in a vain attempt to calm him. Normally she would him give her breasts, but she found Sergeant Harrison both stupid and surreptitiously lascivious- more than once she felt he had been attempting to peer up the slit in her dress. He had tried the phone twice while she had been sitting in the office, and now Margaret decided that she had exhausted the few diversions from tedium the bleak walls offered and was pondering the possibility of walking to the main SecurityOffice. This was less than ten minutes' walk, and she could stop in the Wall's sole remaining park and feed William undisturbed on the way. Harrison looked up from the sheet of paper he had been pretending to complete. It was full of idle doodling he had unconsciously created whilst trying to catch a sneak of the blonde's heavy breasts or up the slit in her skirt. He hadn't had a woman for months, and was trying to decide if his sergeant's rank gave him the power to have this one when she announced *I've had enough of this waiting. I'm taking it to the main office.*

What? Harrison replied, a slight sweat breaking out on his upper lip. He'd had every intention of stringing the woman along until he could decide her availability – the child was nothing, plenty of nubile women had children without formal marriages. Hadn't President Smith himself exhorted the faithful to *'go forth and multiply'* secure in the knowledge that God himself would sanctify their every physical Confederation? The prospect of her going to the main office, and his captain discovering he had done nothing so far, was potentially dangerous. *You sure?* he queried. Then, seeing the steely determination in Helen's eyes, he agreed *Ok, let's go together. I need to do some things myself over at there* And then added *and the captain there is a close brother to me!* just by way of trying to demonstrate that he had power. So, she shouldn't try to make life difficult for him. Collecting his keys, Harrison opened the door to allow his problem out. Then realizing he had forgotten her insect thing on the desk, he stepped back into the office.

The light from the sun contrasted gloomily with the inside of Harrison's office, and Helen blinked as her eyes struggled to adapt to the change in light. For some ten years now the Federals had been pejoratively been called Wuccies. The 'w' stood for western, the 'u' for uncircumcised when the true Brothers had decided to adopt the rite to separate themselves from the unclose, the 'c' for part of the female genitalia that caused some to blush - the rest had been forgotten. It was now one of the foulest words in the language and its use as a term of abuse had resulted in many deaths. It was also used by the Christian forces as a battle cry and to rally the troops when things went badly. As Helen's eyes focused in the light of day, she opened her mouth and screamed as loudly as she could *Wuccies here! To weapons!* Discarding William, she sprinted towards a side street as the Federal troops advancing down the road opened fire. Harrison had just looked up and, despite his sluggishness, managed to press the button activating the alarm network before a burst of automatic fire terminated his seedy existence.

Baton RougeWall and floating facilities.
12.14 UTC March 7th

The word *treason* was spat into Monroe's face. As now, Smith 's eyes tended to turn red and the President spat profusely when angry. *Mr. President..* he began, the sentence remaining forever unfinished as, without warning there was a violent explosion in the innards of the *Greenville* as sea water flooded into its boilers. The explosion punched the hull apart, throwing bodies and debris high into the air, and the ship seemed to heave itself out of the water before sinking from sight in a ferment of steam and swirling water. For a split second there appeared to be a total silence before the air was filled with the agonized cries of survivors struggling to remain afloat in the seething waters. As though suddenly released from their torpor, the *Montgomery's* crew threw themselves into a frenzy of activity. In desperation, some crew dived directly into the water while others threw anything that would float into the water, and Monroe saw lifeboats boats were lowered from both the *Montgomery* and *Memphis*, a regular navy destroyer which had raced to the scene. Taking the com speaker, Monroe ordered the commanders of these and other vessels in the immediate area to provide an immediate report on survivors and estimated casualties- in his heart he knew that the latter must run into the hundreds.

Smith had quietly left the bridge. A temporary reprieve. The reckoning would come later, but later in this world was not now, and there was still much work to be done. The chaos surrounding the *Greenville* had distracted many of the pilots in nearby vessels and, while Monroe himself had been distracted, a potentially dangerous bunching had occurred amongst the ships attempting to make their way out to sea. Taking the com again, he issued a stream of curt orders in an attempt to get the lanes out to the open waters cleared. Within minutes he was relieved to see some greater space developing between the vessels as they navigated into deeper waters. Meanwhile, *Genesis* itself held its position, the pilot clearly awaiting instructions from the admiral and, as Monroe eventually realized, expecting his ship to play a part in the rescue. *Pilot, take us out,* Monroe ordered after some minutes thought. *We are too large and cumbersome to be of any use here.*

Avoiding the rescue sight, and moving into a deeper channel, required keeping *Genesis* unwisely close to the Wall. It was lined with the many thousands who could not be taken- the old, sick, infirm, infertile and what Smith deemed *the useless* who had to be left behind. The President had informed Monroe that these played no part in

God's plan for New Eden, but that He would protect them in the Christian Lands and any who might be lost fighting the unbelievers would be gathered to the Lord's bosom. Many younger people had chosen to stay with relatives and other loved ones, but as the fleet lacked space for everyone this had not been an issue – except for a small number deemed indispensable by the President due to their unique skills or knowledge.

Monroe knew that Smith would take the *Greenville's* loss in front of so many of the faithful as a personal humiliation and, as he had already made clear, revenge would be exacted. To protect himself he had started to identify who he could blame for the incident when a new, sinister, sound developed. The sirens within the Wall started to emit an undulating whine and then to his dismay Monroe heard first hundreds, and then thousands, of voices united in chanting *Wuccies within our Wall! Wuccies within our Wall!* Then came the sound of intermittent bursts of small arms fire. The admiral could see many on nearby ships turn, a shared senses of disbelief on their faces. No Wall had fallen to the Wuccies since Atlanta over five years earlier, and almost every person on board ship had left behind close kin or friends who were potentially at the mercy of Federal unbelievers. If the Wall fell, Monroe knew that Smith's fury would have no limits - the loss of a ship had already been humiliation enough, but the loss of a Wall would be seen as a clear sign that his leadership had lost God's favour. He trained his binoculars and could see gun teams trying to turn their heavy weapons away from the sea and train them on targets behind them. Many emplacements had never been designed with this eventuality in mind, and brute force was required in an effort to move the weapons past their designed limits. In some cases the crews were successful, though in most cases the weapons blocked or slewed at useless angles. The successful crews started firing towards an enemy which immediately returned a fierce, merciless and effective fire. Within minutes, the emplacements

Monroe could see had been silenced, and the Wall was shrouded in smoke.

Baton RougeWall and floating facilities.
12.15 UTC March 7th

As Martinez had planned, within minutes they reached a raised knoll Lang had identified. It was strategically useful. An old   factory complex stood on it, its flat roofs serving as some form of basic settlement which was cleared with minimal resistance. RougeWall was now echoing with the sound of sirens and the traditional *'Wuccie'* chant which Martinez had first heard almost ten years earlier at the Carolinas. In the distance, he could see some   Christian gun crews attempting to rotate their weapons to open fire. These appeared to be having difficulty, but resistance was increasing rapidly. Alpha company had managed to position a group of   short-range launchers, whilst Beta provided covering fire against snipers and increasingly organized, large-scale resistance. In his ear set he could hear Lang barking instructions as the buzzers identified new targets, and then a hurried message, *General, heavy piece almost ready hundred yards to your right.*

We ready? Martinez barked.

Ready General. replied all but two of the teams.

Fire at will then, but first get those guns on our right. Quick! Before they get us! It was an indication of how seriously President Lopez viewed the mission that he had allowed them one M179. The semi intelligent, ambulant hardware had been developed just as *The Troubles* started and was generally considered the most sophisticated weapon the United States Army had ever developed – since then things technological had either   stagnated or declined.   Able to automatically seek-out new targets, walk or run if required, its four barrels could each spit out fifty armour piercing shells per minute. Lacking experience of the device, Martinez's men activated the software and then promptly over-rode it, chewing first one and then a second target into oblivion before the gun Lang had warned of opened fire, destroying the roof the machine stood on.

Almost simultaneously a man immediately to Martinez's left fell, his face grotesquely disfigured by a high velocity bullet, and then Martinez himself was knocked off his feet by an explosion, his armour taking the full force. Lying winded for several seconds, he found himself looking into the dead face of a young woman he recognized as a recent recruit from Vermont, and then found himself dragged to his feet. *Sir, we are starting to take really heavy casualties, I reckon I've lost about twenty so far and ....* the sergeant shouted, the sentence unfinished as both men dived to the ground as another shell ploughed into the side of the knoll, generating a storm of shrapnel and concrete.

O.K. men, withdraw, we've done what we have to here! Retreat! Martinez cried. He waited for a few seconds to ensure his men has obeyed his order and that he could see no injured troopers who he would have shot instantly to avoid their capture and torture by Smith's men. Then, he sprinted down the knoll along the road they had come along. The fire was much less on the far side of the knoll, and the few Christian militia who opened fire were instantly silenced by a fierce barrage from Rangers occupying nearby buildings. Seconds later he joined a small group of his men sheltering in a doorway.

The pause was brief. *General, they're coming this way. Thousands of them charging. Don't think the buzzer spotted them all at SeaWall,* blurted a young private who had glanced out. For a few seconds all that could be heard were the odd shots and some muffled confusion and then, as if to prove him right, a great roar arose from further down the street. Following the Ranger's example, Martinez popped his head his head out of the doorway and instantly realized that his plan risked failing.

The mission's objective had been to lure the Christians into an engagement in which- hopefully- one of their senior officers would take a lead position in which they could be identified and then snatched. It was a desperate, dangerous gamble and relied on the Christian's tradition of senior officers leading a charge – a certain way of achieving sainthood. But what he saw was a confused, seemingly endless swarm of people cascading down the knoll and jostling its way into the street where they had taken cover. There were thousands more than Lang's buzzers had revealed and they appeared totally fearless and intent only on revenging themselves on the WUCCIES who had dared to pollute their home. Rather than proceeding cautiously down a street where they knew their enemy lay, these people were striding purposefully as though on their way to Sunday chapel. To a child they were carrying a firearm. *Shit, these people really are total fanatics* Martinez swore to himself, and then turned with a new urgency to his men. *Alpha company stays here with me. The rest of you. Out, all of you now! Get out through the far end of this building and rejoin Zulu company. Take up positions there and cover us as we come. Pilkow, forget your earlier orders, collect all the men you can as you go and arrange them to provide covering fire just within the Wall. You, what's your name?* he demanded urgently to a Ranger carrying a communications flash on his shoulder.

Randolph sir, communications specialist num…

No time Randolph. You make sure you take up position next to Lieutenant Pilkow. Keep me informed what is happening and get through to Lang and tell him to get me a location for one of their senior officers. I'm not losing men for nothing, and you tell him that from me. Clear? Now go. Alpha, group up here……….men, Martinez said with a half smile to the remnants of the company huddled next to him *I just hope their officers are a bit more intelligent than ours.*

Sir? enquired someone.

Well, we came here to get ourselves someone important and if all their officers act like big heroes and get themselves killed we'll have no one to interrogate – and then all this would have been a waste. Now let's get out of here.

Checking out of the doorway, the square still seemed empty and the four –the remnants of a company- sprinted, zigzagging, down the street. There was occasional fire from behind, but fifty yards down the street they reached their own forward lines and dashed into the open doorway of a food shop. *Everyone falling back as planned lieutenant Pilkow?* Martinez demanded.

Yes sir, as far as I can see. Confusing here - we seem to have bits of all companies. I reckon our flanks have been pushed in a lot, and we've lost contact with Captain Hallman. These people all seem to have done some sharp shooting – they always go for the face or legs unless they have armour piercing bullets. Don't know what they're using for that, but makes one God Almighty mess once through the armour.

OK Lieutenant… *you take command of delta and echo companies and try to give us some space on the flanks. You delegate command to one flank, that clear? You can't be on both sides at once. O.K. now go, pull back as we agreed.*

The Rangers were coming under increasing fire and being outflanked as the Christians infiltrated nearby buildings from other streets and along co-joining passages- they had the advantage of intimately knowing the ground. Their only assistance lay in a thick, white haze of plaster and concrete dust generated by the explosions within the building and which poured through shattered windows. Swirling in the wind, it helped to obscure the Ranger rearguard. Then, they reached the small square near where they had breached the Wall and where Zulu company lay in wait. The Christians were streaming down the roads close behind.

From decades before, it was often said from the 1970s onwards, police forces across the world had experimented with devices to incapacitate individuals and groups without the use of lethal force. Similar systems had been developed for military use in the late 20th century, though most had been abandoned when faced with the practicalities of both trying to manage thousands of prisoners on the battle field whilst continuing to wage war. Death was shown to have major advantages in terms of military efficiency, but the P16 was one of the few machines designed with the original intention which was still in use with the American military when The Troubles had started, and was still used by both sides on an infrequent basis - the development of intelligent camouflage with its powerful electrical fields frequently disrupted the system. Today there was no camouflage as the leaders of the Christian column burst vengefully out of the street and into the square where one stood hidden behind a wall. *Got him!* Martinez heard the edge of excitement in Lang's voice. *Guide fire then Lang.* Martinez replied tersely and then, turning to his men, he ordered them to cease fire and get to the far side of the square closest to the Wall. In front was not the place to be when the P16 operated.

They were still running when Lang gave the order to discharge the machine. There was no noise of bullets, no screams from the injured and dying. The sound was similar to air escaping from a tyre valve, followed by a collective gasp as anyone who had reached the square was hit by a carefully calibrated, near lethal, electrical discharge. *'Near lethal'* was the technical term, and in reality there were frequently fatalities – especially amongst infants and the elderly. Martinez recognized the sound and the yawning silence which followed. *'Please God let's get someone of value alive. Hopefully that Field Major Laing identified,'* he thought. If his plan was working, a squad would immediately be making its way through the mass of bodies in search of any senior officers. Any found would be checked for poison capsules (teeth were still the favourite place), tracking devices, explosive implants and whatever new form of technology Intelligence believed could be secreted in, or around, the human body. Fighting the exhaustion the heat and battle had inflicted, Martinez cautiously raised his head. The square was littered with bodies. Most were WallPeople but there was a scattering of Rangers who had been too slow in making their way back. Some appeared to have no clear physical injuries and had, perhaps, been carried forward as a human shield by the enemy.

The P16 would not fire again for ten minutes it needed time to recharge. This one was on a one-way trip – too heavy and clumsy to carry under fire it had already been booby-trapped and would detonate once they had cleared the Wall. *Got our man and a couple captains.* Lang's voice brought relief. The sacrifice appeared to have brought results. *Suggest you get out while you can General. Thousands converging on your position from all three directions. Your position is not, I repeat not, tenable.'*

Renewed gunfire signaled the arrival of the next Christian wave in the square, stumbling over their fallen comrades and engaging with the Rangers. Despite the fire, a couple of Rangers still showing signs of life were dragged into cover by their comrades. *Zulu company, who's in charge there?* Martinez demanded urgently into the voice piece. Pilkow replied, the only more senior officer killed minutes earlier. Some of the Christian militia had taken positions on the Wall itself and were inflicting murderous fire on all below, though like the Rangers their priority was to target senior officers. The remnants of all the companies were now being driven back towards the Wall. Martinez ordered a squad of some twenty to focus on the militia on the Wall , and then ordered Zulu company to provide covering fire for the others struggling to get back across the square.He saw now that they faced the same problems as they had earlier created for the Christians. Their own firepower was limited by the front afforded by the small square, while the Christians were pouring in fire from a broader front including not only parts of the Wall and square, but also the approach roads and every window and roof overlooking their position.

Pilkow! Martinez snapped. *Get a detachment to take officers through the Wall and then give me as much smoke cover as you can. Say ten RPG rounds.* Several hundred years of use had done little to improve the precision

– or was it luck? - of rocket propelled grenades. A minute later, the first smoke canister fell uselessly into the small fountain in the middle of the square. The second over-shot, rattled down the roof of building, lodging against the gutter and spewing smoke uselessly into the air. The third and fourth canisters landed successfully in the square which began to fill with a dense pall of white smoke into which several more grenades could be seen plopping. Visibility became so poor that an occasional clatter or clang was the only evidence that further rounds had arrived. *Time to move again!* Martinez shouted, his voice breaking with the strain. The first of his men disappeared in the gloom which the late morning sun could barely pierce. There were still wild shots into the mist from the Christians, but overall the white smoke gave an impression of eerie serenity and Martinez found his mind filling with irrelevant images of old sailing ships' bows looming into sight. With a heart rending jolt he re-focused as a burst of fire erupted and his earpiece filled with a violent babble.

Cease fire, cease fire! he found himself shouting into the small mouthpiece on his body armour. In an environment in which layers of command had been mutilated and cast to the wind, he – as supreme commander – had forgotten the fundamental of coordinating his command and telling his final line of their position. He had sent his men to their death. The shooting stopped almost immediately, but the groans and screams of wounded men could be heard distinctly through the haze. *What happened ?* There was a long silence before a terse voice answered. *We reckon about twenty down, General. Could be more. We've got a couple of medics looking. You come across now, we know you coming. Most of the companies already here.*

Taking the lead, Martinez led his remaining men through what was now a thinning white swirl. They moved quickly, but had covered only a few yards when Lang's voice came through Martinez's earpiece. *General, the buzzers have large numbers coming to the smoke from both your flanks and your rear. They're gonna rush you. Suggest you move with maximum speed.* They broke into a run, Martinez reminding of their imminent arrival – two errors in one day were to be avoided. Almost immediately they stumbled across the bodies of their own. A young private lay sprawled on her back, arms thrown back as though basking in the few rays of the morning sun which managed to penetrate the smoke. Her face was only slightly contorted, but a dribble of blood from her nose indicated the trauma her body had experience and a small hole in the chest plate revealed where an armour piercing bullet had pierced. Lying at her feet, Martinez was dismayed to see the body of one of the Christian officers they had captured.

He was about to ask about the fate of the Field General –their main prize-when a Ranger behind him shouted a warning as several forms emerging from the still swirling mist. The first two fell immediately, but next second the Ranger crumpled as a torrent of gunfire engulfed him. The Rangers replied in kind, and had the satisfaction of hearing a number of cries and thuds as their bullets found a target. Next moment they had had cleared the square and were scrambling across the rubble from the gap they had created in the Christian Wall. Encumbered as they were with body armour and weapons weighing some thirty pounds, in a heat which was now well into the thirties, waves of exhaustion were washing across everyone. A Ranger in front of Martinez stumbled, blocking his path, and he bent to help her up. He recognised her from earlier in the battle, despite the dirt and sweat covering her face, though she seemed to have aged several years in the intervening time. *Nearly there. Move on now!* he urged and he found the energy for a half grin. A few more yards and –now well clear of the smoke - they met with the tail of Zulu and a smattering of men from other companies and the HARU which had been left to guard their retreat. It was another semi-intelligent unit designed to act as passive defence units, provide guard duties or act as a rearguard for withdrawing – 'retreating' was never used –units. The army had designated an additional task for the units- for years they had read a tiny chip in soldiers' dog tags, so the machine knew how many Rangers had passed when entering the Wall, and how many had survived to pass it on the way out.

Historically, such battlefield information would have been transmitted immediately to central command via satellite, giving senior commanders data on the disposition of their forces. That was in the 'good old days'. Martinez's pre-mission brief had included the fact that no Federal satellite would be transiting this area for over forty eight hours, by which time the machine would have become no more than metal fragments either through enemy action or when it self-destructed. He ensured the tail of his command were past the gun and scrambling across the rubble and out of the fallen Wall section before he turned to check the counter displayed on the machine's crown. In red letters it simply read '*In: 430 Out: 169*'. He found himself quietly praying that some of the 211 would have found other routes though which to escape. The wounded could be counted as dead if they fell into Christian hands – forced conversion followed by immediate execution was Smith's way. Intelligence reports claimed that he had read about this as the system Spanish Jesuits in South America during the 16th century and had taken a liking to it – '*No scope for recanting,*' was apparently what he said.

Suddenly the the numbers shuddered, the gun firing on a militia group which had come into range. Hot cartridge cases shot out and cascaded over Martinez as he slipped on a loose slab. Then, he was jumping from one concrete or mud section to another, the ground around him spitting dust where bullets missed their mark while his gun's armour popped and crackled under repeated hits. Reaching the crest of the pile, he slid down the scree, the open mud flats before him, and caught up with his group sheltering at the foot of the Wall. Two Rangers lay on the mud flats between them and the first ditch, protruding tatters of body armour clear evidence that one had been hit with a large calibre weapon. Further away, Martinez could see some Rangers returning fire on the Christians on the Wall. *Delta Company. Martinez here. Who in charge there? Why haven't you wasted this Wall section?* he demanded.

There was a pause for a few seconds before a voice, taut with tension, came back. *General, we've lost the heavy gun in one of these ditches. The side gave way and it slipped in. We're trying to get it out now. Keep under cover for a few minutes and we'll be in a position to take them out.*

OK. but make it quick, lots of unfriendly people behind us and....

Look out General! Grenades!! Martinez turned in time to find himself thrown into a hole by a burly form. Even with the weight on top of him he felt the shock from the two blasts and a searing pain in his left ankle. Seconds later he pushed a lifeless form off and started to struggle to his feet. The grenades had wreaked havoc amongst the motley collection of soldiers, many now lying prone – the dead with the living. The thought briefly crossed Martinez's mind for the second time that that the Christians seemed to thrive on this slaughter, but was cut short by a sharp pain as a bullet ripped through his left arm, leaving it dangling useless at his side. He slumped to the ground again, the pain invoking waves of darkness through which he vaguely heard a voice in his ear shouting *Take cover! We're opening up!!* It was an old weapon of the type which the American government once sold to its close allies as the next generation of weapons was developed. Now that things were different, it was a weapon cherished by most commanders. This particular model's weight meant it was not the type Rangers would have used for preference – but then neither were many of the other weapons they had been obliged to bring along on this mission. As Martinez had commented to Anderson on their way south, the state of the Federal army's arsenal was starting to reflect the problems the government was having in raising taxes and supporting essential aspects of state activity. It was an old, simple weapon, but for the next few seconds, lying in a pool of blood-stained water, Martinez learnt to love old. It had taken minutes of desperate activity under increasing enemy fire to get the gun back up the slippery slope and into a firing position, but despite the weapon's age and limitations the effort was rewarded as it chewed its way through both Wall and flesh. A few seconds later a similar fate befell the section to his left.

For one of those brief times which seem to represent eternity, there was a near total silence before it was broken by the screams and cries of the injured and dying. Firing from the Wall had nearly ceased and, as he struggled to his feet, Martinez made some fuddled calculations of the time his men would have before the Christians recovered. Turning, he realised that that he had either been quicker – or luckier – in reacting to the warning. A number of the Rangers with him had been hit, one trooper nearby sat staring into space, her eyes barely registering and a stream of fresh blood oozing from her ear. Near her lay a tall black private Martinez knew from the battalion basketball team. His skull lay open and, mud – or was it blood?- coated his brains. He was still moving feebly. '*Convulsions,*' Martinez thought, but it was clear that on the battlefield he had only minutes to live. A medic struggled across the rubble to the soldier's side. *Leave him! We can't save him*, Martinez ordered. The medic hesitated, shrugged his shoulders and then turned away in search of those with lesser wounds.

All of you, up on your feet. Quickly now!!! Martinez shouted, perhaps hysterically, and some of the injured managed to get up with help. He shook a private roughly by the shoulder and she looked up with tears in her eyes and mouthed *Deaf, Sir. You speak to me?* In a rare moment of personal sympathy Martinez took her by the hand, helped her to her feet with his good arm and pointed vigorously to the mudflats. *Run!!* he mouthed clearly, and then set off to run himself, his hand still in hers. He fell almost instantly. The pain in his arm had distracted him from the ankle injury but, as soon as he tried to run, his left ankle failed with the unbearable pain. Without warning, he found himself scooped off the ground and thrown across the same trooper's shoulders, his face smeared with blood dribbling from her ears. For the next hundred yards, felt the ignominy and honour of being carried by a woman whose name he could not recall whilst the troopers around him fought and died to save him. Despite her body armour he could sense and smell the sweat pouring from the woman's – for he suddenly felt her as a woman - body and mixing with a subtle perfume. Applied when??? Two days ago before they had left? Or had she carried some with her to maintain a modicum of femininity and civilisation amidst the barbarity of the battlefield? What is her name? Would she be a good lover? These and other thoughts far removed from the chattering of guns, the shocks of explosions and cries and shouts washed through his mind as he fought waves of darkness. Then, suddenly, he was dumped back into full consciousness on the churned earth, much as he used to dump sacks of potatoes at the back of his grandpa's shop back in Buffalo. The woman collapsed next to him gasping deeply and insanely he felt profoundly reassured by this.

There was the distant sound of Hamling shouting orders. and next second he was surrounded by medics. It was one of the contradictions of modern warfare that the Federal armed services usually abandoned their wounded on the battlefield – usually with only a small, self-administered trauma kit - until there was a safe haven where treatment could be ministered. Martinez had read somewhere, sometime, that historically medics had accompanied men into combat and the Red Cross was still used to identify medics as it had been when – was it the time of what many now called the First Civil War ? That was before Smith had changed the rules of engagement and had made medics a legitimate target. Now, the deep dip into which private Rosie Lang had carried Martinez constituted the mission's rear field hospital and the full range of modern medicine was being mobilised as Martinez lay there with the third pint of blood pouring from the severed artery in his arm. One hand sprayed the wound with a potent antiseptic whilst another shot two loads of sophisticated coagulants to temporarily stem the flow of blood whilst a fourth almost immediately applied a thick living-gel which simultaneously started to mend the artery and heal the other tissues in the arm. By this time the first hand had inserted a needle deep into the veins in Martinez's leg and a complex mix of blood substitute, anti – infectants, healing agents and pain killers was released throughout his body. Within fifteen minutes the wound would be stabilised, within twenty minutes he would be on his feet-within two or three hours he would be ready for combat again. Within the Wall he would have been left to die – or shot by his own troops to avoid torture.

General. General Sir! Can you hear me? It was Hamling's voice once again calling him back from the sleep with which he was becoming enamoured. Martinez struggled between his body's yearning for sleep and peace and a deeper, more permanent, sense of duty. He forced his eyes open. *What our status captain?* Hamling's face visibly relaxed. His youth combined with a newness in this command post to ensure that he had no desire to lead the remainder of the mission. *We've lost the best part of two thirds of the command sir. Those bastards fought harder than they've ever done before and we got really mauled on the way out of the Wall. The Christs got really hurt by the HARUs – must have killed hundreds of them – and then again when we took out the bridges, but Lang says they regrouping on the far side of the Wall and bringing forward some light artillery. With respect sir, we need to move. Can you make it with help?? You took a really bad one.*

Martinez smiled grimly. *Staying here means being caught by them or drowned in the waters when the tide arrives captain. I think I'll accept your kind invitation to the dance. Maybe the Christians are going to stay with their Wall now -*

repair it before the tide gets in. Now, can you help me to my feet and get me Laing? Do we still have control over some buzzers? Where are our prisoners? And get me that trooper who brought me in. The one who was here a minute ago. Quick now.

1 mile north of Baton RougeWall and floating facilities.
13.54 UTC March 7th

There was a dangerous silence across the mud flats. An occasional shot came from the Wall, but the Rangers had taken to the hollows they had used for their approach and the remnants of the battalion was shambling north towards its boats as quickly as fatigue and the wounded would allow. They were also encumbered by the fettered and gagged Field Major they had managed to get through the Wall. He did everything in his power to slow and obstruct them and Martinez had soon realised the necessity to order that he be given a strong anaesthetic. The other officer had been killed - she was too junior to be of any value. Martinez had briefly considered leaving her to be saved by her brethren, but one look at the grim remnants of his command had changed his mind. Letting her live would doubtless have resulted in the death of more good Federals in the future, but he had not enjoyed pulling the trigger. Killing in the heat of combat was one thing – seeing and smelling death at close range was another. They had also administered a fatal drugs dose to a young private wounded in the final exchanges. In a hospital he would have survived, but out here on the flats every minute's delay was a danger to his command and, without intense, immediate, lengthy treatment the medics had declared his case hopeless.

Martinez himself was still waiting for the full effect of the medication to kick-in. Where the passage was wide enough, he was being helped with the support of a burly soldier on either side. In narrower places he was hopping forward using a carbine as a crutch under his good arm. Those who had remained at the rear had even had the chance to re-charge the camouflage units in their armour and were blending once again into the landscape. Not that this could be relied upon any longer. The Wall would be organising its weapons and electronics even now, and Martinez spotted Laing sliding over the mud with certain alarm on his face.

Good to see you back, Sir. Sir, the buzzers got some artillery being moved this way. I suggest we get our arses out of here before they get blown off.

Martinez hesitated. *How many buzzers now? And what kind of artillery is coming?*

Two buzzers still up sir. The blonde bitch got one, a couple got shredded by fire and we have two still going. I can get them back if you want.

No. Better than that, can you get those buzzers out to those ships they spotted leaving. Any ship will do - though a warship would be better. Get them on the ships and then close everything down – I mean everything – except for the communications beacon. Choose a frequency you know we use and you haven't found them using. Put the buzzers on auto signal, say five minutes every hour, Clear? You can do that on the move, yes?

Laing hesitated, clearly puzzled. *I can do that sir. It'll take a few minutes, but no technical issue to it.*

Good. That way we can trace the movement of their ships.

The mystery resolve, Laing saluted and dropped back to allow Martinez and his helpers space to get through the next gap. They had barely passed the first of the deep gullies when a salvo of artillery buried itself in the mud some one hundred and fifty yards to their rear, spewing a fine spray of sand over them. Feeling stronger, Martinez had dropped back to the rear and was scouring the thin lines for the Ranger who had carried him to safety. He found her and, in a clear breach of etiquette took her hand and pressed it between the palms of his by way of thanks. It was a strange situation. The gulley was barely wide enough for two to pass abreast and yet neither Martinez nor the trooper seemed anxious to break the physical link. Consequently, they shuffled forward – not quite like crabs – with the water swishing around their knees. Despite the grime, Martinez sensed that he saw a deep blush spread across her face and felt what he could only describe as a twinge of sexual interest. Stripped of the filth and blood, and despite a well-cultivated masculinity, there was a certain sensuousness at work here. Her name had disappeared with her breast pocket, and though Martinez knew many of the names in his command this was one that evaded him. *Thank you once again private…private?* he mouthed.

Sir. Mustapha: Lucy   Serial Number 3401289.

Relax private. When we get back I shall ensure you are mentioned in despatches. Promotions aren't easy to get these days, but you – and many of the others here for that matter- deserve to have your heroism recognised. Where you from with a name… and a second salvo of shells came screaming in. They both ducked, and in so doing slipped and fell face first towards the brackish water. The fall brought the pain ripping back into Martinez's leg and he gritted his teeth before clambering to his feet again. Mustapha had beaten him to it. *Grandfather was from Turkey, Sir. He came to the States before Istanbul and my father was already a Colonel in the Marines when….* but she had already lost him. Martinez was looking away and was scouring the horizon anxiously.

Lang, how the fuck are they getting the range on us like this? he demanded into the mouthpiece. *Have they got buzzers on us or what?* He had to repeat the question a number of times, and then hit on the simple expedient of hitting the device. A couple of drops of water fell out, and - magically – communications were re-established.

Sir, been busy trying to get our own buzzers on a ship, but nothing on the automatic systems. I'll have a look now.

Martinez was about to turn back when a thought hit him. In a decision which was to change history, he turned the piece back on. *Lang. Turn the buzzer control off immediately. They must be targeting us through your signals. Turn off now! We can reactivate later.* Despite Lang's protests that the buzzers had not settled on a target, the Christian gunners suddenly found the signal they had been following disappear.

There was much unchristian cursing before the battery commander turned to his maps of the flats and proceeded with a creeping barrage across the route he believed the Wuccies would follow towards higher ground. With an incoming tide, he was convinced they would have no choice but to follow that route or to drown. There was no reason for him to know that the Rangers had paddled for miles through the creeks and gullies of the flats, and that their boats were now neatly stacked on the damp mud, unaware that over eighty percent of them would not be used again. Nor could he know that his final salvo following the signal had killed yet another two men, catching them at the very rear of the column and blowing them lifelessly high into the air. The rest of the column plodded on, its prize securely trussed and carried at the middle of the line. There was a confidence that the Christians would not follow them on foot. Martinez had ordered their withdrawal be seeded by mines, and they had already heard the distant, muffled explosions and screams which had aborted the Christians' pursuing foray. For now, all eyes were nervously flickering across the sky- if vengeance could not come on foot, he would probably use his wings.

Chapter XI
Raising the Stakes

90 degree west. 30.0 degrees north.

17.40 UTC March 7th

Monroe and Smith found themselves sitting, once again, in the room where they had addressed their assembled captains earlier that day. This time they were absolutely alone. Even Tuckman, whose ever-presence at times extended to sleeping in the same room as the President, had been left outside at a discrete distance. They sat facing each other, a tightness in both their faces and the silence broken only by the gentle, distant rumble of the ship's engines.

Smith's fury had already been unleashed on the crews of the two dirigibles which had been on security patrol. Both crews had been so engrossed in celebrating the departure of the fleet that they *had disobeyed their orders and failed in their duty* as Smith insisted. To Monroe's amazement, he had ordered that they should both be landed rather than sent north to hunt down the Federals. As soon as they touched ground everyone above the rank of lieutenant had been arrested and summarily convicted of dereliction in the face of the enemy. Smith was always attempting to establish his biblical credentials and on this occasion he hit upon the novel idea of having these officers crucified. Even now, he was assured, the crucifixes were being constructed within the Wall ready for the morning. Monroe felt that by then Smith might have softened slightly and would have the remainder of the crew executed in a less painful manner.

It was Smith who broke the silence and, despite years of deep friendship, in their anxiety both men reverted to formal forms of address. *It's certain then Admiral? Habbard was definitely alive?*

Mr. President. To the best of our knowledge Field Major Habbard was still alive when the Federals left the Wall and he was not amongst the bodies found later. He may have been able to commit suicide later – perhaps they even kept his body *as a bluff- but I believe we have to assume they have him and so …. *

And so may learn something of our plans Admiral. Habbard was not privy to everything, but he was a cunning old man and will have guessed… and in his guessing he may have guessed correctly. He certainly knew both the weapons we took aboard and the disposition of the fleet, so he will have used his military experience to make some very, very educated guesses.

How do you want to deal with this then Mr. President? As you are aware, even I am not aware of the ultimate objective of this trip. I, and the other officers, have planned on the basis of the knowledge afforded us by The Lord through yourself.

Smith hesitated, closed his eyes momentarily, and then leant forward.

That is how it should be for now John, and this, John, is what we must do…

Roughly forty minutes later two jets were launched on a logged reconnaissance mission from the deck of the *Genesis*. Their departure was something of a surprise. The use of so much fuel early in the mission was not a good omen, but the word rapidly spread that they were hunting for Wuccie dirigibles to the east and north. Some of the flight deck crew contested this, saying that they had seen the aircraft flying out armed with missiles and not the usual, more economical, machine guns. Some ten minutes into the flight the pilot of one aircraft reported engine trouble, an on-going problem which reflected the quality of the aviation fuel the jets were now using. He turned back, banking into the setting sun in the west and then sweeping back as the remaining aircraft sped north.

Martinez was looking at the setting sun as their boat sailed slowly through the deepening waters leading to the rendezvous with the *Minneapolis* and *Jefferson*. The gentle, westerly wind was enough to fill their sails, and he was allowing himself the luxury of thinking once again about the woman who had saved his life. For reasons he could not understand, she had evoked feelings which he believed had long been killed in him, and Martinez found himself mentally mulling through the military code and reminding himself that sexual relationships were not allowed amongst the ranks in his army.

He was disturbed that there was no sign of their contacts. By now, one or both of their rendezvous should have been visible, but all the dying rays of the sun revealed were an increasingly dark and stormy sea. They were keeping as close to the coast as they dared, but if the sea continued to rise like this they would have no choice but to make landfall again. Habbard, that was the name of their man, was lying securely tied on the deck of the boat. He was tied low and tight to make sure that he could not capsize them by starting to rock from side to side, and had said nothing since regaining consciousness fifteen minutes earlier. His gag had been removed to assist his breathing - there was no one to hear him out here. Martinez looked at him, and once again checked his bonds. It was then that he sensed, rather than saw, a focusing in Habbard's face- a searching in his eyes. He appeared to have seen or heard something, and Martinez followed his gaze out to the east just in time to see a jet at high altitude flying away from them, briefly illuminated by the sun, and then disappearing into a bank of cloud. Martinez's first thought was that it had failed to spot them.

Goodbye General. May your soul rot in hell where it deserves, were the first and only words he heard Habbard utter. It took several seconds for the significance of the words to penetrate Martinez's brain, and several more seconds before the last of his command had reluctantly jumped into the sea. The seconds were irrelevant. The unseen missile, which Habbard sensed had been launched, added its own illumination to the evening sky some hundred feet above where the last of Martinez's command had been. The nuclear warhead instantly vapourised the surface and those within it, the boats disappearing in a flash of ash and molten resin. Those at RougeWall simply noted a flashing glow in the sky.

Smith was standing on the bridge of the Genesis as the aircraft came in to land. Sadly, the other aircraft's engines had failed before it had returned to the *Genesis*, and the pilot was missing, assumed dead.

Only the ever-observant, ever-present Tuckman noticed that, as the plane's lights became visible in the distance, the President put his hand in his right pocket and fumbled with something. Tuckman had seen Smith do this before, and each time it had been associated with what Tuckman neatly summarized as *'bad news resolution'*. He was therefore unsurprised when a small ball of fire replaced the aircraft's blinking navigation light, and noted how unmoved the President was as the ball of fire plunged towards the ocean swell. Tuckman had often wondered if he should be impressed or frightened by the President's willingness to kill for their cause, and had resolved that question through the simple expediency of deciding that he would never incur Smith's ire. As a trained killer he had long ago abandoned any pretense at morality and had come to summarise death through a simple creed: *'The faithful to The Lord, the Wuccies to Hell.'* However, Even Tuckman's blood would have chilled had he been able to follow the drift of Smith's thoughts as he gazed out through the armoured glass. *'At this stage there can be no risk of them finding out we have gone nuclear,'* Smith repeated to himself once again. He had not wished to lose a loyal pilot, a trustworthy brethren and a good aircraft. As he turned away from the bridge he reassured himself by putting things into perspective. *'That was, after all,'* he told himself repeatedly *'only one life amongst the millions which will soon be lost.'*

To the north, the transporter *USS Jefferson* rode at anchor sheltered in a river inlet. The crew had been working on the engines since they had been forced to separate from the *Minneapolis*. They had heard nothing from their sister ship for a day, but as Captain Joseph Weizen watched the small mushroom cloud to his west he felt chillingly confident that he would never again see either the Minneapolis or the Rangers he had been charged to carry.

Chapter XII
Hesitation
Washington Federal Wall
23.42 UTC March 7th

President and Mrs. Lopez had been in bed for about five minutes when the phone rang. It had been a long, hard day in a long, hard week, and Mrs. Lopez looked sympathetically at her husband as he hesitated before picking up the receiver. She listened with only one ear to the conversation whilst struggling to complete clue 12 in her crossword, but that was enough for her to note the change in her husband's voice. It started with a controlled note of slight irritation –he hated being disturbed so late- before becoming one of deep concern. She stopped looking at her crossword magazine, closed the cheap, recycled pages, and looked intently at her husband. There was a whiteness in his face which already told a disturbing story, and she had no need to even ask when he put the receiver down. *That was the Pentagon.* He blurted, struggling to control his voice. *It appears that Smith has gone totally insane. The army sent in a raiding party of Rangers to one of the Christian bases this morning. It seems that Smith used nuclear weapons to eliminate them.*

Ah Dear Mother of God, are they sure? she demanded.

Almost certain. We had a ship in the area waiting to collect the troops and the captain saw what he is convinced was a nuclear weapon. They also monitored a rise in radiation levels. We are going to send in a search party from that ship in the morning to locate any survivors and take more measurements. But yes, they are almost certain.

Where are you going ....? but Mrs. Lopez knew the question was redundant. Her husband was already clambering into the clothes which had been set out for the next day, and in which he would almost certainly be spending the rest of the night ensconced with his senior commanders. He reached the door and then, standing with his hand on the handle, he turned. *Susan, I want you to collect the children from their rooms and take them down to one of the bunkers. Try not to worry them too much. I shall arrange for you to be escorted and made comfortable. If Smith has gone this far I think we need to consider that he may do any number of reckless things. For your own safety, and for theirs, accept my advice this time. And tomorrow we shall have a long talk about what to do with the children. It may be time for us to send them somewhere safer. For now, goodnight my old friend.* Turning,he walked back to the bed and for the first time in over three years kissed her gently on the lips.

Washington FederalWall.
11.06 March 8th

By dawn, Washington's defences were moving to a state of full alert. Elements of the Federal Atlantic Fleet had set sail two hours earlier and had been swiftly carried out by a combination of benign winds and tides. The fleet had already launched a series of balloons which were sweeping to the south, and was awaiting permission from Lopez to launch aircraft to probe further out to the eastern and northern seas. Other naval and marine elements were still loading weapons and fuel on the FarWall, whilst the missile batteries which ringed the Wall, and the local garrison, had both been fully activated. Lopez sat alone in the Oval Office at the White House. He had always had a strong sense of history, and this morning he had found this flooding his mind. Looking up at the Presidents who stared down at him from the surrounding walls, he was reminded of the symbolism of Washington and the White House. *Why White?* He struggled to remember before his basic history came flooding back. *Because it had been burnt by the British during a war around about, when was it again? About 1812 or thereabouts. And then it had been stormed and damaged during the First Religious War – or riots or The Troubles as some preferred- so that had been some eleven years earlier. And Washington itself had always been the symbol of the Federal Government – the Federal District which the Founding Fathers of the Constitution had carved out as special land, free from the narrowness and special pleading of any individual state. Washington had survived the British, the Civil War – only just – and had emerged damaged but triumphant from the barbarity of the Religious Wars. Consequently, it is only logical that Smith will wish to attack Washington again*, he found himself concluding.

The failure to take WashingtonWall was one of Smith's few, clear set-backs. His supporters had not appreciated that the majority of Americans continued to support their constitution and government rather than a religious dogma which many considered had been dragged out of the seventeenth or eighteenth century. The irony was that the same people who had rallied to Washington's defence with guns in their hands were the very ones criticising the national government for excess taxation and *'interference'* in their daily lives. *Perhaps an attack here is the objective of the armada intelligence said Smith has been constructing for the past years.* But a doubt lay at the back of Lopez's mind. *Why all the civilians and children? Either the intelligence was faulty or perhaps Smith has changed his plans.*

The next few days would tell and Lopez found himself cursing the parsimony of an electorate which denied him the money to properly direct national defence. He turned to a memo brought in by a courier an hour earlier. It outlined the cost of a series of aircraft launches and its implications for the strategic fuel and fiscal reserves. His brow furrowed as he studied the note, and finally he made his decision, picked up a red phone and spoke directly to the Operations Room some twenty floors below where he was sitting.

Having ascertained that the satellite links were still down – and might be so permanently – Lopez closed his eyes and then decided. *Please inform Admiral Cutler that his aircraft are only to sweep south along the coast and out for a 100 miles. Smith will not have been so stupid to have gone far out to sea only to have to tack back in. He can send reconnaissance flights down to the southern Carolina belt but no further without my permission. Understood? In the meantime, I want the complete dossier we have on Smith – everything from every agency and source. And be so kind as to instruct the head of the intelligence agencies to join me – and could somebody bring me another coffee. Real coffee. Thank you Captain.*

Washington FederalWall.
23.00 UTC March 8th

Lopez sat in the same seat he had occupied during the meeting three days earlier. He clasped a cup of steaming RealCoffee in his hands, and sat back deeply in the chair. The same officers were also there as had attended the first meeting, though this time there was an added tension in their features and voices, and a fatigue resulting from having been called from their beds shortly after midnight and then dragged to a breakfast meeting which had continued for nearly six hours. The coffee was much needed, and there were many silent prayers that the long-promised bagels or some late lunch or early dinner would soon make an appearance.

Lall was looking particularly strained. He had taken the loss of his Rangers at RougeWall, very personally, especially the loss of Martinez for whom had had possessed great respect. He had also forgotten to bring his medication with him, and a rider had been sent to his home as a matter of urgency to collect it before he fell into a diabetic stupor. Air force Commander Nielsen and Admiral Cutler, both sat in the same chairs they had occupied three days earlier. The army was again under- represented, many of its senior commanders still tied down in the fighting in Oregon, though there was a swarm of lesser officers and intelligence people seated around the room, none of whom had been invited to the earlier meeting. Lopez had noted the tension from the first arrivals -this time there was none of the schoolboy rivalry and inter-service point scoring which had rendered earlier meetings so frustrating and pointless – they were either scared or shocked, or possibly both.

So, ladies and gentlemen, he proclaimed loudly, *exactly what have we concluded? It seems to me that we have made little progress and have spent a long time doing it – if you get the drift of my rather poor English. We do not know what Smith is doing, apart from moving as much equipment and people as possible out into the Atlantic. What I have heard so far are theories about him planning to sink the entire fleet in mid ocean – a million martyrs so to speak – through to a grand plan to invade or attack the Confederation. He has not done the same thing in the Pacific- it seems- but we don't know why he has done it in the Atlantic, so he may choose to move his people on the west coast later. We don't know his motives or his target, and we have almost no satellite capacity. What are we down to again? Six operational, two very iffy, four over which we are still tussling with the Christians was the last I heard. Or is there any more bad news that I haven't caught up with yet?*

There was restrained laughter followed by silence. Lopez had clearly intended the question to be a rhetorical joke but, given the quality of their current intelligence, all that Lall could do was to look up with an almost boyish sheepishness. *Now Mr. President, you shouldn't take things like that. There isn't a man or woman in this room who is not full of respect for the way you have led this nation during the past years. We are all trying to do the best with what we have at our disposal.*

I really appreciate your sensitivity, but cut the shit and get to the point. Lopez stopped Lall in his tracks. *What should I know that you have decided I don't need to know?*

It isn't like that Mr. President, but perhaps we have been too slow and too soft at times. Perhaps we should have used our military capacity more forcefully before it was weakened by the economic situation and internal divisions.

Lopez put his head in his hands for a number of seconds, leaning heavily on the table. *Reminds you of the First Civil War in any way does it ?* he mumbled. Then he lifted his head and looked around the table. *If my memory is correct, many of the Confederate officers then were allowed to ride away freely from West Point, only to return to slaughter their Confederation fellow officers within a matter of months. Is my history correct?*

Lall paused. *You may be right Mr. President, perhaps we have all been too soft, but that was a policy with which we all concurred.*

And what about now? Lopez demanded. *What exactly do we still have that can give us some intell on this area?*

I believe that we still have control of one bird Mr. President Anderson replied. *It's in rather an erratic orbit, but we can monitor parts of the Eastern USA and Atlantic.*

So, if this satellite is not in geostationary orbit, just how often can we see this part of the Atlantic?

Anderson paused. *Mr. President, this is an eccentric bird- the fuel has gone so it's no longer geostationary. I understand we have surveillance of different areas of the western Atlantic at least twice a day for about an hour at a time. The coverage is very variable.*

And of the area where Monroe is sailing?

I'm not sure we can answer that Mr. President. Can we answer that Gentlemen? Do we actually know where our Christian friends have gone sailing?

No Mr. President, we cannot, Admiral Cutler replied *which is why I think you should re-consider your decision to limit fly time. I know that logically Smith will not have sailed out only to come back on himself, not unless he has a hell of a lot of fuel to burn, but Smith is not a logical man. Anyway, he may have chosen that as a way of throwing us off. He's a cunning bastard as you know Mr. President, and evil enough to destroy thousands of his own men if he thought it would serve his ends. So please do re-consider. Give at least another hundred miles leeway for security's sake.*

Lopez hesitated, and then turned again to the calculations on the memo he had received earlier that morning. *John, I'm really sorry,* he concluded after a few seconds *but I have to take the bigger picture. Since we lost the Mexican fields we have been really struggling for fuel and we need to shepherd what we have until the bio-fuel plant at Rochester comes on line in the summer. And, before you go any further, we also have a problem paying for the damned stuff. Our tax take is so low at present that paying for the military is a drain. A real drain. Even with conscription wages we are struggling to pay our troops in the field, let alone replace their equipment. So, my answer is no.*

But Mr. President...

But Mr. President nothing John, Lopez interjected *my answer stands.*

However, I have a question ? I spent the morning reading Smith's file, and it appears that he spent some time at some form of theological seminary in Cambridge, England when he was younger. According to the National Security Agency reports, he shared a house with some English student – younger than Smith- and the two of them used to spend their nights getting drunk and discussing big theological and religious issues…Anyone here tell me what the difference is? Ok, so what I want to know is if this English man is still alive. If so, was there anything that Smith was burbling about in those drunken exchanges which might help us?'

You want us to get in touch with our men in London Mr. President? Lall asked eagerly. The army's inability, or unwillingness, to risk getting useful troops back from the European theatre was a major embarrassment to the military command. This was a rare opportunity to do something useful with the London garrison.

Lopez hesitated. *No, let's see if we can get something useful by using our English friends. Anna, you are Secretary of State for Foreign Affairs, so see if you can use some of your Brit. contacts to track down this fella and extract whatever might be useful from him. Do it quickly though. Is that clear?*

Yes Mr. President, Anna Fulbright replied happily. This was one of the few occasions when a meeting had not ended with total dominance by the military, and she felt cheered by the possibility to exercise the skills of her department.

And now ladies and gentlemen, Lopez intoned *if there is no more bad you have hidden from me, I do believe there is some much needed food coming through the door and probably some beds to hit. Meeting is over.*

Ten minutes later Lall caught up with Cutler in the toilets, and they quickly checked the stalls. *What do you think John?* he demanded.

I think Lopez is well intentioned but taking too limited a view. Smith definitely used a nuclear device, we have the data on that now, so we are in a new game. My gut feeling is that he may try something really dramatic now, and this entire fleet he's assembled maybe intended to attack the thing he hates most – us.

So why all the kids and women? Lall replied.

Audience perhaps? You remember that the Congressmen brought their wives and children for a Sunday picnic at the battle of Manassas at the start of the Civil War? A bad mistake because we lost. But perhaps Smith wants an audience for his victory. He has the type of ego that needs an audience and remembers what he will see as eternal glories.

Mmm perhaps, but I'm not convinced by that John. Lall replied thoughtfully. *I don't think we understand what Smith is doing and that truly worries me. But perhaps the army can help you here. The President made it clear that your aircraft were not authorized to do the extra flying. But, just by good fortune, the army just happens to have a couple of new powered dirigibles we are in the process of commissioning. A bit of reconnaissance work would be a good way of testing them out for airworthiness. You tell me where you think the gaps are in your surveillance flights, and I'll do my best to ensure that those two machines are out in the next two, say three days at the very latest.*

The two men smiled at each other. *Fuck the finances John, there is a war to win.*

Chapter XIII
University Times

London Wall Strategic Governance Area
We apologise for the break in Channel 8 transmissions.
Full services will be resumed as soon as possible.
Remember, Channel 8 brings you the best of adult 24 hours a day.

03.02 UTC March 10th

It was three in the morning when Henry woke. He had enjoyed the meal with Macgregor. It was not only that the food has been good – perhaps the best Paul had ever produced -and for the second time in three days Faz had been apoplectic. No, it was also the way in which he felt more comfortable by the end of the meal – Macgregor was showing him the old affection. Not for the first. La Fontaine found himself thanking a God in which he did not believe for the fact that Macgregor had no children of his own. *'Was it this alone which has kept in post?'* he found himself asking yet again. Or was it possible that he, Henry La Fontaine, had abilities which Macgregor had identified but which had passed their owner by. *'Or'*, and the thought crept unwillingly into his mind *'are the rumours right and he does fancy me? If so, that is going to be difficult to deal with.'*

The Cabinet meeting later that afternoon had been something different. The tension had been almost tangible from the outset and within minutes of starting all the personal advisors had been cleared out of the room. There had been no precedent for this in the years Henry had worked with Macgregor, and he found himself sitting in a chair-lined corridor with a group of equally confused and disconsolate officials. Even in the corridor, raised voices could be heard through the thick, padded door, and Henry quickly noticed that everyone was attempting to identify the voice of his or her master.

There was a young, ginger haired woman from Foreign Affairs sitting opposite him and, between efforts to hear Macgregor's voice, it increasingly appeared she found him attractive. Convention was that advisors did not speak to each other, but the way she showed her cleavage and thighs was a fulsome communication, and one which Henry struggled to deal with. He was still aroused when he returned home and found Rachel alone – the boy was with grandma – and willing. *'Too willing,'* he found himself thinking after they had made love, and he was tempted to ask if she was trying for another child without his agreement. The thought made him shiver slightly –the rations would be stretched with a fourth mouth to feed. Rachel must have sensed something as she lay in his arms, for she suddenly rolled over and looked at him with a quizzical expression in her eyes. *You O.K. Hen?* She'd asked, and a long discussion about the day's events had followed. What left both of them feeling somewhat apprehensive was the simple fact that Macgregor had refused to discuss anything with Henry after the meeting, and had simply ordered him to go home and enjoy himself, and then to meet him at Chez Paul's for dinner at eight.

This was so out of character that Rachel had demanded she hear the sequence of events several times before their conversation had been interrupted by the door slamming as John returned home. They had found themselves dashing out of bed and attempting to clamber into something decent before he came charging into the bedroom, his hand waving an old glass container before their eyes. *Mum! Dad!* he had shouted, oblivious to their embarrassment. *Look at this. I found it in grandma's house. She says it's a thing called a fly. Have you seen one like this before?* He had held the jar up for closer inspection.

Henry had just managed to get his shirt down his trousers, and was walking awkwardly across the room in his bare feet, when his mother-in-law joined them, breathlessly, at the bedroom door. Her embarrassment was immediate, but she restricted her comment to a simple *Rache, this boy of your needs to learn to wait. He went charging ahead of me and all to show his dad a silly fly. And don't you go making any comments about cleanliness in my house. I don't know how it got there.*

But grandma, I've never seen anything like this before. John protested. *Why was it in your house? Why don't we have any in our house? Can I keep it as a pet?*

Henry looked carefully. There was a bluebottle flying desperately in a vain attempt to penetrate the glass. He grimaced, his mind immediately full with the images of fly-blown corpses which had seemed to dominate, and blight, his youth. Corpses had been everywhere – fly-blown and bloated on the land, bloated and fish – nibbled bobbing in the sea and bumping against the early Walls. Early Walls had been such primitive, hastily constructed things that many of the corpses had been thrown against sharp surfaces by the waves and the air filled with a disgusting stench. He hadn't seen a fly now for at least ten years. *'How had this one's ancestors managed to escape the mass purification?'* he wondered.

He looked directly at his son. *John, you have to kill this thing. It's a dirty, disgusting thing and soon it will lay eggs which will need to eat off something either dead or alive. Leave it in the jar to die – without food it won't last more than a couple of days and won't be able to breed.* One glance at his father's face was enough to ensure that there were no protestations. For Henry the incident had provoked such strong memories that seven hours or so later, even after an excellent meal with Macgregor, he found himself sitting bolt upright in bed, his mind still filled with the images engendered earlier that evening. The evening should have erased his memories. Macgregor had been really pleased the way the cabinet meeting had gone – not that any firm decisions had been made, but at least the ones he most feared had not been made. Paul had excelled himself –real venison from the Sheffield forest he claimed, and Rachel had even been happy for him to take her for the second time that day. She seemed satisfied enough, though Henry suspected that he'd drunk too much red wine to have performed particularly well. Now, she was snoring gently by his side, a gentle smile on her lips and a strand of her long blonde hair trailing across her a cheek and into the corner of her mouth.

He heard the gentlest of taps at the door. Or at least they were gentle at first but, when he disregarded them and attempted to push them into the further recesses of his mind they grew in force and frequency. *'Work!'* yes, it had to be work. Security would have stopped anyone entering the building at this time of night if they hadn't been carrying priority clearance. Swearing under his breath, he slipped out of bed, padded down the corridor and cautiously opened the door. His jaw dropped.

Why Henry, you don't seem at all pleased to see me. Not enough leg showing? the girl from Foreign Affairs giggled coquettishly. She was wearing loose fitting trousers and a neck-high top in contrast to the sexually suggestive outfit earlier in the day. *Aren't you going to be polite and ask us in?* and she inclined her head in the direction of two heavies who were clearly her escort. Without another word the three walked into the flat and Henry lead them into the kitchen, his head spinning with questions.

Coffee? And an explanation? And what is your name? We didn't get that far this afternoon, he demanded. He immediately regretted his abruptness as the Foreign Affairs girl bridled and snapped back.

Yes, white with honey. Amanda Brown. A very boring English name. Not interesting like yours. They, she said indicating to the security *will have nothing.* She stopped there. Answering the most important part of Henry's question was clearly going to be delayed as a punishment. She could match his rudeness with the anguish of uncertainty. The water for the coffee – RealCoffee, Henry had decided despite reservations about the cost, was starting to boil when the conversation re-started.

Amanda assumed the coquettish mode again, and it occurred to Henry she might be one of the famous women one heard about from time to time who relied on what was up their skirts as the prime route to promotion. *We're here to make your life more interesting dear – to take you on a little holiday - somewhere where you might feel at home,* she added meaningfully.

And where do you propose to take my husband at this time of night may I ask? Rachel had woken, sensing the activity in the house, and stood at the kitchen door with her dressing gown loosely wrapped around her. La Fontaine saw the ginger haired woman – he still couldn't decide whether woman or girl was right for her – stiffen, and her body language shifted into a more formal pose. If she had done her homework she would know that Rachel's father was not without influence. However, there was an instant antipathy between the two women and Henry was slightly thrilled to be at the center of this potential rivalry. He found himself reflecting on the fact that he might be his boss's servant, and certainly not a fully free man, but he still had the work status, or the looks, or the something, to attract women.

Sorry to disturb you at this hour Mrs. La Fontaine, but your man is required on state business as a matter of urgency. Minister McGregor has transferred him to Foreign Affairs until such time as his contract expires - or until we have not further need of him. It appears he's an important man. Perhaps I should have got to know you better this afternoon Henry, she added in a manner clearly designed to irritate Rachel. *Jones, Wilson, please help Mr. Fontaine to pack. Oh, and please do try to travel light and include something for hot climates. You will be outside the country for a while,* she added with considerable emphasis.

Outside the country? Rachel gasped. *How long is he going to be away for? Where is he going?*

Sorry, I'm not authorised to reveal that, Brown replied curtly, her enjoyment of the situation barely concealed. *Perhaps I could accept your offer of the coffee while your husband is packing. He said it was RealCoffee. Wonderful stuff.*

Henry heard nothing else. The walls of the flat were sound-proof, and even if he could have heard any conversation taking place his mind was too busy wondering what exactly was happening. *'Was this the reason McGregor had let him home early and treated him so well that evening? Had he planned this from the time of their abortive meeting earlier in the week?'* he found himself asking. *'But no, that didn't make sense. He had done a good job of the briefing for that day – the previous day he found himself correcting. What was happening and where was he being taken?'*

He packed a few things in a shoulder bag, hesitating as to exactly what he should take. *Exactly how hot is it going to be?* He asked the one whose name was apparently Jones. *No idea mate,* was the less than respectful reply. *We ain't going on holiday with you, but you might be unlucky and have missy go with you.* Both Wilson and Jones smirked. It was typical of security personal who were confident that their new charge was not of any great, permanent importance and might even – unknowingly- be on their way to prison.

Almost before he knew it Henry had given a sleeping John a goodbye kiss, was at the door embracing a tearful Rachel and then found himself walking quickly down the stairs with the two heavies as escort. As he turned a corner on the stairwell he heard Brown's voice half-heartedly attempting to reassure Rachel. Though his mind was still befuddled with events, he was sure he heard her say *Don't worry, he may be away for a month or three, but he'll be back before your daughter is born.* Then he was down the stairs, past the inquisitive security guards at the front desk and barely had time to sniff the night air and note the armoured escort before he found himself sinking into the padded leather seats at the rear of a government car.

Chapter XIV
A Change of Plan

Latitude 27.30 degrees north. Longitude 83.2 degrees west

12.00 UTC March 12th

Monroe had only once before been called for a working breakfast with Smith, and that had been six -perhaps more- years previously. At the time Monroe had been a simple captain commanding a small cruiser the *Phoenix*. There was nothing special about the ship, and for Monroe life had been about doing his duty to God and the fledgling Christian Confederation which, even then, was slowly building its naval strength at what was to become CharlestonWall. The reason why the federal government had waited so long before striking at Charleston had always puzzled Monroe, though he was reminded of it again as he squeezed through the crowded galleys towards Smith's executive cabin. Then he pushed the question to the back of his mind, and again focused on the immediate concern as to why he was being summoned.

On that occasion, years before, halfway through the most sumptuous breakfast Monroe had ever eaten in his entire life, Smith had suddenly diverted the conversation away from polite nothings to a discussion about the history of punishment in the navy. Though Monroe made some gentle protestations about the value of loyalty as a motivator of military personnel, Smith had kept insisting that the historical dominance of the British navy during the eighteenth and nineteenth had reflected the ferocious discipline inflicted upon crews. And then, without warning or explanation, Smith had insisted that Monroe follow him on deck. There was something important he wanted to show.

It had taken Monroe a few moments to adjust his eyes in the light of that morning sun, and when he did the instant was burnt permanently into his psyche. While they had been breakfasting Smith had executed a fair part of his senior naval command in the traditional 18th century British way of hanging them from the ships' rigging. A couple of admirals and twenty or more other senior officers swung gently with the wind and rocking of the ships, their heads lolling uncontrollably. Before Monroe could say a word Smith had turned to him and said in a quiet firm voice *They were not strong enough in their beliefs John Christian. You have been clear and honest. Now, I want you to be my admiral.* And so it was that Monroe had suddenly found himself with complete command of the Atlantic fleet – or at least those parts which had not stayed loyal to Washington – and survived by doing exactly what he was asked, when he was asked.

He stopped. *'Why is Smith calling me now?'* he asked himself, and leant against the bulwark, a cold sweat breaking out on his brow. The President had been furious over the botched departure from RougeWall and then the Federal raid into the Wall itself. Losing the *Greenville* had been the type of signal which Smith always attempted to avoid – he looked for signs showing approval from God, not a loss of pleasure. Monroe had been adept at blaming the loss on the ship's captain. A shame. He had been a good man and Monroe had grown to know him well during the year they had been at the Wall, but Smith had wanted a scapegoat and it had taken Monroe only twenty four hours to establish the Board of Enquiry which was going to hear the evidence and find Waine guilty.

Monroe privately thought that it had been the responsibility of the *Montgomery's* captain, but Frisk attended Smith's church so Monroe had decided blaming him could be unwise. He had not attended Waine's execution. Nor had he watched the execution of the dirigible commanders. In what was widely, but privately, considered a major miscalculation, Smith had ordered the crucifixions be recorded. He had then risked a crew and valuable fuel in sending a seaplane back to RougeWall to collect the recording and had ordered it copied and distributed throughout the armada.

Even in its carefully edited version, Monroe had yet to find anyone who has watched more than a few minutes of what some were saying - even publicly- was an hour long example of excessive brutality, but it seemed to have cheered Smith. The attack on the Wall and the seizure of Habbard had been unexpected setbacks which Smith had taken very badly. It was a sign of disapproval from God he had said, though it had taken him nearly two hours to explain so. Both men knew that the Wall had been expendable from the time they had cast off, and might well have fallen with time, but the impact on the armada's morale had been dramatic.

Thankfully, Smith had not blamed Monroe for this, and since then things had gone well. They had sailed out into the Mexican Gulf with no opposition, and the weather and wind had both been favourable. They were now tacking south east towards the Strait of Florida, and God had been kind enough to provide a fresh westerly to help. Though the hurricane season was theoretically months ahead, Monroe had been dreading one of the unusual events which was becoming ever more usual. As it was, the fleet was holding its formation well. No breakdowns, no collisions, no major problems and Smith had been in a good mood the evening before.

So why had he summoned him for breakfast? He was still pondering this, and the memories of his last breakfast meeting as he turned the final corner and stepped through a bulkhead leading to the President's suite. As usual, there were four Presidential bodyguards and a squad of marines stationed immediately outside the door, but this time there was also young *'Who?'* standing, breathless, with an envelope in his hand. He had clearly run to intercept Monroe, and made a futile attempt to tidy his hair and uniform before saluting briskly. *Admiral, Sir, Commander Lewis asked me to ensure you received this*, he gasped. *He thought it might be of value to you before meeting the President.* Then, nervously, he saluted again.

Lewis was one of the very few intelligence officers Monroe trusted entirely. Not that it helped either man at this juncture, because Smith was constant in his refusal to provide details of what exactly they were doing. However, if Lewis said he should read it before meeting Smith, then he should read it. Informing the bodyguards that he would need a few minutes before entering the President's accommodation, Monroe slowly walked a few yards down the galley and opened the sealed dispatch. He read it twice carefully, his lips parting as he did so, and then folded the paper in two and carefully closed it within his breast pocket. He turned back. *Lieutenant, thank Commander Lewis for his professionalism. Tell him the Admiral appreciates it. You may go now.*

Minutes later, and after the obligatory weapons search, he was sitting across the table at breakfast. A heavily pregnant Mrs. Smith – the fifth by Monroe's reckoning- slipped through the room on the way back to bed, and warmly bid him good morning. Then, a naval valet served coffee, muffins with jam and honey and a plate with bacon rashers, eggs and hash brownies. It was all good, traditional-looking food, and may even have been genuine. However, the coffee betrayed the fact that it was being produced using some fairly radical systems and no longer came from what had become The Brazilian Scrubs. Monroe just hoped that the rest was genuine and that the President was living according to his anti-genetic principles. He had heard that bacon made from genetically treated sewerage was now served to Federal troops, but the source was not one upon which Monroe cared much to rely.

How are you today John Christian? Smith asked warmly.

Very well thank you Mr. President. I trust you and your lady are both well.

Very well too, thank you John Christian - and I feel I shall be even better in a few days. From experience, Monroe knew that Smith always felt better after he had reached an important decision, but thought that the President could not surprise him at this point with one of his dramatic, whimsical changes in policy. He was about to be proven wrong.

John Christian, I know that our original plan was to meet with the fleet out of SavannahWall before continuing our pilgrimage. Monroe focused carefully on what was about to be said. '*Pilgrimage'* was not a term he could remember Smith using before, though he was constantly changing terms and objectives. '*Perhaps he has used it and then disregarded it for something else,'* Monroe thought to himself.

I also know from speaking to some of the captains, Smith continued *that this wind is helping us greatly. So, following the Lord's guidance, I have changed my mind and our plans.*

Changed your mind? In what way Mr. President? Monroe asked tentatively, trying to make the question as non-challenging as possible.

The Lord has told me that we shall attack WashingtonWall before sailing to New Eden. Smith stated, with a finality that brooked no potential challenging. *It's time we taught those Wuccie bastards a good lesson, and it would raise the morale of every good Christian soul here if we could crack their Wall and kill that evil, heathen, son-of-a bitch Lopez!* Smith's rising voice revealed an edge of hysteria, and he had half risen from his chair, spilling his coffee over the table as he did so.

Monroe's lower jaw dropped visibly for the first time since that other breakfast many years before. Internally, he was unsure whether he was more shocked by Smith's newly announced intention or by the obvious hysteria in the President's tone. He had heard Smith angry many times before, but never so overtly uncontrolled. It seemed to Monroe that the pressure was clearly telling on the man. Or was there something else that he did not know? *Attacking WashingtonWall Mr. President?* He questioned hesitantly. *But I thought the idea behind this great project - your project - was to move as many Christian souls as possible to the safety of our new home — to the New Eden land the Lord has revealed to you as ours. With my limited understanding............I don't understand why you would want to stir the Federals now? They could inflict huge damage on us with their fleet and air force and.....*

Can they now Admiral? Can they now? Smith interrupted. He was shouting now and instinctively Monroe sought to find a way of defusing the situation. Not that he had actually challenged the President, but simply reminded him of what he had stated as a priority a hundred fold. *If they can cause us so much harm,* Smith continued *why have they been so weak in attacking us up to now? The Lord has told me that we should strike at the heart of evil in the coming days and can there be anything more evil within our reach than the Federals?*

Monroe hesitated. He thought back to the message he had received a few minute before his meeting with Smith. Should he tell the President that he knew nuclear weapons had been used against the Federals outside RougeWall? No, if Smith had wanted him to know, he would have told him. It could be dangerous for him to think that Monroe was spying on him. But, assuming the Federals had received the message from – what was the name of the ship again? – the *Jefferson.* Yes, if they had received that message, wouldn't they be gearing themselves for retaliation even now? Timidity won.

If the Lord has spoken to you Mr. President, then the Word of the Lord must be done. This wind is carrying us well, and by tomorrow evening we should have cleared the Strait. The southern Florida lands are either loyal to us or under water, so there is no threat there. What is left of Cuba and the Bahamas are military irrelevancies, so my only concern until we approach Jacksonville is herding the Lord's flock though the Strait without damage. For that, we need to pray to the Lord for continued good weather and remind our captains that they need to keep alert. We do not want a repeat of ... and he stopped mid-sentence as, seeing Smith's reaction, the realization dawned that a reminder of earlier events would be most unwelcome. Monroe paused nervously, and then continued rapidly as if this would hide his error. *Our... your plan was to join with any additional ships coming from Savannah and Charleston after JacksonvilleWall. Intelligence tells me that communications have been very poor, but that a number of ships have been prepared and are awaiting your command Mr. President . And after that, we were to await further orders from yourself. Is that correct?'*

Orders from The Lord, John, Smith replied, his voice and demeanour having returned to normal. Monroe was relieved to note Smith's continued use of the informal. It was difficult to deal with the constant switches between first names and formal titles, though it was a useful indicator of Smith's mood changes.

Mr. President, the Lord's Will Be Done, Monroe continued, using the safest structure he could identify. *May I make the observation that we are not disposed as a battle group to attack from the sea, so can I assume you are thinking of an airstrike of some form? And what kind of distance are you thinking of? Every mile in the air reduces our aviation fuel reserves. And would I be correct in believing that you would wish to split the armada?'* Smith smiled for the second time that morning and perhaps for the tenth time since Monroe had known him. *'He seems to be thriving on the violence,'* Monroe thought to himself.

My thinking exactly John Christian. Smith beamed. *I was thinking that an airstrike would make a very nice breakfast call- could be exactly what so-called President Lopez needs. Perhaps something in the form of a very cold Atlantic bath,* and Smith laughed quietly at his own joke. *Can you see any problems in splitting the fleet? If we allow the ships with the pilgrims to continue out with the wind, we can put a battle fleet under power without too much use of energy. We don't have to go too close to Washington – say take the aircraft carriers within fifty miles or so, that way we preserve the aviation gas.*

I can't see any problems with that Mr. President. We can still leave enough armed vessels with the pilgrim carriers to protect them against any Wuccie ships which may have strayed this far out. I'm a bit concerned about submarines, they could be out in the deeper waters.

Does Lopez still have any? Smith queried.

I'm afraid we have no intelligence on them at all, in fact I'm unsure there are any operational, Monroe replied tensely. *However, we do have some good ships with anti-submarine capability, so I don't think we need worry about that more than any other unknown. Importantly, if the wind and weather hold we should be in range of WashingtonWall ready for a strike say around dawn on the 18th.*

or 19th. I've always been convinced that dawn attacks give the attacker a psychological advantage, and in the case of WashingtonWall we'll have the sun behind us just in case anyone is physically scanning the horizon. We can rocket - launch some Stealth IIs for the first wave, so their radar will almost certainly be useless. And with what type of weapons Mr. President? I assume we are staying with conventional? he added, trying tried to keep his face totally neutral. Smith eyed Monroe carefully, looking for any revealing weakness or indication of hidden secrets in the other man's taught face. *Of course John Christian. You wouldn't want to be the first to use non-conventional weapons on a fellow American would you? Not even on a Wuccie Wall. No, a good, traditional conventional strike at dawn. Something like the Japanese at Pearl Harbour. You remember from your history? They launched some kind of surprise attack in, when was it now? Sometime in the 1940s, at the start of the Second World War if my memory is correct. Only now, we are already effectively at war so no one can say we lacked honour. However, I'm not going to allow use of the Stealths. I know they are getting a bit old, but we have nothing with the same technology, and once they are launched from a carrier they are lost – and we can't deliberately sacrifice any more crews. Bad for morale that.*

But Mr. President, their use could be crucial in the success of this mission and.. *No 'Buts' please Admiral,* Smith replied tersely. *I am clear about that - we shall need those aircraft later. For now, please draw-up a range of scenarios for me by this evening- and then arrange a meeting with the full complement of senior captains. Please do finish your breakfast. It must be getting cold.*

Chapter XV
Unwanted Guests

Bordeaux Forward StrategicWall
EuropaWall Complex: European Confederation of Democratic States
19.00 UTC March 12th

Captain Marie-Claire Heinz hated waiting. That she had been waiting for more than six hours for some lousy English official to arrive had made her temper even worse. That she already engaged in this exercise the day before had kindled her fury, and she had repeatedly asked herself with heavy sarcasm how many thousands of kilometres away was this LondonWall. She been told that this one could speak some French – miracle of miracles – and that she was to show him around the base and make him feel at home. Not to take him anywhere too secure – and certainly not to make him too much at home she'd been told. Not that she would ever sleep with an English - sleeping with the enemy was not her style. *'So why is he being allowed here?'* was, and remained her question.

Her anger had grown during the latter part of the morning when the damage report for her craft arrived. It was worse than had first been thought, and she was now grounded until a detailed examination of the damage had been completed. Now it was night, the patrols had already returned, and she was still waiting at the train terminal for the express from ParisWall. More technical problems she found herself thinking, and partly hoped that the train had fallen off its tracks into some water-filled ditch where the Englishman could slowly drown. Then, in the distance, she saw the lights of the train snaking across the marshes, its progress and speed limited by the need to negotiate the remaining dry land or embankments constructed across the marshes which had enough stability to take the strain. She looked at her watch. *'Nearly eight hours late. Things must be getting worse around Paris,'* she told herself, and not for the first time she asked herself how much longer the capital –her home city -could be kept standing above water in the Seine Delta. Some of the Germans had been really irritating her recently by making cruel jokes – that was what they called them - about how *'Insane it was to protect Paris from the Seine.'* It had taken her a while – and some pronunciation lessons - to understand what she concluded was pathetic, Teutonic humour. One of the problems with everyone communicating in better or worse English was that jokes did not travel, though English – or was it American? – was the lingua franca of the Confederation despite its abandonment by the English. Unfortunately her attempts at developing jokes about *'Boggy Berlin'* had been abandoned - near to perfection - when parts of Berlin's Wall had collapsed, and she had been left in the conflicting position of neither wishing to make poor jokes about the dead nor to let her German colleagues feel that they had got one up on her and the other French pilots.

Finally, the train pulled slowly into the station area, the doors opening almost immediately to disgorge a wave of visibly tired and relieved travelers onto the platform. Most of the passengers wore military uniforms, but it took her only a split second to identify the Englishman from the rest of the civilians. Everyone had been obliged to compromise on their dress because of rationing, but the English appeared to have done so with some enthusiasm. She had always heard that they had a history of dressing in what her mother had described as rather casual and dull clothes, but this one – in his greyness - seemed to have come straight out of an old black and white film. He was good looking though- tall and strongly built with a certain immediate charisma. It took her a few more seconds to realize that there was a ginger-haired woman with the Englishman. Initially she thought that she was another mainlander, but then the clothes and shoes gave it away again. For a second she felt something flash through her system. Perhaps some basic sexual jealousy? Reluctant though she was to admit it, Heinz did find him quite attractive - though the clothes did nothing to add to this she reminded herself. As for this other woman, she checked her papers again and there was no mention of her. *'She must have the right papers to have got this far,'* Heinz told herself, and she stepped forward to meet the couple who were now standing hesitantly on the platform.

It was then that a military policeman stuck his head out of the train door and smiled apologetically. *These yours?* he asked in a French whose singsong immediately revealed their Italian owner. *Sorry. I fell asleep. You English naughty. You promised not to escape without us.* He laughed, disappeared back into the carriage and then reappeared with a sheet of paper.

So these two are not to be trusted on their own after all, Heinz reassured herself, recovering from the perplexity of having two enemy government officials wandering around on their own. Then she reminded herself that, officially at least, the English were no longer formally enemies – but certainly not to be trusted.

You sign here please captain, the MP said once he had delivered the document to Heinz. *You be careful with these two. They very dangerous,* and he laughed. *She attack you with her vomit if you no careful.* The ginger haired woman's eyes flashed and Heinz's English was good enough to catch a torrent of swearwords and some uncomplimentary comments about travel sickness, French trains and why the Europeans were so bloody tight that they couldn't have provided air transport. She pretended not to understand, saluted stiffly, introduced herself and then lead the way to the exit with the Italian MP in tow, and another who had finally emerged with sleepy eyes from the train.

You coming with us? Heinz enquired.

No, captain, the Italian smiled *but you take us to center. You have car, no?*

No. No car. I walked, you walk, and, seeing the disgusted look on Brown's face – ginger head now had a name – she added with pleasure *They walk too. You be gentlemen and carry bags?* and without allowing time to protest she handed the two light travel bags to the

MPs.

It was about one kilometre from the rail station to the square where Heinz had left the official car. She was always reluctant to bring it into the heart of the Wall- it simply used too much fuel for such a short distance. Anyway, it was a pleasant evening and these two could probably do with stretching their legs after hours cooped-up on the train. She glanced at them both as they walked slowly up the steep hill which led from the station. The moon was rising and was powerful enough to cast a pale light across the waters and countryside which could be seen from this side of the Wall. In places the view was sufficiently clear and detailed to reveal the wind rippling the waters and a slight mist exhaling from the tufts of land which protruded irregularly from the shallows. The man, she now remembered he was called La Fontaine, stopped and looked back when they were about half way up the hill. She was more than surprised when he complemented his comments about the beauty of the vista by reciting a few lines from a poem she vaguely remembered studying at school. Despite the name, she'd forgotten that he was supposed to be fluent in French, but ginger head appeared to be struggling to keep up. Heinz's mother had always told her that the English solved all their communication problems in foreign languages by talking more loudly, and she had a mental comic-image of ginger head's hair standing on end as she shouted loudly in a vain attempt to control events. Her instincts told her that, of the two, the woman was more dangerous. The man seemed just a little bit too relaxed, lacking the killer instinct, to be a real threat. But ginger head –she was something different.

Two hours later they were sitting in the base briefing room. Heinz had decided to dump the military police as soon as they had reached the base. They had been nothing but a problem. Cramming them and the English into the car had been difficult, and then she discovered that the English had not eaten since soon after leaving ParisWall.

The MPs had eaten the rations they carried, but had offered nothing to their *prisoners*. Even ginger head's French had been good enough to catch that, and there had been a furious row in which both the English had threatened to leave immediately and inform their government of their mal-treatment. Heinz still had no idea why the two were here, but they seemed important enough to ensure that they were kept happy, and had ordered a meal – a good, real meal, not rations- be taken to their rooms immediately. That had delayed things a lot, and then ginger head had insisted on a shower, which had delayed things to the extent of infuriating the base commander and the other officers who had assembled for their arrival.

Now is was nearly eleven and the lights would be going out in another hour. After that would mean more paperwork explaining why they had used the room at that late time, how much electricity and gas had been used etc. etc., and she had the strongest of feelings that the reports would fall to her. She had learnt years before that junior officers always did the reports. Then, to her relief, the room was suddenly full. She was surprised to see another group of pilots enter the room with the senior officers. One of two she knew quite well, and other she recognized vaguely from flight school. The others were unknown to her, but their uniform flashes indicated that they had been drawn from a large number of member states. She was wondering to herself if they had been involved in some form of pre-briefing, and if so why had she been excluded, when a Major General from the Austrian liaison unit took the floor. He briefly introduced everyone present by name, and then handed over to a colonel who had just been introduced as coming from military intelligence. The occasional pronunciation and grammar mistake was enough to suggest Portuguese as a first language, but Marie-Claire's focus soon shifted from an analysis of his language when he started talking about the English. *You may all be rather surprised to find that we have two English officials with us tonight. As you don't need to be reminded, we have not enjoyed the best of relations with the English for some years, but I would ask you to focus professionally on the task we are dealing with at the present.*

She could have sworn that she saw one of the Dutch officers stiffen. *'Perhaps that had been addressed to him?'* she asked herself. *'They have good reason to hate them.'*

The intelligence officer interrupted her thoughts again. *It is known to only a few very senior people that we have managed to maintain - how shall I say this – a 'working' relationships with some people in the Washington government. You will all keep this information to yourselves. Washington has their sources for intelligence and we – very fortunately – still have a few friends. Our English friends are better in this way – they are very friendly with Washington.* A titter of laughter swept the room before it was stopped by a withering glance from the Austrian. *But we both have a problem, now.* The intelligence man continued. *We both know that something big is happening between Washington and the Christian peoples. It used to be simple disobedience, but every day it looks more and more like open war. We also know that the Christians peoples are doing something big. Very big it seems. And our sources say that we are involved. All of the European.* He paused. *It seems that they don't even like their English friends any more.* There was a more overt roar of laughter this time and Marie-Claire saw ginger head turn red with – was it anger or embarrassment? – though she would have sworn that the man had a quiet inward laugh. *So, even the English are a little worried and have asked us to play with them this time,* he continued. Amidst the laughter, Marie-Claire wondered what had happened to earlier comments about professionalism, but was more than surprised when ginger-head stood up without any introduction. *'How powerful is this woman?'* she asked herself.

Brown waited until there was complete silence and then turned to the previous speaker. *Thank you Captain Suarez,* she said acidly *that was all very entertaining. My name is Miss Brown and I work in the intelligence section of Foreign Affairs. There are plenty of other intelligence services as you doubtless know, but they are a little – shall we say, too close to the*

Americans even for my government's tastes. Now, what I would like to say to you all, on behalf of the English government, is that we have concluded on the basis of our intelligence – and what we have borrowed from yourselves - that the American Christians appear to be planning some form of mass migration. We are not sure where the Christian Americans are going, but the east coast people seem to be sailing towards either Africa or Europe and…

You said 'the east coast people' one of the other intelligence officers interrupted. *Does that mean that nothing is happening in the west, or don't you have no information for that?*

There was a pause for a few seconds, and Marie-Claire realised from the angry flash in her eyes that Brown was not accustomed to be being interrupted. Nor was she good at recovering her composure, for when she started talking again she clearly struggled to re-find the thread of her ideas. *What…that means is. … er that we have less data on the west than the east. As do you,* she added almost triumphantly. *But it does appear that nothing is happening on the west coast at present. Perhaps Smith has no power there, or perhaps the Californians are too strong. Or..*

Or there may be another reason, the same officer interjected *like there is nothing of religious …..how you say – important? - for them that way, in the Asia. All their religion talk is about Europe and the Middle East land - you say Holy Land area. I read nothing from Smith about Asia.'*

Again Brown's face registered her irritation at the interruption. Marie-Claire craned forward to catch a better glimpse of the speaker between the two figures seated immediately in front of her, and she found herself cursing her stupidity in having sat at the back like a guilty school child. The young man who had been talking wore the flash of the Greek contingent, but no sooner had she made a quick calculation that this classic beauty would be worth getting to know than she spotted the army chaplain's cross immediately above it. She had no idea why a religious should have been invited to this meeting, but she made a mental note to check the child-producing status of Greek religious officers, and then turned back to focus on

Miss English.

Thank you Captain …?

Heraklios lady.

Thank you then Captain Heraklios lady. Brown struggled to control her face, pleased with her own joke. *You may be right, it could be that the religious issues is important. That is why we are here tonight. My government, and your government, feel that what is happening in America is so important that we need to know what their intention is. Our reports, and your reports are not very different, indicate that there is some kind of armada carrying many thousands of troops and civilians coming out of the west coast. We don't know the destination, the exact numbers, or the reason, but none of us have the spare food or energy to take in thousands of Christian refugees. This is why we think we should work together on this. The Americans have such a huge advantage over us in all the intelligence areas, and we are limited in what we can do in London by the presence of American military.*

Which is why you need us. True? one of the older Dutch officers interjected. *We can do your dirty work and then you can betray us as usual.*

That would be a negative way of seeing things Brown replied soothingly. *Why can't we work from the premise that none of us want to suddenly find ourselves with tens of thousands of unexpected and unwanted guests, and that each has something to offer. We still have some satellite capability, as do you, but we also borrow information from the Americans – an unwitting present from them to their best friend. However, you have the advantage of being further south and west than our units, so what we are looking for - and our governments, I repeat, have agreed to this – is that you use your air and sea reconnaissance to probe deep into the Atlantic until we find their fleet, discover its composition and work out what on earth they are doing.*

Ah, so that is why we are here! Marie-Claire could barely restrain her anger, and looking round the room she saw that the other pilots had also realized the reason for their presence -they were about to be sent out into the Atlantic deeps to hunt for American ships. Marie-Claire made a quick calculation. There were some twenty pilots in the room including herself. Given recent experience, between ten and fifteen of these were unlikely to return from this mission. There was an immediate interruption from one of the younger pilots. The precision and clarity of her English, re-enforced her initial suspicion, generated simply by a mass of blonde hair, that she was probably from one of the Confederation's Nordic provinces. *Excuse me Major, but don't we have any satellite capacity for the Atlantic? I thought the English lady said we had. With all due respect, it seems to me that if we are down to this level of military preparedness that we are all in great trouble.*

What we have at the moment is a very limited satellite capacity, Flight Lieutenant. Suarez who replied. *We do have a couple of old birds, but they are in a relatively erratic orbit above the equator with no fuel for major navigational activity. So, they go nowhere. They are ...how you say 'stuck'. If the Americans go south enough, we can see them. If not, we see nothing. Miss Brown says the English have the same problem, but I not so sure about that,* and another acid glance exchanged between the two. *So, we work with what we know we have. We are trying to get another satellite in orbit, but since we lost our launch sites in Russia and Guiana this is very hard. The Chinese and Indians are not organized to this now, and we all know the problems of trying to launch from the sea.*

Not that this has stopped the American Christians. Henry spoke for the first time, and all eyes turned inquisitively to focus on him. He hesitated for a second and then continued. *There must be something truly important about this activity. From what we can understand Smith is risking the lives of hundreds of thousands of his followers by going out into the deep seas. Admittedly he has chosen the best time of year – there shouldn't be too many storms at this season. But, and this is a really big 'but', we all know how unpredictable things are and if a really big one developed he could lose most of his ships. So, whatever this is, it is big and..*

What kind of ships has he?' interrupted another pilot. *It might be useful for us to know what air defence capability we might meet. After all, it would be kinda good if some of us got back.*

Brown waited for the nervous laughter to subside before she chose to reply. *Our intelligence – and this is basically what we have been told by Washington- suggests that he has everything from a few regular Federal navy warships through passenger ships to old scrap heaps which probably won't make the journey. In between there's everything from oil tankers which have been converted to aircraft carriers down to bulk carriers which are being used to carry people and supplies. I don't know if that coincides with whatever information you have.*

There was a pause. *So, if we know all this, why don't we know where they are going and why?* Marie-Claire had spoken without thinking and was left almost shocked to hear her own voice.

A good question Captain …. Heinz, Henry replied, struggling to remember the name. He paused, smiled and added *And may I thank you for organising the meal* as a way of compensating for his social gaff. Almost immediately he regretted his words. Heinz blushed visibly and there were some hoots of derision whilst Brown gave him a scathing sideways glance as though to say *'Fancy her do you?'* before she enquired *And Mr. La Fontaine, you want to talk about something other than the food?*

It may be, Henry continued after a moment's hesitation *Brown*

Actually, Mr. La Fontaine doesn't know very much about the intelligence side, Brown interrupted abruptly. She was too late to avoid the querulous incredulity which swept the room. So here was a man who claimed to know Smith, who had actually met Smith. Smith the man who had helped bring the once most-powerful military country in the world to a state of near-anarchy and internal division. And the Smith who had threatened death and damnation to anyone and everyone who did not share his religious beliefs.

That Brown's abruptness was evidence that she feared La Fontaine was going to reveal too much was obvious to everyone in the room 'I briefed Mr. La Fontaine on some of these things during our trip down,' she added hurriedly to try and cover her mistake. 'So perhaps these questions should be addressed to me. Henry – Mr. La Fontaine – is here partly because he studied Smith as part of his doctoral thesis and partly because he actually met the man briefly. He is, therefore, our 'expert' on his beliefs and behaviour. He is also, I must say, somewhat braver than I had been led to believe – out of duty to country he has volunteered to join us on the flights as an observer / advisor.'

The hostile titter which swept the room was cut short as the normal lighting went out and the curfew lights kicked in. Long distance pilots hated carrying anything more than the basic crew. In an emergency it reduced their manoeuvrability and the extra weight was a drain on fuel. If a flight hit bad weather every litre could make the difference between reaching home safely and being swept by the winds to who knew where. Marie Claire personally knew a pilot whose crew had been reported lost, but some of which had managed to make it back to Europe a year later after being carried onto the African coast. Brown paused in the face of this new hostility and then, with a grim smile which was unseen in the emergency lighting added: *Smith is also one of my specialisms. You will doubtless be pleased to know that when I said 'us' it was because I shall be coming out with you too. This is part of the agreement between our governments, so I regret to say you are obliged to enjoy our company.*

01.27 UTC March 13th

The military police escort south had been an irritating joke, though sitting for hours without food while their escort had stuffed themselves had been extremely unpleasant. It had confirmed warnings in their pre-departure briefing – *'Expect hostility'* – though otherwise the freedom and courtesy extended them by the Europeans had shocked both La Fontaine and Brown. The windows of the train had been left open, not closed as they had been briefed in London. Consequently, they had been free to observe the countryside, waterways, towns and cities as the rain rumbled along. In security terms they had been free to see whatever there was to see, and both had been surprised by the quality of life they observed as they passed. It was certainly much higher than they had gathered from their desks in London, though for miles after leaving the coast at AmienWall they had passed over what seemed to be interminable expanses of sea, marshes and villages which were flooded to a greater or lesser extent before starting the slow climb towards the concrete masses which constituted ParisWall. La Defense was the terminal for this section of line, and whilst Brown was adamant that this was connected with the Wall defences, Henry was sure that he had somewhere read that there was an older origin for the name.

Now, they were both walking freely inside a military installation. Technically the European were no longer 'enemies' though the terms tripped of the tongue with remarkable ease. There had been no major hostilities for over seven years – not since the American Atlantic fleet had helped lift a blockade in the Channel. Then, in one of the great ironies of life, a large part of the fleet had been sent to the ocean's floor in the greatest storm thus far in the century. Many of the survivors had been driven back to England, and there had stayed, fearful of venturing out to sea again.

La Fontaine and Brown were walking freely on the grass border at the perimeter of the base. The lack of lighting was compensated for by a radiant moon which was only fleetingly covered by scurrying clouds. It was mild enough to require only a shirt and they had both coated their bare skin themselves with anti-mosquito cream; though the injections in London might save them from malaria the cream was proving highly effective in protecting them against incessant bites.

They had both expected some sort of escort on the base. Instead, as soon as the meeting had finished, they had been abandoned by the French officer who had collected them from the station. She had stopped only long enough to confirm that they knew their ways back to their rooms – she had made a point about single rooms Brown had noted – and then scurried away. Clearly, she was less than happy about the prospect of carrying passengers on the mission and Henry hazarded a guess that she was probably being really unpleasant so that they would ask to go with another pilot. She had, after all, been quite civilized all the way up from the station. They stopped under the branches of the sole tree in the area. Its height, and the age evidenced in its tortured branches, clearly showed that it had survived the construction of the base. *Do you think we can talk here?* La Fontaine whispered gently.

Brown looked around and shrugged her shoulders. *I have as much idea as you.* Brown purred to Henry's surprise. *It all looks very empty, but they could have the place full of bugs and nanos and all sorts of exotic security and listening systems. There's nothing showing on my detector, but… Tell you what though, the French-German bitch seems to think we are – shall we say, doing nice things together. Did you notice her comment about the rooms? How about you and I proving her right and having a good snog?*

Before La Fontaine could respond, she drew him forcefully to her, kissed him passionately for uncountable seconds with her tongue darting boisterously into the depths of his mouth, and then let herself hang close to him. *Get too randy before I say so and I'll cut your balls off later,* she whispered, feeling his embryonic erection. La Fontaine's latent passion drained away instantly. *Now Henry,* she cooed lovingly in his ear, *we may appear to be alone, but I'll bet you my pension they have our rooms bugged. We have to take our chances here. So, what was it you were going to say in there about Smith? Letting too much information out reduces our value and that could be a really serious mistake at this stage – and we don't like serious mistakes do we darling?* Brown drew away slightly and looked him directly in the eyes. *So be careful what you say darling. Otherwise, your precious wife and child could have a nasty accident at home. A very nasty accident. Understand darling? Remember that these people are not really our friends, and that we are here from necessity to protect our country. Oh, and do keep your eyes off the captain woman. I know she's pretty, but don't get too close – I may find you useful in that way if we are away from home long enough,* she said, pushing La Fontaine gently away.

La Fontaine found himself standing shaking. Brown had deliberately raised her voice each time she had said 'darling' in a primitive ploy intended to confuse anyone eavesdropping on them.

She would doubtless be carrying some form of counter measure, as was he, but his raised voice was no pretext. *Listen to me you bitch. I don't know who you think you are, or what powers you have, but this is not England. And even if it were, if I find anything has happened to my family I shall find a way of getting to you. You understand? Whatever security you, have I shall find a way of getting to you. So listen, I shall do my job, but you keep the threats out of this.*

With each sentence he prodded his fingers into Brown's ample bosom, before turning and blindly storming off in the general direction of their accommodation block somewhere on the other side of the base. In his haste, and in the darkness of the curfew hours, Brown heard him regularly swear as he tripped or walked into things. She stood under a tree for a few minutes laughing at la Fontaine's comic progress, but became more thoughtful as his curses faded away. La Fontaine's file has suggested he would be an easy, malleable subject with no real loyalties and no great courage. Macgregor had been mixed towards him, both being reluctant to let him go, but also describing him as …*a bit of a loose end with a love of good food, wine and women*… Certainly his wife would be a bit upset to discover how many junior staff he'd already screwed that year. However, the force of his reaction to her words had revealed that he was not without loyalty or something to Rachel and his son. Or was he simply ratty because he was tired? The fatigue of the day's journey's catching up with her, she decided to leave these thoughts to the morning and made for her own way to the accommodation block by a route she had decided was both shorter and easier than Henry's.

Some twenty minutes after she had left, two figures slowly emerged from the growing mist. They wandered nonchalantly across to the tree where Smith and La Fontaine had been standing and, while one coughed amateurishly on a cheap cigarette, one extracted a small device from his jacket pocket and gently manipulated a series of controls. Almost immediately, a small moth flew from the trunk of the tree and deftly settled into a slot on the device itself. The man connected a set of earplugs whilst staring intently at the images on the small screen mounted on the device.

Any luck? Both started as Marie-Claire arrived silently. She looked in amusement at the private struggling to master the cigarette. *What do you think is happening? Are we spying on them or do you think they are hiding somewhere and spying on us? Stop it with that thing before you catch the cancer.* Relieved, the private dropped the smoking cigarette and ground it viciously into the ground with his boot. *Have a look yourself,* the sergeant suggested with a broad grin. *The English woman is – how do you say it?- a real bitch – I almost feel sorry for the man. I'm pleased with the way the system has worked. They were both wearing jammers, but we have really good audio. These English always under…what the word again? understand, no ….underestimate? us.*

Heinz grimaced. She had met the English in combat and had learned that they should not be underestimated. *That may prove to be a mistake one day. For maintenant –now- do we ave anything useful on this?*

I don't know. So far she is being not kind to him. Here, you want to listen? and removing the ear pieces he handed them to Heinz.

She looked at them with some disdain and them, with a wry smile, put the plug in. *Sergeant, I hope you washed your ears recently and that was regulation wax,* she added. The two men tittered and stood watching her as she listened with increasing intensity.

At the end she took out the plugs, a grimness replacing the smile. *Sergeant Moulin, I'm formally taking responsibility for this and will ensure that it goes directly to security. You two are dismissed for tonight, but report for duty demaine — tomorrow — at 08.00. These two need to be controlled. I shall speak to the commander first thing in the morning. I, for one, do not want to fly with people we cannot trust.*

Chapter XVI
Eastern Clouds
WashingtonWall.
23.19 UTC March 13th

Lieutenant Gary Ragler spat again into the dust outside the bunker which served as the newly re-formed Army Aircorp's WashingtonWall base. He had been planning a Friday night out with some fellow officers. A few beers, perhaps some bowling, perhaps picking up some nice women. Then he'd suddenly been ordered down to this hell- on- earth to fly a night surveillance in a piece of canvas strips held together by wire and cheap wood, but with enough ammunition on board to blow them all into another hell if anything went wrong. The C22 had been out all day, one of Ragler's friends having drawn a lucky straw for the day flight, and was now coming in late – it had been held up by some strong head winds so the ground crews informed him.

Despite its slight build, the C22 was an impressive piece of technology, and it wasn't really accurate to describe it as canvas and wood. The main struts were built from some of the strongest and lightest alloys the Federal government could produce, whilst the ships armaments ranged from heavy machine guns for close defence to sophisticated air-to-air and air-to ground missiles for attack purposes. Ragler and the other five crew would much rather have been spending the night with some beautiful woman or man, but a sudden canceling of their leave meant they would be stuck several thousand feet in the air over the Atlantic monitoring radar and comms screens. He watched uninterestedly as a couple of land anchor were dropped from either end of the craft, the engines cut, and the C22 winched down into a secure berth. The hatches opened and the crew hauled themselves out, whilst a team of engineers and technicians moved in and fuel and oxygen lines were connected and activated. The senior pilot, an elderly captain Ragler vaguely knew, looked around, spotted Ragler and walked stiffly over.

You taking this son? he demanded, deliberately disregarding Ragler's failure to salute.

Sure am Sir. Must have done something wrong to have deserved this one on a leave day.

Wouldn't say that Lieutenant. Haven't you heard, all leave has been cancelled, so we are all in the same position. You know what this is all about?

All I know is that we are taking this thing on some kinda proving test. Apparently we have to do a test of the night systems. But why are we going so far out and why she fully armed for that Sir?

The captain drew slightly closer, looked around, and continued in a slightly hushed voice. *This is off the record and you are instructed to say nothing, not even to your crew — that is an order. Officially this is approving test. That's the reason on the fuel authorization slip. Unofficially, and believe me I never said this, the army is doing a bit of unofficial scouting for the navy. They haven't got the fuel slips to fly out past the one hundred mile mark, which is why you are going to be flying out far beyond that mark and patrolling overnight.*

Patrolling Sir? What we looking for?

What I understand from my briefing is that a large number of Christian ships set sail a few days ago. The top command have this idea that they might be coming this way, but seems the President doesn't. Or at least that's how I read it — otherwise he would have authorized the fuel slips. So that's why the most of the navy boys have set sail and why we are helping to cover their ass by covering this area here. And he pointed to a zone on a map in his hand. *The C23 is covering the area immediately to your north, but I suspect that if there is any trouble coming it will be in your area.*

Why can't they use radar or satellites to this job, Sir? I can't see no reason to spend the night freezing when this could be monitored from a secure site.

Three reasons Lieutenant, the Captain replied glumly. *First, the Christians have some damned sophisticated stealth systems — we been hit before with no radar warning. Second, we have no satellite cover any more. They took our last birds out a few days ago- don't know how, but seems they got into the SAC control in*

Colorado or something like that. Thirdly, and here the older man started to prod Ragler vigorously in the chest with his fingers *you are a regular soldier and this is your duty. You should be ashamed of yourself to be wearing your country's uniform and talking like some spoilt kid. What do you think this is? The last Friday to lay some broad? Come on soldier, get yourself and your crew on board and get this thing fueled and airborne.*

31.02 degrees north. 83.3 degrees west.
23.22 UTC March 13th

Monroe sat in a large leather chair in his cabin, nursing a large glass of vintage Kentucky whiskey. He didn't usually drink anything so strong, and Smith, as a wine man, probably wouldn't approve. Today he didn't care so much. He had been suffering from flu-like symptom for the past twenty four hours and so felt justified in slugging down a glass or two or three of something strong – clearly for medicinal purposes. He could feel the very slightest tremor of *Genesis* as she moved north, and when he placed his glass on the table the oscillation of the whisky made this even more evident. He closed his eyes for a few seconds to savour the fiery taste sliding down his throat and when he opened them again it was to scrutinize the large map of the eastern seaboard hanging on the cabin wall. The journey through the Florida Strait had gone more smoothly then he could have dared hope. There had been no sightings of Federal ships or aircraft, and a small Cuban fishing boat had been the only vessel sighted. He had felt some compunction about ordering the sinking of this, but he daren't risk it returning to its home port and reporting on the size and movements of his ships.

His main concern at this point was the way the armada was increasingly spreading like a long thread across the ocean. The original plan at RougeWall had been that the entire fleet would be shielded by an outer skin of warships and more heavily armed vessels. However, that departure had been more chaotic than he had dared inform Smith, and he had barely managed to create the formation he had intended when course changes going through the Strait had again disturbed it. Above all, it concerned him that having chosen *Genesis* as the flagship, Smith insisted that it led the fleet. Having what was essentially an aircraft carrier lead without any forward protection was against the accepted wisdom of naval strategy, and Monroe felt deeply uneasy.

A further difficulty arose from Monroe's own insistence that wireless communication be kept to a minimum in order to reduce the risk of Federal interception revealing his position. Consequently, the armada was operating using a system of semaphore relays sending messages down and across the line. With the best skill and will in the world there were inevitable errors in the process. *'Not,'* Monroe thought to himself *'that we are doing so badly. With some 322 ships in the armada there aren't many similar examples in naval history.'* What was now going to be problematic was the integration of the ships coming out of JacksonvilleWall. With an existing tail back of nearly fifty miles, finding the right stations for the new vessels was going to be problematic and he was just about to pour himself another glass when there was a knock at the door.

Come in, he ordered. A middle aged ensign opened the door, a large crucifix advertising his loyalty, and his face instantly demonstrating his disapproval as the smell of alcohol hit his nostrils

Sorry to disturb you Admiral, but the Captain requests your presence on the bridge. He tried calling you and he inclined his head to the phone Monroe had deliberately left disconnected to get some peace *but there was no reply.*

Problem ensign? Monroe queried.

I'm not in a position to say Sir. I was simply asked to invite you to the bridge at your earliest.

Monroe hauled himself reluctantly from the luxury of his chair. *Tell me —who's the duty Captain now? I've forgotten — tell the Captain that I shall be with him immediately.*

Captain Wallace in on the bridge Sir, the ensign said, with what Monroe felt was a touch of criticism that the admiral was unaware of who was currently in control of the armada flagship. *I shall inform him that you are on your way. Permission to leave, Sir!* and he saluted smartly as he left the room and closed the door.

Monroe turned to the small sink in the cabin and threw a handful of cold water over his face before adding a blob of toothpaste to his brush and giving his teeth a perfunctory cleaning – just enough to remove the smell of alcohol. Minutes later he walked onto the bridge, his uniform fully buttoned and smartly returning the salutes of the crew stationed there.

'*That'll stop any rumours the ensign might start to spread,*' he thought to himself, and then, catching sight of Captain Wallace he addressed him in Smith's new style. *Christian Brother, how can I help?*

Wallace was several years older than Monroe, and if he had been more able would probably have been of sufficient seniority to have been executed in Smith's purge. As it was, he was a plodder of no great ability who had eventually worked his way through the ranks through effort and praying with the right people. He turned, and Monroe saw worry writ large on his face. *The Lord has been bountiful to us Brother Admiral, but I fear I lack the skills to respond to his generosity.*

The problem then Alf? Monroe responded in a less formal and more efficient manner.

One problem is that, Wallace indicated, pointing to their starboard bow.

Good God! Monroe declared in astonishment. Looking out through the glass, the ocean was full of navigation lights from ships bearing down on them. He had expected twenty, perhaps thirty ships out of JacksonWall, but a quick glance told him there close to a hundred, though their size and nature would only be clear come dawn.

I'm not sure this a problem Alf! This is wonderful! Monroe exclaimed. *Does the President know?*

The President has been informed admiral, as per his own instructions. He should be with us within the next few minutes.

And the other 'problem' Alf? I hope it is as pleasing!

Well admiral, these new ships are bearing down on us with the wind behind them. I trust you have noticed it has suddenly shifted to a northerly and greatly increased in strength. As you can see, much of the fleet is in the process of taking down their sails and shifting to motors but things are becoming rather muddled. How are you proposing to integrate the two groups without radio communication? I cannot see a way.

Monroe's concerns rose immediately. Wallace might be rather slow but he had anticipated a problem which Monroe had not. Indeed, variations in technology, skill and experience on ships within the armada were becoming increasingly evident. Some vessels, a minority, had no sails even for auxiliary power. The majority had automated systems which raised, lowered or tacked the sails according to either human or computer judgement. Finally, there were those which relied exclusively on human labour and calculation to control the sails, though some of these ships had been in the process of modification before leaving RougeWall and work was continuing – at a very slow pace – as they sailed north. To compound these complexities, some of the less experience captains were starting their motors as soon as they felt their sails were adequately stowed, and were beginning to bear down upon slower ships in front of them. Monroe broke into a cold sweat as memories of the chaos outside RougeWall flooded into his mind. There was no choice. Looking rapidly at the disposition screen on the bridge, he issued a series of precise orders to the comms teams seated at their stations, and within seconds the airways between the ships were awash with encrypted messages.

Chapter XVII
Distant Sounds

Latitude 35.8 north. Longitude 77.7 degrees west.

01.13 UTC March 14th

Ragler was still smarting from the dressing down he had received at base. It wasn't that the captain had been wrong – it was the fact that he had both been right and that he had faced down in front of his own crew. To add to his ill humour, the internal heating system on the C22 wasn't coping with the −10 Celsius they were reading externally. Despite the thermal suits the entire crew had felt increasingly miserable since a couple of hours after take off. Something to put in the trials book which the engineers would probably do nothing about.

Initially, they had met a strong northerly wind which had pushed them south at a speed which their navigator/gunner calculated would take them far into enemy territory before their shift was over. According to the air force weather reports they had been issued with, there was a change in wind direction at ten thousand feet and when they reached that height Ragler had allowed the wind to carry them north with almost no use of engine. For some reason which they would have to discuss with the test engineers, they found it difficult to stabilize at that height and continued to rise until external icing started to weigh them down; hence the internal cold. They had actually been carried so far north that they had had a brief radar contact with the C23, provoking a rapid exchange of recognition signals to avoid being fired upon, and some cutting questions from ground control as to who was navigating that day.

Then they had turned south west and started some routine exercises, the engines pushing the craft easily forward helped by an incessant, increasing tailwind. Realising that they were again being pushed too far south, Ragler tried to counter the effects of this by first increasing their altitude and then, finding this made matters worse, trying to find calmer airflows and various heights. He could see from the growing anxiety on the navigator's face sitting next to him that he was growing concerned about the amount of gas they were using with all the changes, but he felt unusually optimistic that they have enough to get home or get to Norfolk if pushed -though when he thought about the latter option he remembered that there was occasional Christian anti-aircraft fire there.   Finally, to their relief, they found a layer of calmer and relatively warm air at around the three thousand feet mark and decided to stay at that height. There was some discussion about this, the radar /comms operator complaining that the height really cut down her view to the horizon and the armaments commander warning their low height greatly reduced maneuverability in the event of an attack. Ragler was still in no mood for argument and cut them both short.

The next hour was spent trying various trim maneuvers and practicing the length of time it took to go to battle stations in the dirigible's cramped, dimly lit core. By the time they started to roll the missiles into their bays for the third time, Ragler was beginning to feel that this could prove to be a good ship. He was in the middle of the exercise when the radar/comms operator came through on his earpiece, and he glanced up to see her waving him over to the monitor bay. *'Shit!'* he swore to himself. *'Why do I always get rookies on the crew when we're trying out new gear. Fuckn crazy.'*

Ya? he enquired.

Sir, have a listen to this. It's really faint and I ain't not sure if it's background static or encoded stuff. Ain't ours if it's encrypt - if I get the manual properly. Reluctantly Ragler made his way to her bay and took the headset. Almost immediately he found himself regretting his criticism. Faintly, against waves of static, was the dimmest, fragmented echo of a digital signal. True, it could be so distorted that even the onboard computer software couldn't identify it as friendly, but the battlefield computers rarely made mistakes of that nature. It continued for a few seconds and then stopped.

Well done Collins, he beamed, priding himself on his instant name recall even on the first flight with a new crew. *Make sure the recording of this is double saved, and try and get a rough fix on location ….and yes I know,* he added seeing the concern on the corporal's face. *I know it'll only be a rough fix, but do your best. See if you can use the log history if the signal doesn't come back.*

Shall I send it through to Washington as a message Sir? Collins enquired enthusiastically. *You think it important?*

Could be important or could be a Christian porn channel Ragler replied with a laugh, *but it ain't gonna survive another transmit and we'll risk setting ourselves up as a target for the Chrisies. Store it and we'll hand the unit over to intelligence when we land. Our orders are to continue testing out this baby and we got another six hours or more of that crap. So well done, and keep your ears and eyes open for anything else. If this is good you could get yourself a nice bonus or even a promotion. Who know, we might all get boosted! And pigs do indeed fly!* He gave Collins a friendly pat on the back and, laughing, returned to the missile practice.

WashingtonWall
11.00 UTC March 14th

Ragler brought the dirigible in to land with at least an hour's gas. He was as proud of the fact as his crew were amazed, and was unsure whether he should attribute it to his flying skills or the quality of the C22. He decided to go for the former. They had radioed ahead when approaching Dulles airbase, and a couple of intelligence officers were standing, anxiously, waiting in the wind and rain. They took the data-box like it was their latest, best ever Christmas presents, though Ragler insisted they sign for it before he would let them go. Then they headed for their transport as Ragler and his crew walked through the driving rain towards the mess – he had promised the entire crew RealCoffee in gratitude for what he believed had been a good night's work.

31.90 degrees north. 80.12 degrees west.
11.10 UTC March 14th

'413,' that was the number that kept going through Monroe's head. With the additional ships out of JacksonvilleWall the armada now totaled 413. Neither Monroe nor Smith felt happy about the 13, and Monroe was already considering how they could change the number by abandoning some of the less valuable vessels. Obviously Monroe had not had the opportunity to inspect all the new arrivals personally, but since first light his officers had been flitting along the lines of the new arrivals, stopping to quickly check crew capacity, cargos – including humans of course- and weapons with their captains. Simultaneously, an eye had been run over the boats to decide their seaworthiness, power and size.

Consequently, Monroe already had a reasonably clear picture of the pluses and minuses he had acquired. On the positive side were four large coastguard vessels from the former Federal navy. These were welcome for their armaments and speed, but worryingly demanding in terms of fuel- no one had considered the possibility of fitting them out with sails. Of greatest concern were the twenty or so ships which were essentially no more than large yachts, but each of which was crammed with thirty or more people, most of them camped out on the open deck. They reminded him of historical films he had seen of evacuating troops clinging on to whatever was available. There was a very old one about a place called Dunk something, and more recently the American and European evacuations from Istanbul. The captains of the newly arrived ships clearly had no inkling of the journey ahead and would find controlling the vessel in poor seas impossible with the encumbrances on deck – assuming that the passengers were not washed overboard. This could prove an academic discourse however, for if he guessed Smith's intentions correctly they would be soon be dead from lack of water. The order had been to ensure a minimum of a month's water per person, and none of these could be carrying supplies for more than a few days. Smith's refusal to divulge his full plans was becoming a source of increasing frustration amongst his officers, and Monroe was on the receiving end of a stream of extremely polite, but increasingly concerned questions. Shepherding resources was now second nature for even the youngest child, but for the military it was essential to know how long resources need to be shepherded for. Glancing at his watch, Monroe felt a further wave or irritation. Smith was arriving later and later for meetings, and to Monroe this was both an indication of diminished respect and an enormous waste of time when important decisions needed to be made. They had been moving north under engine power for nearly eleven hours now. The engines had been working at low levels in order to allow changes in the fleet disposition, but valuable fuel was being consumed by the minute. There was no hope of the armada tacking under sail given its current size, disposition and changes in the weather. Monroe had proposed that they either go to anchor at a spot near where Brunswick had once stood, and which was partly sheltered from the increasingly powerful northerly. There they could ride out what were now nearly storm force winds. Alternatively, they could at least tack further to the east so that they were heading less directly into the wind. Smith had opposed both suggestions, but had promised to discuss them further on the bridge with the charts and other senior officers. Finally, twenty minutes late, he arrived.

Good morning Christian officers, he beamed with a genuine warmth reflecting the elation he felt from the increase in numbers. It was an enormous boost to his ego. *How are we progressing?*

Rather than repeat the same arguments and risk appearing inherently opposed to The President, Monroe had briefed his duty officers as to the problems he identified and the potential consequences. They did well, in part thanks to the goodwill arising from the fleet expansion and –unknown to them- in larger part thanks to Mrs.

Monroe accepting that Smith service her three times overnight. Her advanced pregnancy seemed to increase his excitement, rather than generate any consideration on his part. The combined result was that Monroe found his initial suggestion of sailing in a more north-easterly direction almost immediately accepted. Sailing due east would have been potentially dangerous for the stability of some of the smaller vessels, but Monroe calculated that sailing some twenty degree east of the northerly would be both safe and would result in their being well located geographically for the units he was planning in preparation for the attack on WashingtonWall.

He used the opportunity to slowly change the disposition of the armada, which now snaked in an unwieldy tail for some thirty miles behind *Genesis* and approximately twenty miles across. The exercise was a double nightmare because of the return to semaphore communications, the content of which seemed to be inevitably garbled despite repeated practice sessions. Monroe felt they had been extremely fortunate not to have been detected in their brief use of radio comms off JacksonvilleWall, and was unprepared to repeat the exercise either until there was an emergency or they were many hundreds of miles further off the coast.

He had managed to obtain two important sessions from Smith after much pleading. Tactically, he had gained agreement that Monroe could deploy a mixed force of heavily armed vessels forward of the *Genesis*. At least the huge vessel would now have some forward protection if, or when, they encountered Federal forces. Secondly, Monroe had at last confirmed that there was no intent to land again on the mainland, nor was there any intention to sail south and retrace their steps. Monroe was still bemused by Smith's ultimate intention, but this new strategic certainty enabled him to order a special team he had assembled to start engaging in another slow redeployment of the fleet.

In addition to creating a hard core forward of the *Genesis,* additional vessels were slowly re-positioned on the starboard side of the armada with a view to their being detached for the attack on Washington. A further, less substantial, screen was being deployed on the port side of the fleet in the hope that any threat would appear from the landward side rather than the deep Atlantic. Following the same logic, a heavy battle group was being created at the rear of the formation, reflecting Monroe's firm belief that, whatever the level of success in the attack on Washington, Smith was about to stir the wasps' nest.

Finally, within all the other shifts in deployment, Monroe was slowly detaching the vast majority of his ships so that they were slipping slowly eastwards. This was one of the reasons why the Genesis had lost its lead role. Given its speed, power and air capacity it was only logical that it should be involved in the attack, so the *Genesis* followed its own battle group in detaching from the fleet. Smith was to transfer his flag to the *David*, a heavy battle cruiser, and the two groups were to reunite again several days later at a time and place which, Smith informed Monroe, would be communicated by The Lord in good time. Smith was about to leave the bridge, and had already asked Monroe to join him for some RealCoffee, when one of the comms lieutenant looked up and urgently addressed the admiral.

Admiral Sir, the Lee V is breaking radio silence. She is taking in water and the captain believes she will sink within the hour. He is asking for immediate assistance.

The Lee V, what exactly is that? And you lieutenant, I want those transmissions silenced immediately. You are not to reply except to order the ship's captain to cease all transmissions.

Captain Miles was one of the officers who had been assigned to log and control the disposition of the fleet, and within seconds he had pulled-up the computer data and identified the vessel as one of the small ones out of JacksonvilleWall. It had twenty five souls aboard including two infants.

She breaking radio silence Admiral Sir the comms lieutenant babbled, the confusion and concern clear in his voice. *The captain is begging for help and keeps changing channel to ask for assistance, but she is being left behind the fleet. No one is responding to her signals.* Miles, Monroe and Smith looked at each other with knowing, but troubled, eyes. There was silence for nearly a minute until Monroe spoke. *Captain Miles, what is the nearest armed vessel we have to the Lee V?*

The Charity Miles replied almost immediately. *Bout three miles ahead and increasing distance.* Monroe hesitated for a second. 'Charity' was an unfortunate name in the context of what he and Smith had already agreed and informed all officers of captain's rank and above. Lieutenant, is she still broadcasting?

Yes Admiral, Sir. She's sweeping all the old emergency bands now.

Mother of God, Monroe mumbled she'll have the Federal around us like bees to a honey pot. *Lieutenant, you are to break radio silence with the Charity and order it to sink that vessel immediately using whatever weapons are required. There is to be no, I repeat no, turning back to collect any survivors.* A wave of faces on the bridge turned in total disbelief, several individuals daring to murmur objections. Monroe hoped that Smith would support him at this juncture, but the President looked down at his feet. He was clearly giving Monroe the responsibility for this, although the two men had agreed the policy.

Ladies and gentlemen, Monroe found himself saying *we are in a state of war, and we cannot – I repeat cannot – allow the weakness of some to threaten the safety of the majority. The President and I have agreed this policy in consultation with other officers. Now lieutenant, I am ordering you to communicate that order. Or do I have you removed?'* he added, inclining his head to the bridge marine guards. The lieutenant swallowed hard, blinked and then opened the communication link to the *Charity.* Meanwhile, Smith stormed off, all thought of coffee forgotten.

You fucking bastard, Monroe found himself mouthing silently. *You wanted me to be seen taking sole responsibility for this.* Leaving the bridge, he walked down onto the flight deck, alone apart from a marine bodyguard. A growing unease filled him. Past a certain level in the officer corps Smith was infamous for his paranoia and lack of trustworthiness. *'I wonder what he has in mind for me at the end of this journey?'* Monroe asked himself. *'Once we make landfall he doesn't need an admiral, and certainly not one who can share the glory of a successful pilgrimage.'* He stood pensively as the sound of the Charity's first shell could be heard in the distance.

WashingtonWall
17.00 UTC March 14th

Ragler cursed as the phone in his Officers' Accommodation room penetrated the depths of what was proving to be a highly satisfactory and stimulating dream. There was this blonde serving in one of the bars on West 22nd who had the biggest tits he had ever seen and, this being Saturday, he had pencilled in an evening trying to get her into bed. As the squeal finally dragged him into consciousness, he cursed again and then swore down the mouthpiece until a voice at the other end of the line silenced him. Ashen faced, within minutes he was in the shower and was just finishing the last touches to his uniform when there was a loud knock at the door.

Lieutenant Ragler? enquired the MP, checking his uniform name for confirmation of the reply. *General Lall's compliments. He is waiting for you in the briefing room.*

General Lall? Ragler queried incredulously, thinking back to the stream of profanity he had just heaped on the caller. Seconds later he was marching down the corridor, flanked by two MPs, whilst fellow officers glanced at him uncertainly. He was unsure whether to feel important or threatened by events, the only certainty being that this urgent meeting had something to do with the mission he had completed only hours earlier. There was a squad of marines standing guard outside the briefing room, and a larger group of officers milling around with no clear motive other than to try and discover what was happening. The lead escort knocked at the door. A captain opened it and looked around critically. *Clear these people away sergeant*, he instructed with a volume intended to be heard by all *and if anyone tries pulling rank on you send them to see me. Lieutenant Ragler, this way please.*

Lall was sitting on a desk, holding a bundle of documents. Ragler thought he looked as exhausted as he felt, but this didn't stop the general standing briskly to attention to return Ragler's salute. You've got a good range of vocabulary there son, Lall started with a smile. *I assume your ma doesn't normally call at this time?*

No Sir, not normally Ragler replied, struggling to remember exactly which parts of his very extensive bar-based vocabulary he had used. *My apologies, Sir.*

Accepted Lieutenant, though I fear I may have to apologise to you for what I am about to say. You and your crew brought back some very useful data from last night's mission – the trials shall we say. Intelligence is still working on the codes, but your navigator and comms did an excellent job in getting a fix on the origins of the signal – perhaps a bit rough, but excellent given the circumstances I've been told. You appreciate this is all top secret, yes? and he waited for Ragler to nod his head vigorously. *Now the bad news is that we need to get a more idea of the enemy's location and, as you may already be aware, all of this is happening in what others might describe as an unofficial way.*

Sir? Ragler queried. *To be clear, this is connected with the rumour that these are officially craft trials but we are really doing work the navy and, or, air force can't afford? That the rumour at least.*

You have it exactly Lieutenant. However, sadly for you, your crew did such a good job last night that I want you out again. On paper you are very inexperienced, but in reality you either performed brilliantly or were very lucky. I need both, so I'm taking a gamble with you. That means you lose you leave for today, and perhaps there will be no leave for any of you until we find these fanatic bastards and discover what the hell they are doing. Come back with some more intell for me today so that I can get the President's permission for more activity. Ragler's face failed to hide his disappointment and anger as Lall spoke. For the second time in as many days his plans had been frustrated. *Listen son,* Lall continued *I'm sure not pleased to have spoilt your evening, but we are not playing games here. These fuckers are a danger to the United States, so do your best tonight and for however long it takes to find their ships. I've stopped here on my way to the Whitehouse – I was literally passing the door, but I wanted to meet you in person to stress the importance of the C23's work. I shall be talking to the C22's crew later today. For now, I suggest you get some more sleep – the C23 will not be back for another five or six hours, and who knows, they may already have all the information we require. If so, you can go and get as drunk as you want. If not, I'll leave it to you to talk to your crew- their leave has already been cancelled and they've been informed of that. Is that clear? Any questions?*

No Sir, Ragler replied. *We shall do our best, Sir.* Lall walked slowly to the door, opened it, and then turned. *Thank you Captain Ragler, and good luck,* he said as he closed the door behind him.

Chapter XVIII
Positions

34.23 degrees north. 76.81 degrees west.

19.11 UTC March 15th

Monroe sat alone in his cabin. Thanks to God there had been no problems for several hours now, and he felt unusually relaxed and content. He had even managed to finish a couple of glasses of bourbon in peace. Throughout the day, his plan to slowly ease the main body of the fleet eastwards, whilst tightening the formation of the battle group to attack WashingtonWall, had gone remarkably smoothly. Reflecting another of Smith's whims, the honour of being the armada's flag ship had now been transferred from the *Genesis* to the *Reliance,* a former Federal navy destroyer which had been with them since RougeWall. By now she should be a good forty miles to their east.

Monroe's good mood arose in part from his pleasure at seeing Smith disappointed by the number of ships which had joined them out of CharlestonWall. The experience of SavannahWall was not one that Monroe believed could be repeated. It was too small, too close to enemy lines and had been subject to repeated attacks over the years. He was thus surprised to find another twenty good vessels had joined them, though only two of these had any meaningful military capacity. Smith, by contrast, had raised expectations of another huge 'joining' as he had termed it, and had clearly felt humiliated by the lesser number. *'The dead cannot join you here on earth,'* Monroe had found himself thinking, and he had been secretly pleased that he could avoid the earlier logistics nightmare of positioning dozens of new ships.

Not that he could totally disregard the problems that were coming, not least of which were those which might arise from Smith's insistence that he stay with the battle group rather than sail eastwards with the main armada. Monroe dreaded another improvised change of plan. He was also continued to be baffled by Smith's ultimate intent and – as with all senior officers- was none the wiser following Smith's cryptic instruction that the battle group and armada were to rendezvous several days later in mid ocean. Monroe found himself asking the dangerous question as to whether Smith had indeed been guided by God, or whether he had simply decided that 35 degrees north and 35 west had a good ring.

To you Beth, he sighed, looking at the picture of his deceased wife next to his bunk. Monroe had genuinely loved Beth with all his heart, though he had loved his career in the navy marginally more. That was probably the reason they had never had the time for the children they both longed for. It was certainly the motive for his passing-up his leave furlough in order to command a ship during operation *Flaming Torch* during the First Saudi War. True, it had ensured him his captaincy and the command of a ship, but during his years-long absence Beth had fallen more and more under the influence of one of the most radical evangelical churches in New Jersey. The pastor was obsessive about abortion, and it was during a violent demonstration outside what the he had deemed an *'abortion death factory'* that Beth had fallen victim to the growing tensions within American society. True the police had difficulty dealing with the crowd, but a private security guard had decided to unleash her anger and frustration as radical feminists by emptying both magazines of her guns into the demonstrators. Beth had not died immediately, but Monroe had been on an air force jet to her bedside when the news came through of her death whilst he was mid-way over the Atlantic. Always a religious man, Beth's death had itself changed Monroe's outlook and evoked a more critical view of what he saw as the shortcomings of the society he was sworn to protect. That Beth's killer was given only a brief prison sentence on the grounds of self-defence was the final straw which convinced him to join the local evangelical church and subsequently be drawn into Smith's sphere.

It was also true that at one time he had loved Smith as the spiritual saviour of The United States, though he was increasingly coming to fear him as a deranged demagogue. He was, however, the only capable leader the Christian Confederation possessed. Given the atrocities committed against the Federals, little mercy could be expected if the Christians lost this war – which was the likely outcome given their military superiority – or failed to find a new home. Monroe was content with this option, though exactly where and how this was to be achieved was a mystery. *Who is to be eliminated to make way for us?* he mused for perhaps the hundredth time that week.

He gently kissed Beth's picture, and then looked at the data screen on his cabin wall. The screen replicated some of the significant data from the bridge control and showed that the wind was, unusually, still blowing strongly from the north west. Monroe had been a keen yachtsman in his youth and he knew the traditional Atlantic wind patterns well –or at least the ones that had become dominant in the last twenty years or so. Northerly winds were the norm until spring, when they were usually been replaced by more southerly flows, though in recent years higher temperatures appeared to have changed this and southerlies had become more dominant.

This calculation had been one of the factors in the decision to sail at this time, and while the main armada would be able to tack with this wind, he cursed his luck in having to sail with an opposing northerly. He and Smith would need to decide if they were to tack northwards using sail power, and this would mean a very considerable delay, or risk using their fuel reserves at a time and place which was outside their planning. His good mood had dissipated instantly with the realization that he would have to face another of Smith mood swings. He poured another long glass of whiskey, and then picked up the cabin phone and rang the president's number.

35.68 degrees north. 72.11 degrees west.

04.16 UTC March 16th

Ragler sat in the pilot's seat of the C23 with a mixture of sentiments racing through his mind. The entire crew had been promoted by a rank, and the anticipation of additional salary, status and power was mixed with the immediacy of having lost another night's leave. It was Saturday too -the hottest night in WashingtonWall with the near certainty of being able to make-out with the man or woman of your choice.

Whilst the Christian – Federal split had been born of differences in social and political values, religious beliefs and the like, the ensuing conflict had driven both sides into a living caricature of what they stood for. Federals had become increasingly hedonistic over the years, especially following a series of unexpected defeats which had tapped into the traditional cry of carpe diem. By contrast, many of the Christian communities had become sufficiently radicalized to introduce capital punishment for offences such as adultery and pre-marital sex. Tall, strongly built, and with what were generally deemed to be good looks with penetrating blue eyes, Ragler hardly ever failed to find a woman to bed on his leave nights.His thoughts turned again to the blonde barmaid he had planned to seduce over the weekend.

Captain Ragler, Sir! his co-pilot exclaimed, saluting with the humorous exaggeration the crew had exercised since arriving at the airfield. *We have arrived at the coordinates you instructed. What are your orders? Captain, Sir.*

Ragler smiled at the newly made lieutenant sitting to his left, and pointed to the row of red buttons with yellow crosses on the console which separated them. *Aimes, you remember from training what these are for?* Aimes hesitated momentarily, struggling to recall all the complexities of the C23. They were sitting in an environment of new and old technologies, relying on the ancient technology of hydrogen balloons for their lift and engines, but with state-of -the art intelligence capability and a nasty sting in weapons terms. Aimes blinked and then giggled as she squirmed in her seat. The pod slung beneath the balloon was made of a light composite designed to reduce both weight and radar image, though Ragler had his own doubts about the image of the balloon itself. Whilst traditional aircraft used ejector systems to escape in an emergency, all the current dirigibles relied on a simple drop system which sent the crew seats plunging towards the ground before the seat chutes opened. It was a simple, but effective, system if there was adequate height and the balloon itself – as sometimes occurred- did not ignite and drop with the crew. *But Captain, you ain't gonna drop me in this nasty sea are you? Not without you buying that drink you promised? That could spoil such nice things.*

They both laughed. Aimes had already been identified as the C23's potential diva and whilst military law strictly forbade intimate liaisons between crew members the main barrier was probably that her great humour was –as she was the first to acknowledge-nearly matched by her lack of looks.

Well private Aimes, note I've just demoted you, and the rest of you fuckers in the back, with this wind we ain't getting back to Washington tonight without burning one heck of an amount of fuel. Unless you can think of any tests we have forgotten to do, I suggest we slowly drift over to NorfolkWall. This is not scheduled, but we can get checked over and fuelled by the navy. What I want do for now is to take her up and check the heating has been done. And then we can come in low north of NorfolkWall keeping clear of the Chrisie ground fire. Collins, you see if you can do your magic of last night and get us all another promotions.

You and Collins did magic last night Sir Captain? Aimes interrupted. Why you not do magic with me? Her giggling continued despite the light blow Ragler landed on her shoulder.

Good to hear you two having a good time up there, Collins interrupted. *I can give you magic OK. The sea down there is lit-up with friendlies over place. I got the C22 and six other diris out west and north. What the game Captain? And we ok going into Norfolk? I heard the marshes just south of there swarming with rebels with anti-aircraft missiles.*

You never study Pearl Harbor at school Luce honey? Fleming, the chief armaments officer cut in. *The bosses are shit scared that our ships are gonna get shot up in harbor, so they are sending them out into the open sea to scatter so that our Christian friends don't get them.*

Not what I'm seeing Karl honey, Collins replied emphatically. *You sure bout this? These babes are joining up, look like a big battle formation coming together from us here. Somebody going to get a surprise if they bump into this lot. And where is this Pearl place, I..*

Sorry ladies, Ragler cut in. *Don't want to spoil your chatter but can we just focus on the task we have. Ames, can you take her up. Collins keep an eye on the radar and comms status. Keep the chat down too. If we can hear them, then they can hear us. And I don't want to be shot down during my first day as captain.*

Bordeaux Forward StrategicWall
EuropaWall Complex: European Confederation of
Democratic States
Annual rain 190 c.m. Annual sundays 270. Average summer
day temperature 33 centigrade. Average winter day
temperature 14 centigrade.
Average wind 11 knots. Maximum recorded wind 240 knots
Garrison: Elements of the Free Dutch Marines
3rd Division European Tactical Corp
1st Franco-German Strategic Corp
3rd and 7th Confederal Air Corp Squadrons
Elements of the Confederal Atlantic Fleet
1st Italian Strategic Squadron
4th Swedish Strategic Air Squadron
1st, 2nd and 5th French Strategic Air Squadrons
7th and 9th German Strategic Air Squadrons
06.00 UTC March 16th

Henry stood, observing the growing military presence, with the rising sun slowly warming the back of his head. He yawned, making no attempt to conceal the half – eaten mixture of real bread and real jam which he had stuffed into his mouth accompanied by a gulp of welcomingly hot CoffeeSubstitute. There was no point in manners at this point. Everyone within sight was busy checking some piece of equipment or another. There were armourers still loading ammunition belts and missiles onto the aircraft and the machine guns mounted in the dirigible ports. He understood from talking to the crews that these were old weapons, nearing the end of their working lives, which could be regarded as expendable ballast if extra height were required or the balloons were abandoned. After a lifetime calculating the implications of resource shortages for government policy, Henry considered this an enormous waste of resources until brought to harsh reality by one of the Swedish pilots. *Would you prefer waste or death?* she had asked with a dead pan face. The aircraft themselves were checked and checked again by other technicians and pilots. He knew that this procedure would be repeated at the end of this – and every other - stage of the flight, but for the time being each aircraft was being loaded as heavily as possible with spare munitions and filled to their limits with aviation fuel.

Rather than the customary one balloon, for this trip each of the aircraft was supported by a triad of gas balloons. Each was some thirty metres long and fifteen in diameter and were distanced from each other by a system of metal spacers, which were then attached to the dirigible which contained the air crew. The dirigibles varied in size and, according to this, a fighter or fighter –bomber was integrated into the dirigible in a manner Henry had still to understand. He had seen a few aircraft like this before, mostly from the American base at London Central, and he had actually seen one take-off when he had been waiting for Macgregor the first year he had been working for him. *'A week's lighting gone every second,'* he had thought at the time, and his figures had been about right when he had eventually checked. He could also vividly remember the evening on the Yorkshire coast when he had first seen a system like this being tested. Shortly after his entire life had been thrown into turmoil.

He had a worrying impression that the entire system would prove highly unstable if they hit turbulence, and had asked one of the technicians about this earlier in the morning. After eyeing him cautiously for a few seconds he had replied in a garbled French –and another language Henry couldn't identify – which had left him with a clear impression that he had been asked something about arriving with or without underpants. He had given up at that stage and returned to his coffee. Not that he considered this morning's activity to necessarily mean anything. This farce had been repeated for three days now, with a morning ritual of preparing the aircraft for the long haul down to the Portuguese and Spanish provinces, and then a cancellation around nine when the weather reports had come in and it was decided that the winds were unfavourable.

What changed each day was the number of aircraft being prepared on the tarmac, and the daily arrival of new craft from the north. Some of them were of designs had had never seen before, and he had heard rumours that the Norwegians and perhaps even the Finns or Russ might join. He had deep doubts about the latter, the last he'd heard they were struggling desperately to deal with economic and climate changes, and he wondered whether the delays were simply a ruse to keep the aircraft grounded until they had all assembled- but this was just idle speculation. It had all become idle speculation from the second day when he thought about it. Once it had been concluded that he didn't have the information to make any informed analysis about Smith's intentions, their welcome had become even frostier. Even the French – or was she German?- officer had become much cooler after the first night, and he wondered if this was a woman-

woman thing involving Brown. All that was clear was that the decision had been made at some level to use the Spanish and Portuguese bases as a scouting shield on the basis that any threat to the Confederation would likely come from the south west or west. As English government officials, both he and Brown had found it ironic that England was totally removed from any consideration.

Morning Henry darling. It was Brown. Since their exchange three days earlier he had done everything he could to avoid her. The threats had been too clear to have been anything other than deliberate, and he had spent much of the previous day trying to contact Macgregor in London in order to find out exactly what power the bitch had. He had failed. The few lines available were either engaged or –when he did eventually get through –Macgregor was out of the office or otherwise unavailable. Clearly there was something wrong. He knew Macgregor's routines better than his own family's, so for the old man not to be at his desk at a certain time meant he was ill or worse. And why had he let him go in the first place. It was not at all like him to let one of 'his' be prized away from his control, not least to Foreign Affairs.

Morning, he replied with a fleeting, half-smile *you sleep well?*

Not bad. she replied, and watched Henry's face carefully as she added *I slept so much better after I'd had that Greek Captain. You know, the gorgeous one with the theology bit.*

His theology was good then? I must remember that for the future, Henry replied with an alacrity which surprised himself. Ironically, he'd been drinking less since arriving in Bordeaux, despite the survival of some good vintages.

We have many different countries here. Perhaps you want to try them all before you go back to boring London?' Neither of them had seen Marie - Claire emerge from the still rising sun, and La Fontaine had to suppress the laughter he felt welling inside him at the sight of Brown's obvious discomfort. *Good morning to you both. A good day for flight then. You have both been up before?* she continued. Henry felt that, having branded Brown a total slut, there was the slightest smile on Marie-Claire's face as the nuance registered.

Good morning. No, not in one of these contraptions, La Fontaine replied. *I flew in a conventional airliner once when I was quite young. Got a government scholarship to study the American economy and political system and how they linked to the growth of the Christian extremists. That's when I met Smith and got interested in what he was doing. And what about you Amanda, you ever flown?*

Before Brown could reply Marie-Claire interjected *Miss Brown has undoubtedly flown many times. She appears to be able to ..how shall we say it…. get into many places. No?'* and she giggled gently. *Now, I shall see you in the office in ten minute. Today we are definitely flying – the wind is with us. We –I– have things to discuss with my commander,* and with that, she swept away leaving the English woman's apoplectic face almost merging with her flaming ginger-red hair.

I shall kill that cow before we go home, Amanda snarled, and stormed off leaving Henry bemused that people seemed so offended by the reality that they created for themselves. Twenty minutes later Amanda re-appeared, apparently fully composed, in the base commander's office. No one looked up as she entered, and Henry noted her indignation re-ignite at this deliberate snub. Not that there was much to repeat for her benefit. The meteorological forecast for today was good, with a strong wind blowing from the north. Tomorrow the wind was supposed to shift to a more north-easterly direction, so, -all being well- they would have two days of easy travel. Henry noted with interest that he had been assigned to Marie-Claire's craft, whilst Brown had been assigned to a Dutch officer who was somewhat less attractive than her recent Greek conquest. As they left the office, Henry wondered both if the two would survive a day together, and if it would be the Dutch officer or Brown who would react more aggressively to hours in the confined and hostile space of a dirigible.

It was ten minutes later that they realized that things really were going to happen today. The two of them were led back into the headquarters buildings, passing a stream of aircrew dressed in a style which reminded Henry of the old World War II films he had seen on television in his youth. They were led into separate rooms and he momentarily worried that they were about to be interrogated or –for the briefest of seconds- executed as spies. His fears were almost instantly allayed when a short, tanned technician entered the room carrying one of the suits he had passed minutes earlier. *Strip to your unterhosen – your under clothes and put this on,* he ordered, with a range of stress and intonation which left Henry guessing for a home region. *Make certain that the joins are pressed together and closed and that the tubes – you have seen the tubes?- are not, are not…'* and lost for English *'geslossen', 'obstaculo', 'ferme'* and a number of other alternatives were offered with an accuracy he was unable to guess.

What are these for? Henry enquired, holding a collection of pipes of various colours and sizes.

Immediately, the technician grabbed the collection and sorted them, holding each up for Henry to see. *This oxygen, this for bad gases, this for heat and this, –* he added triumphantly for piss, *so make your thing go inside it in the clothes.*

And if I need to poo? Henry enquired, already fearing the answer. The technician looked puzzled for a second and then followed the logic of the conversation.

You –poo?- here now or wait until tonight. You not say crap? Poo, poo, poo! he tried with increasing humour, leaving Henry wondering if he was ignorant of some meaning in his language. *And then put shoes and helmet on. Ready to go. Five minutes,* and with a few more *poo, poos* he walked out of the room. Henry heard him burst into laughter in the corridor. Minutes later he was in the sun again. Both the boots and the helmet had been a struggle until he had mastered the simplicity of the universal closure system. The Brown woman must have struggled more, or had fashion or hygiene issues, but she eventually emerged with a posse of female flight crews and pilots. Looking at her, Henry was immediately reminded of a cross between a woman aviator from the… -1930s was it? Called? Was it Amy something?- and an astronaut from the old International Station.

What are you doing to amuse everyone? Amanda demanded with a touch of bewilderment.

No bloody idea Amanda. Does 'poo' mean anything in any of the mainland languages? he asked with a smile. It was an atypical attempt at civility between the two, but he received only a loud guffaw by way of reply.

You two, your attention please! Marie–Claire Heinz's voice cut across the conversation. *As you can see, the first craft have already taken off, and we shall be joining them in a few minutes. Miss Brown, you will be with Captain Leader van Ryan. Just to be clear, you are entering extremely hostile environment. You must listen carefully to the instructions on your suits, emergency procedures and everything else. Understand?'*

They both nodded, and within seconds Amanda was walking across the landing pad with her new Dutchman. Henry asked himself if they could do 'it' in one of these flying boxes and concluded that Amanda would doubtless try to find out. For several minutes he stood in increasing admiration – and some trepidation- as one after the after the gas balloons reached a critical mass, rose steadily into the air, strained at the haws tethering their cargoes, and then rose slowly into the air. For the first few hundred feet they seemed to remain stationary above the base until the hidden hand of wind currents started to carry them effortlessly south. That was the key word – effortlessly- for each mile or kilometre travelled saved priceless aviation fuel, and there were how many aircraft? *Two hundred,* Marie-Claire said as though reading his mind. *We do have others, but this is all the government is willing to commit at this time. They are not sure if it is all a waste of time. Or even an English trick?* she said with a little laugh whilst her eyes searched piercingly into Henry's. *So no questions about weapons or anything like that. You stay in your seat and wait for me to tell you to move. We are sitting together, so we can talk a little if you want – this man Smith is interesting, so you tell me about him. OK?*

Henry smiled. *And Amanda will be in the same situation? She will enjoy that.*

Marie-Claire laughed. *No, I told the Dutch officer to dump her out if she caused problems. He believes in God that one, and has a good wife. She will have a tough day I think. Now come, it is our turn. Be quick.* Later Henry found it hard to remember exactly when he had found himself seated in the dirigible. There was a sudden jolt as the full weight of the load was absorbed, then they seemed to hang in the air just above the ground for what seemed an eternity before rising slowly into the air. With the exception of the occasional hiss of gas, there was total silence for the first few minutes as the crew made some minor adjustments and he had the chance to look through the forward portal at the – what were these supposed to be, squadrons? Whatever they were to be called, the sky for miles was littered with enormous balloons carrying their cargoes southwards. Soon, he realized that *'littered'* was totally the wrong word to describe the scene. There was a distinct order to the way they had taken off, and the craft were managed. The foremost balloons carried what was clearly some form of radar or intelligence array beneath them. Immediately behind these were lines of fighters which Henry guessed were probably primarily interceptors. The fighter bombers had been assigned a position in the middle of the formation. Henry wondered if there was a similar pattern on their flanks and rear, but felt that this was not the time to ask.

You know how to fit the helmet and get oxygen? Marie-Claire asked, looking up from one of the consoles. *And heating?*

Heating?

Yes Monsieur La Fontaine. The meteo have found a strong wind at forty thousand feet. If we travel with it we can be in Portugal by tonight. Look! We can already see the Pyrenees. But if you have no heating you will be a frozen Henry – not useful to us. Let me show you, and leaning across she ensured that one of the tubes was connected to a port on the dirigible wall and showed him how to adjust the temperature. *A question, for you,* she proclaimed, sitting back in her own seat and adjusting the buckle. *You English are very strange. Xosha, the Albanian technician who helped you at the base, is very confused. He is trying to learn English and is using this very old book about a bear – he thinks for children. He wants me to explain why you call a bear for children 'Shit Bear'?*

Shit bear? queried Henry. Then he started to laugh uncontrollably. *Poo bear,* he managed between fits of laughter. *He must be trying to read Winnie the Poo, a very old book. Very old even when I was young. Shit bear indeed.*

Chapter XIX
Battle Stations

38.9 degree north, 72.3 degrees west

10.00 UTC March 18th

Monroe anxiously scanned Smith's face. The tension writ-large there showed that the President had been more than upset by the battle squadron's slow progress in taking up position for the attack on WashingtonWall. Once again Monroe had endured several hours of Smith's hysterical self-doubt until he had finally concluded that the head winds were not in fact a sign from God that the attack should be abandoned. However, his patience had finally snapped and Monroe had been ordered to take the engines up to full speed regardless of the fuel expended and to sail almost directly into the increasingly strong north westerly wind. At one of his more illogical points, Smith had suddenly decided that he wanted to attack on March 17th and had only been dissuaded from this with great difficulty when shown the figures for the impact on reserves of aviation gas- they were simply too far from the coast. They had rapidly sailed closer to the coast throughout the night and were now, for the fastest aircraft, only about twenty minutes flying time for their target.

Monroe's hope was that one day Smith's emotional 'fits', as he termed them, would be witnessed by other senior officers and that this would raise the question of Smith competence without Monroe himself being isolated and endangered. In the meantime he had been incensed as a naval professional by Smith's constant changes and by being publicly berated when he had asked to discuss essential strategic and tactical issues. Finally, to Monroe's horror, Smith had carried his *Commander in Chief* role as far as insisting on shutting down all what he deemed *'unnecessary electronics'* including all the long range radar. It seemed that the President was alternating between depression and despair, associated with a feeling that God had abandoned him, and an alternative in which God was now offering special protection and consequently human action was unnecessary. A simple message from the rump at RougeWall that they had successfully traversed the New Orleans marshes tipped him in one direction. Bad winds sent him in another. Somewhere in the back of Monroe's mind was memory of a biblical extract which talked of trusting in God, but not testing him unnecessarily – he would have to look for it when time allowed.

The crews already aboard their aircraft, the final checks were being put in place by the *Genesis's* armourers to the armaments while it and the last of the carriers turned into the wind to assist launch. Three waves of slower-flying ground attack aircraft had already taken off from the *Houston* and were no more than dots in the darkness of growing storm clouds. Minutes later, the first of the fighter-bombers was catapulted into the void at the *Genesis's* bows, their engines roaring as they climbed. In good conditions the ship could launch three aircraft simultaneously, the central aircraft of the trio flying straight ahead whilst the two on either flank had greater freedom to bank and gain height. Monroe preferred not to use this system, especially with the increasing wind, but again Smith had over-ruled him and his judgment seemed to be vindicated by events.

Within minutes the huge ship had launched its contribution to the attack of some forty aircraft, and Monroe gave the order for the squadron to turn back on an easterly course and make top speed. The Christians were relying on the classical combination of low flying and surprise to hit their targets, including flights which had the White House and Capitol Hill as priorities. Monroe knew that, whatever the outcome of the attack, all Federal ships and aircraft in the area would soon be hunting them down, and he wanted to put as much distance between himself and their retaliation. *It has gone well has it not John Christian?* Smith enquired, suddenly happy with events. *Some excellent seamanship and piloting I would say as an amateur. With God's guidance you have done very well.*

Thank you Mr. President. Monroe hesitated, unsure how to respond either to the unexpected warmth of the praise or its potential naivety. *However, doubtless much of the credit must go to yourself and the wisdom of God Almighty* was the delay, prudent reply.

True John Christian. The Lord has indeed been showing his favour to us. But something tells me that you still feel uneasy – you want your electronics back I suspect. True? If you feel any happier you can put them back on now – that way we shall be able to observe the progress of victory all the better. Captain, the admiral would like all the surveillance and radar systems back on line instantly. Please see to it and inform the rest of the squadron. Out of the corner of his eyes, Smith saw Monroe's obvious discomfort as he struggled to cope with the reality that this command was no longer fully under his control. It gave him a degree of satisfaction which he determined to develop further in the near future. Admirals were, after all, expendable.

38.5 degrees north, 72.9 degrees west
10.11 UTC March 18th

Ragler was the first to admit that going to NorfolkWall with the C23 had been a total disaster. Not that he could have known beforehand the full extent of the carnage wreaked by the Christians in their last attack. He had heard rumours, but the official news had not prepared him for the major warships which lay like gutted carcasses in the dry docks or lay stranded in the flowing tides. Anything which could be taken had been taken, though both rumour and the official news claimed that most of the Christian fleet and its booty had been sunk in exchanges during a running battle to the south. The majority of the military building had also been destroyed, though some of these had been replaced by new, stronger fortified emplacements.

It was the lack of crucial skills and resources which were the issue. Unwisely, he had assumed that the Norfolk aircrews would have the knowledge and equipment to do what was essentially a simple service on the C23. He soon found that neither assumption was correct, or may have been correct but the local resources were focused on a couple of very elderly AWACS which the Pentagon had recommissioned and demanded should be made airworthy.

Finally, Ragler learnt that it had been decided to scavenge parts from one to make the other operational, but in this time consuming process he found his own craft being crawled over by kids he was sure had just been released from a technical school. He finally ordered them all away after one had accidentally vented much of his main reserve gas reservoir- there was no re-supply. By the time they were scheduled to resume their flight, the final result of a day of indifference, incompetence and confusion was that the C23 was less airworthy than at the time of its arrival. The crew was equally reduced, having managed little sleep during the day and expending substantial energy and time in trying to achieve simple things. With a sense of frustrated relief they eventually obtained clearance for take-off late in the evening and resumed the patrol. Almost immediately, problems became apparent. Whilst they had been unable to obtain lift-gas, the secondary diesel propulsion system had been totally filled. This, and the accidental venting, were causing an imbalance which left the crew with a craft which tended to be nose-up, extremely sluggish in exercising maneuvers and with barely enough lift to ensure a safe return to base. Having discussed the situation with base, he was ordered to return home using, if necessary, diesel power. The logic was clear - burning through the diesel would reduce weight and give them the lift they need to return. Later in the night he received a message from the Pentagon, warning of the approach of a major storm from the north, so it was that around three in the morning Ragler had found himself almost shouting *Time to turn for home!* There had been almost total silence in the aircraft for hours previously, the atmosphere betraying the simmering resentment at how his frustrations had reflected in his treatment of the crew earlier in the flight. He had made a mental note to take them for a drink that evening by way of apology, but knew that his behaviour could backfire by way of an official complaint.

As dawn approached they were making good speed to base, assisted by Ames locating a slight easing in the wind around the two hundred feet mark. Suddenly, Collins broke the icy silence. *Captain!* she exclaimed, her angry inattention having caused her to miss a minute of radar contact. *Unidentified aircraft on the horizon almost dead ahead. 1.0.0 miles and closing. I have approximately sixty high-speed contacts making directly for Washington.*

Have they spotted us? Ragler demanded tersely. He was no natural hero and was acutely aware of the fatal vulnerability to aircraft of a single dirigible.

Sir, no sign of radar activity and no aircraft coming our way, Collins replied with unusual alacrity.

Right. Ames, take us down to fifty feet and hold our position. I don't want to fly into the middle of a fire-fight. Comms, I want an immediate, priority encrypt giving location, direction and speed of the unidentified aircraft. Looks like we may be upsetting a surprise party by our Christian friends.

Time and chance have always been important ingredients in the history of warfare. Two minutes earlier and the Christian aircraft would almost certainly have detected the C23 before Ames took it down like a stone to within fifty feet of Virginian farmland. She had never lost so many feet in such a short time before, and was probably the most surprised person on board when they did not crash. Minutes later and Monroe's squadron would have brought its intelligence systems fully on line, detected the C23's transmission, and have attempted to break the encrypt. None of this happened.

WashingtonWall: The Pentagon
11.16 UTC March 18th

Army Specialist First Class Ronaldo Pezzi had been on duty since 20.00 the previous evening. The security state was at the highest he had ever seen and the night had been full of messages and background chit-chat from the Atlantic fleet and the defence systems and airbases on the Drylands. There had been a number of false alarms, Christian ships having been sighted close to the coast on at least two occasions, and then subsequently being identified at their own coastal patrols. Later, all aircraft and vessels had been ordered back to base or to seek shelter in a port as reports came in from the Northern Atlantic Fleet of a huge storm and winds exceeding eighty miles an hour sweeping south. Consequently, communications had eased in the previous hour or so, and all but the immediate WashingtonWall defences had ceased to provide any intelligence cover.

Pezzi lay back in his chair, rubbed his neck to ease the cramp and glanced around the room at the banks of other intelligence specialists. He had a vain hope that someone was going to have the initiative to make a fresh pot of coffee- perhaps even RealCoffee. He looked back at his console when a bleep notified him that an urgent encrypt had come in. It was from one of the army flights which had been out on test flights for the last couple of days and took some fifteen seconds for the message to be decoded. He ran it through the system again to ensure there were no errors and to validate the authenticity of the sender and immediately took out a key from his uniform breast pocket, inserted it in a small box on the right of his console and sounded General Quarters. As a colonel dashed over to his console, he found himself praying both that he had made the correct decision and that the encrypted information had been wrong.

WashingtonWall: The White House
11.20 UTC March 18th

Lopez had been up most of the night in his office with his team of intelligence advisors. They had tried working through the various options which Smith might be considering, and as the night had progressed he had ordered cup after cup of increasingly strong coffee to help the group stay awake. Finally, they had decided that all that could be done had been done, and Lopez had decided to change into his pyjamas and get some sleep. So it was that, when the sirens started screaming, he was standing emptying his bladder in the toilet which abutted his bedroom. Realising what was about to happen, he was still struggling to stem the flow of urine when the first bodyguard dashed into the toilet, and was still trying to overcome the ignominy of his wet trousers when he was hustled along the corridor into the nearest lift.

My wife and children? he demanded.

Already down on another lift, Mr. President, a bodyguard assured him, and he was left reflecting on the damp warmth around his groins as the lift sped down to the safety of the deep bunkers.

WashingtonWall
11.23 UTC March 18th

Flight Commander William Oakdene was one of the few who had crossed the theological divide from Quakerism to being a true warrior in the New Christendom as Smith sometimes liked to call his flock. Oakdene's parents had survived the first religious violence to sweep Pennsylvania, but they had been denounced as unbelievers by William himself shortly after the defeat by Federal troops outside Pittsburgh. For a few months the Christian 3rd Army had managed to control a thin sliver of land before being forced to abandon the state and embark under fire at Lakewood on ships sent from the south. It had been a messy, bloody affair and in retreating to the coast the 3rd had, for the first time in the religious wars, pursued a scorched earth policy which included executing all known unbelievers or opponents to the faith. As a new recruit, and as a test of his fidelity, William had been ordered to join the execution squads. He had not been in the squad which had shot his parents, but has seen his father's body slumped to the execution stake as they had marched out of Trenton on the way to the coast.

Then he was a young nobody. Ten years later and he was a Flight Commander in an old F69 Airhog of the the Christian Confederation's airforce. Charged with leading the attack on the 'infidel's nest', as President Smith had called it in their briefing that day, Oakdene's six feet six frame sat uneasily in the pilot's seat, his helmet barely clearing the cockpit canopy. His was a relatively slow craft designed for suppressing and destroying ground installations, anti-aircraft missiles, radar sites and anything else which an enemy was unwise enough to point its way. The prototypes had been developed after the third Iraq conflict and had been nicknamed *'Hogs'* for the simple reason that they seemed to 'bristle' with armaments of different types – a simple play on words which had appealed to the military at the time, and which became more firmly rooted as American military policy became more fervently anti – Islamic in the years of the oil wars. Though relatively old and lumbering, the aircraft could cut a swathe of death before it for several miles in a hundred and eighty degree arc.

Before launch, the crews had been briefed that Washington's air defences would almost certainly be disabled. A combination of excellent counter-electronics by Confederacy scientists, some hoped-for intervention by Brethren inside the Wall, and the Hand of God would, President Smith had assured them, ensure a surprise attack such as had been unknown since the time of Pearl Harbor. Later, there had been some negative comments about the Pearl Harbor comparison – no one wanted to be considered as a treacherous, cowardly aggressor – but it was reassuring to feel that Washington would be caught unawares. The city had once been ringed by the most sophisticated ground –to- air systems in the world, and there was no desire to try the effectiveness of the current system. Rumour was that Monroe had wanted to launch a wave of attacks, hitting the Wall's defences first and then going for the main targets of the White House and Pentagon. It was clear that God had given the President wisdom on this, for President Smith had explained in the briefing that their main target was the death of Lopez and the other leading infidels in the Wuccie military. The Whitehouse was, therefore, the main target. The President had proclaimed that, with its destruction, the Christian brothers left in America would be able to live in God's peace. Not that anyone had the slightest illusion that Lopez could be harmed if he managed to reach the deep shelters, but the surprise factor meant that he might be caught above ground.

Oakdene was re-assured to see the flashing green light on his console indicating that his electronic warfare systems were coping with the enemy's radar and other electronic systems. There was a nagging fear of being seen by an airborne unit, but the storm clouds gathering to the north probably meant that the Federals were busy grounding everything. Suddenly, he tensed in his seat as a flashing amber on his console indicated that his aircraft was being interrogated by the Pentagon's computers. Praying that the Confederation's technicians had loaded the correct codes, he felt his breathing become more intense and laboured, the sound echoing in his helmet. Then the green re-appeared. Checking the distance to their target, by way of a pre-arranged signal, he dipped the wings of his aircraft and dropped the nose slightly to decrease his height and increase his airspeed as he neared the outer Wall. Radio silence had been maintained since their launch, but he felt secure that President Smith's plan was working perfectly.

He stared again into the darkness of the eastern horizon, and then, as if born directly from his worst nightmares, the warning light flashed from green through amber to red. With no warning, the near horizon burst into activity as dozens of defence balloons shot into the sky before gyrating to an abrupt stop as they reached the end of their tethers. In the seconds it took them to stabilize, orientated themselves, and identify potential targets, Oakdene's squadrons had broken communications silence and a hail of fire was unleashed. Oakdene's finger rarely left the fire position on his control pad and he felt a rising sense of exhilaration as one balloon after the other exploded or crumpled to earth in a trail of burning gases and munitions. A quick check showed that only one aircraft had been lost, and several voices commented that, if this was the best Washington could, do the success of the mission was assured.

As if to counter this optimistic chatter, the ground directly in front of them suddenly changed, orange pinpricks revealing the launch of waves of short-range missiles bolting out from the Wall's defences. The warning system on his aircraft squawked threateningly, and he was forced to bank violently as one of his own fighter-bombers fell across his path, its port wing dangling uselessly. One aircraft after another peeled away violently, puffing anti-missile shards into the sky and Oakdene realised that all sense of order and co-ordination was being lost. He spoke urgently into his voice com. *This is Alpha One. All aircraft, I repeat all aircraft, have The White House and Pentagon as priorities. All other objectives aborted. Independent attack on your own initiative. God be with you.*

43.8 degrees north. 68.33 degrees west
12. 07 UTC March 18th

Though the medi-pad was rapidly stemming the flow of blood from the gash on his forehead, Admiral Joseph Mustafa Kemel Torgut continued to swear with a vehemence which even the hardened sailors on the bridge found embarrassing. Despite its ninety thousand tones, the United States Federal Ship *Constitution* lurched heavily once more, and then rolled menacingly to port in the same fashion as had had thrown Torgut off balance minutes earlier. To officers and crew on the bridge it was unclear whether the torrent of oaths were caused by the humiliation of an Admiral with some thirty years war service being injured by high seas, or the encrypt which had been handed to the Admiral minutes earlier. The encrypt had certainly had an instant impact on the Admiral – something more dramatic than those who had served with him for over ten years had ever seen.

Torgut's verbal onslaught halted, and using the chart desk for support he inched his way to better view through the bridge window. Even with the wipers working at their highest speed, the glass revealed little. The sun was largely obliterated by banks of thick cloud being driven down by the north easterly wind, and blinding curtains of spray were thrown into the air each time the ship's bow ploughed into the valley between the enormous waves. Despite this limited visibility, he could see his fleet dancing like toy boats on the ocean's surface. What had amazed him this time had been the speed and ferocity with which this storm had developed. In his early days in the navy seas like this had been a great rarity, encountered only in hurricanes and full storms which had passed across each of the earth's oceans perhaps five or six times a year. Then there had been days of warning as the winds and oceans slowly built their force, and the developing threat was tracked carefully day and night by satellite. Now, not only was the satellite system down, and deep ocean meteorological flights restricted, but the frequency and development of storms had taken on a totally new character. It was only as a result of warning from the *Vancouver,* a Free Canadian destroyer some two hundred miles to their north, that they had been able to lower their sails and shift fully to engine power before being engulfed by this fury. Outside he could vaguely see another Free Canada frigate *Ottawa* almost disappear beneath a wall of water, whilst in the distance the larger Federal destroyers *Chicago* and *Massachusetts* were faring only slightly better.

Torgut looked again at the encrypt in his hands. Though the internal wars had been waged intermittently for over ten years now, he still found it hard to believe that the Christians had launched a full military attack on the old national capital. He had always hoped that

Smith and his followers were still – in their deepest hearts – misguided, but sincere in their talk about respecting the Confederation. Unofficially, he had heard from Pentagon friends about the use of a nuclear device on Rangers who had attacked RougeWall, but he had tended to see that as propaganda by Lopez and his cabinet.Years earlier he had decided that politicians were fundamentally egoist self-fulfillers and had never been impressed by Lopez as a man of vision and charisma in his country's time of need. Despite his loyalty to the Confederation, and the office of president, he had considered being sent out to sea to hunt for phantom Christian ships a waste of fuel and time.

Consequently, he had initially taken the easy option of sailing with the wind and currents once out to sea. Now he was off station, too far north to help anyone, and was struggling to ensure he lost no ships. The encrypted contents told him both that he had badly miscalculated and that Lopez seemed to be proving a President of greater ability and foresight than he had ever imagined. He looked again: *Washington under attack. Provide all possible air support at earliest.* was the simple message which ran under the Defense Department banner.

Admiral Sir, a message from the Vancouver a grizzled comms captain broke into Torgut's thoughts. *They are reporting some minor structural damage but the main body of the storm appears to have passed. Sir, they are also asking confirmation..* and he paused. *They are asking confirmation that WashingtonWall has been attacked and breached. Their Prime Minister has ordered them to place themselves and other vessels in the area under your command if this is accurate. Awaiting your orders, Sir.*

Torgut blanched. 'Has the Wall been breached?' he asked himself. He had no news about that. *Captain Dray. Make a priority encrypt to Navy Command at the Pentagon. Ask them their status and orders for us. Explain our status and inability to help. Give them – give them my apologies for being unable to assist immediately.* He turned away again, trying to hide his face on the packed bridge. The Canadians had developed a reputation for often knowing more about the United States than the United States did; an ability generally attributed to their deserved reputation for computer and communications expertise. Whatever else might be said about Smith, his rabid attacks on what he had deemed *Canada's European perversity and corruption*, had served to generate considerable empathy for Federal America in the liberal provinces. Not that he believed that the Federal United States was itself a bastion of liberal sentiments. Over thirty years earlier, before he had applied to join the navy, he had added *Joseph* to his name by deed poll to avoid anti-Islamic sentiments. He had decided that the Americans would almost certainly not understand the secular nature of his first names and, seeing only his Turkish family name might fear that he was the archetypal, potential terrorist. Though his parents had fled Istanbul after the battle, they had been opposed to his dishonouring their fatherland's culture by adding a Christian first name. However, 'Joseph' had indeed proved a strong enough signal for the recruitment panel to appreciate that this would potentially be a young man of some loyalty to the United States, and someone , somewhere, had also spotted the significance in Turkish history of Mustafa Kemel and its link to the secular reformer Ataturk. Unknown to Torgut and his family, this simple change had been enough to sway the selection panel, and was a more decisive factor than his father having fought with the American and European Confederation forces against the fundamentalist armies. Having always prided himself in the loyalty he had shown to his newly adopted country and the navy. Today he felt a failure to both.

Chapter XX
Hunting

38.7 degrees north, 71.9 degrees west
13.19 UTC March 18th

Smith had left the deck as soon as the attack formation had broken radio silence. Monroe had seen his growing agitation as the squadron's sensors had come back on line and detected the sudden surge of electronic probing. The change had almost certainly been too fast and sophisticated to have been identified by the simple on-board flight computers, but the ship's large tactical computers had instantly evaluated them as signaling WashingtonWall was going to battle stations. Monroe had wanted to warn the attacking aircraft and had even ventured to suggest aborting the attack in the face of Smith's growing fury. Then, he had been left to bear the pain and anguish as terse conversations from the aircraft bore witness to the carnage being wreaked in the skies over the Easton Marshes. Radar showed two pilots aborting the mission. It was indicative of their fear of what awaited them on their return that, instead of flying back to the fleet, they had flown south west in a desperate attempt to reach friendly areas before their fuel gave out. The fate of the others was clearly revealed by the growing radio silence as the attackers were whittled down. Total silence followed.

Judging from the voice communications, there did appear to have been some success. Perhaps two or more Wall sections had been destroyed and the White House itself had possibly been damaged. But it was evident that, if the surprise element of the attack had failed, then President Lopez himself was unlikely to have been caught unawares.

Whilst Smith appeared to have left to indulge in one of his mood swings, Monroe's thoughts turned immediately to the survival of his squadron and the armada itself. Washington would be sure to launch a counter attack. It might take them some time so scan so far out, but they would undoubtedly check all potential sites within flying range of the attacking aircraft. *Vice-Admiral Wood, what do you consider the fastest speed we can make given our current disposition?* he demanded.

Wood looked through the windows of the bridge at the storm clouds building in the north. *With this weather Sir, I would say around twelve knots, perhaps slightly less. If it gets any worse, we may be down to below eight. It depends which route you plan to take Sir. Going straight into this will slow us further.*

Monroe hesitated. The Federals might expect them to keep out to sea, avoiding the rougher waters nearer the coast. *'But where is their fleet?'* he asked himself. *'Is it still in the Wall? The attacking aircraft had provided no useful information at all on this, but while there had been no mention of the fleet neither had there had been any mention of aircraft. Were they destroyed solely by Washington's ground defences? Where were their aircraft?'* Finally, after a pause of several minutes, Monroe decided. *Order the squadron to sail due east at maximum possible speed while maintaining battle order. We have an appointment to keep with the main fleet. Whilst I have as much idea as you about our final destination, I do know we have already used valuable fuel and time which I do not intend to waste be being sunk. Please communicate my order to all captains in encrypt and as a matter of urgency.*

Is the President in agreement Admiral? Wood demanded immediately.

Monroe's face contorted with unrestrained fury. *I command this navy Sir. Unless you are given a direct order to the contrary by the President, in his role as Commander-in- Chief, you will obey my orders. You understand Sir?'* Wood's *'Yes Sir,'* and immediate communication of the order indicated clearly that Monroe had re-asserted his authority for now. Satisfied, he left the bridge and made his way to the main War Room some four decks below. Tuckman and several presidential bodyguards were standing outside the door. Without speaking, Tuckman indicated to Monroe that he could enter the room. He hesitated at the door for a second before turning the handle, and then stepped into the gloom inside. Smith had dimmed the lights to their fullest extent, and it took several seconds for Monroe's eyes to adjust to the gloom. Only then was he able to make out Smith's form, prone on the floor under the main speaker console.

For an instant, he thought the President had collapsed before realising that Smith had assumed a prostrate praying position facing – Monroe did a quick check – yes, east. The empty room contained only three sounds. The first was the gentle background hiss of the air conditioning. The second, a not dissimilar but less regular hiss came from a comms receiver which had been left tuned to monitor the attacking flights. It was now dumb except for some background static. Finally, there was a steady murmur from Smith himself. The more closely Monroe listened the more he became convinced that there was no sense to the stream of words issuing from Smith's lips. He had heard that Smith could Speak in Tongues as the Bible described it, but as Monroe listened he was struck by the similarity in sounds between Smith and a young sailor he had once encountered in an engagement with a Federal ship. She had been totally traumatised by the blood and gore of battle. To Monroe's mind there seemed - for the first time - no difference between that and the behaviour of his Commander in Chief. He turned silently and left the room, closing the door behind him. He glanced briefly at Tuckman and there too, for the first time, he saw something new -absolute hatred and disdain.

WashingtonWall
14.59 UTC March 18th

Lopez stood, trying to control his emotions, on the lawn in front of the White House. The area was swarming with military personnel from different ranks and services, the Secret Service guards nervously viewing even their own as potential assassins. The wind twisted an umbrella held by a marine guard in a vain effort to keep the President dry, but Lopez hoped the lashing rain would hide the tears on his face. Remnants of the far east wing of the White House were still smouldering after a direct hit from a ground- to- air missile. The Secret Service had lied in their haste to get him to safety. His wife and youngest child had been killed before they could reach shelter.

Two large craters spotted the lawn, the debris from their impact spattered across much of the White House's shattered frontage. Outside the White House rails, on the far side of what remained of the gun emplacements, a Christian aircraft still burned, its last charge exploding an hour or so earlier in the heat of the blaze. *They were nothing if not determined* Lopez concluded to no one in particular, looking at an aircraft which had crashed into the lawn. There were no armaments visible on any of its racks and it seemed that it had been attempting to ram the White House itself, though the entire structure was so riddled with holes that it must have been flying on air itself for its last few miles. The pilot still lay slumped in the cockpit, the navigator sprawled backwards in his seat with much of his face missing. Lopez walked slowly to the cockpit, his slippers and pyjamas besmirched with a mixture of squelching mud and foam from the fire hoses. He reached in through the smashed cockpit. *Careful Sir,* cautioned a marine guard.

Lopez looked carefully at the still figures and then looked up the foot or so necessary to meet the marine in the eyes. *My thanks for your concern, but I don't think these two are going to cause us too many more problems. I just want to see .....yes here it is.* and he reached into the shattered cockpit and ripped the dog tag from the around the pilot's broken neck. *Oakdene W. Flight Commander,* he read slowly before the tears started to well in his eyes. There are times in the life of every individual, however powerful or glorious they may be, when the human replaces the image of super-human which may have been deliberately constructed over many years. So it was that a young marine colour-sergeant and a couple of Secret Service men witnessed the President of the United States of America burst into a torrent of tears. In their embarrassment they looked away, but their ears were filled with a torrent of oaths and curses as Lopez beat his fists in a mixture of anger and despair against the shell of the aircraft. Some of the larger audience ceased doing whatever it was they had been charged with, and looked on. Finally, there was silence and then a more controlled and dignified voice spoke. *My apologies. I realise that I am not the only one to have lost dear ones tonight. The main Wall has held, but I believe that there have been over twenty thousand military and civilian casualties counted to now. I am therefore not alone in feeling this anguish. But I promise you…* Lopez's voice faltered for a second before he continued in a tone which he had used regularly in election speeches and which seemed totally out of context addressed to a sodden group standing in a growing storm. *I promise you that tonight shall be revenged. I promise you that the deaths of our soldiers at Baton and elsewhere shall be avenged. This pilot and his like have brought our faith, our country and our democracy into disrepute. Wherever they have gone, our attackers will be pursued and destroyed using all means at our disposals.* And, to his surprise, Lopez found a ripple of applause burst spontaneously from his audience.

42.17. degrees north. 69.24 degrees west
15. 04 UTC March 18th

Dray almost ran from his console with the new encrypt. Without opening the sealed envelope, Torgut could tell immediately from his face that the news was good. The encrypt was simple: Washington*Wall intact. Make fullest speed rendezvous. Fleet to refuel and rearm. Priority to locate and destroy enemy.* A tremor of relief passed over his face and his muscles relaxed into something close to a smile. *Thank you Captain. You had family in the Wall too?* Dray nodded his head. *I pray they are well. Please signal that we shall comply at the earliest, but that I am reluctant to try and turn the fleet in these conditions.* As if to make a point the deck heaved again as the *Constitution* dived into a new trough between the waves. *And Captain. Please ensure a change in the encrypt codes. We don't know where the Christian fleet is and the nature of its* *composition. They may be having the same problems as we have with this weather but there is no reason for us to advertise our limitations. Vice-Admiral Larkin, Commanders, the Battle Room in five minutes. Captain Dray, be so good as to arrange an inter-ship conference on a secure frequency as soon as you can. For now, despite the weather, I want all ships brought to battle stations.*

38.7 degrees north, 71.9 degrees west
16.19 UTC March 18th

The remnants of Monroe's RealCoffee splashed over the edge of his mug as he stood on the bridge of *Genesis*. He had already changed the course of the squadron several times to reduce the roll in the swell and the ship had twice taken up position to receive the pitiful few aircraft returning from the attack. It was a tribute to the skill of the pilots that three had managed to make it back and land safely on the *Genesis's* rolling deck. Whilst wireless contact with the main armada was being minimised, it was already clear that it was far enough ahead in the ocean to have escaped the full fury of the storm. Even so, a number of the yachts and one of the smaller supply vessels had been reported lost.

However hard he tried, he could not help cursing Smith for his unadulterated egoism. If they had not engaged in the stupidity of the Washington attack they might have completely missed the storm and would not have lost the vast majority of their precious aircraft in a futile raid which would have served only Smith's ego. He was not sure exactly what the Lord had told the President – that was for Smith as God's speaker to know -but he did understand that it involved the ultimate loss of the impure lands of the eastern coast. So, the attack had simply been a diversion to maintain Smith's face following the earlier mishaps. And that was all they had been – simple mishaps. Considering the hundreds of ships and hundreds of thousands of souls aboard them, the losses thus far had been miniscule. But Smith insisted on taking each and every loss as a personal affront- as an indication that he had lost the Lord's love.

They were sailing eastwards with the greatest speed Monroe dared inflict on the squadron, and he looked grimly at the two, young seamen controlling the rudder. It was usually a physically demanding job, computers did most of the work, but today the storm's violence required human intervention to ensure they maintained position and course. He felt a need to speak, to somehow release his anxieties, to purge himself of his concerns in a cathartic discourse with people who would not have the immediate ear of the President. *Christian Brothers, a question please* addressing the two in the least formal manner his rank would allow.

Both looked at him with evident surprise, and there was a pause for several seconds as they inwardly considered how to reply. Finally, the younger sailor responded timidly: *Your question Christian Commander? Have you ever heard of Pearl Harbor brothers?*

There was a pause for several seconds until the same seamen replied. *An attack by Asian terrorists on the Pacific fleet during the Second World War in the late twentieth century I believe Christian Commander. Is that not correct Sir?*

Monroe smiled. *I see that our schools are doing a good job of educating our young. One hundred percent correct. What I am trying to remember is something that one of the Asian admirals said after the attack. An unsuccessful attack that one, as you will remember. And what he said was ......* There was no response to Monroe's pause. *And what he said was that the Asians had succeeded in arousing their enemy, the old United States you know, without destroying it. And that this would ultimately cause their downfall.*

For a minute there was a silence, and then the elder of the two spoke. *With respect Brother Commander, that has nothing to do with us.*

Why do you say that? Monroe demanded with greater conviction than he had intended.

Three reasons Brother Commander Sir, the man replied cautiously. *Firstly, God is with us. Secondly, President Smith knows the will of God and has promised the eventual defeat of the unfaithful.*

And the third? Monroe interjected.

And the third Sir, he said formally but in a way which brooked no opposition, *is that we are sailing for New Eden. President Smith knows where we are sailing in the end. But I know that, each time I touch the steering, God in his mysterious ways, is taking us closer. The Federals may try to destroy us, but fail. God will protect us and bring us to our new home.*

In the darkness of the storm a silence bore down upon the three men standing together on the bridge. Monroe found himself admiring the blind loyalty which Smith could still evoke, even after a blatant failure such as that day's. He also knew that his questions were on the brink of disloyalty and that he should speak no more. He could see nothing, but at an animal level he sensed something behind him and felt certain that Smith had stirred a potent foe he would have been well advised to leave dormant.

At the Time of the Presidents' Wars: *Aftermath*
Is available on Amazon and Kindle

WashingtonWall
22.48 UTC March 18th

Lopez had insisted in holding the meeting in the old Oval Office, despite continued concerns about a second attack. The constant trickle of news revealed that, whilst the Christians had failed in their assumed primary objectives, breaches in Wall sections and other damage had caused several thousand more civilian and military fatalities than first reported. However, the damage to strategic military facilities had been minimal and the White House itself was still functioning despite the damage.

For the umpteenth time that evening he looked at the picture of his family on the desk in front of him, and then turned again to the small pile of dispatches. Inevitably there was the message from Vice President Howard, nestling in the safety of California, asking of Lopez's well being and offering to assume the Presidency whilst Lopez mourned the loss of his family. *'Give him the Presidency and I'll never see it again,'* Lopez mulled to himself, whilst struggling to decide what level of desperation had forced him to embrace such a despicable individual as running-mate. Equally inevitably, there was a scattering of messages from some of the South American states. Lopez was intrigued by the speed with which the news had spread and wondered if, or when, he would hear from elsewhere.

What had attracted his attention was a curt message from Premier Yang-Laval which read simply: *'The Government of Free Canada communicates its condolences on both your personal and public losses. I have ordered our armed forces to cooperate with you in locating and destroying the perpetrators.'*

What do the Canadians have Andy? And I trust your family is well? Lopez asked as soon as Admiral Cutler had taken his place at the table.

My family is safe thank you Mr. President. As for the Canadians, may I ask why are you asking? And you mean naval capability? If not, perhaps we should wait for…

No, naval intel is what I'm after. Can they help us in a meaningful way to track down and destroy Smith?

Cutler sat back in his seat and gazed thoughtfully at a new crack in the ceiling for a full minute before replying. *They have a few good ships Mr. President. Like us, they were weakened by both religious and secessionist wars, but they appear to have come through better. Didn't have as many religious crazies from what we understand, but you need to talk to one of the intelligence agencies rather than me about that. What I can tell you is that they may be able to help a bit - and if they are being friendly, then I would take the offer. We need all the help we can get.*

Anderson's arrival concluded the conversation. This was a decision Lopez was going to make on his own, and later that night he made a discrete call to Montreal on the secure line.

Printed in Great Britain
by Amazon

84255373R00139